Published by Vintage 2014

2 4 6 8 10 9 7 5 3 1

Copyright © Lawrence Osborne 2013

Author Q&A copyright © 2013 by Random House, Inc

Lawrence Osborne has asserted his right under the Copyright, Designs
and Patents Act 1988 to be identified as the author of this work

First published in the United States of America in 2012
by Hogarth, an imprint of the Crown Publishing Group,
a division of Random House, Inc., New York

First published in Great Britain in 2013 by
Hogarth, an imprint of Chatto & Windus

"Off the Grid: Beyond Marrakech" originally appeared
on Fodors.com (October 2012)

Vintage
Random House, 20 Vauxhall Bridge Road,
London SW1V 2SA

www.vintage-books.co.uk

Addresses for companies within The Random House Group Limited can be found
at: www.randomhouse.co.uk/offices.htm

The Random House Group Limited Reg. No. 954009

A CIP catalogue record for this book
is available from the British Library

ISBN 9780099578932

The Random House Group Limited supports the Forest Stewardship Council®
(FSC®), the leading international forest-certification organisation. Our books
carrying the FSC label are printed on FSC®-certified paper. FSC is the only forest-
certification scheme supported by the leading environmental organisations,
including Greenpeace. Our paper procurement policy can be found at
www.randomhouse.co.uk/environment

Typeset by Palimpsest Book Production Ltd, Falkirk, Stirlingshire
Printed and bound in Great Britain by Clays Ltd, St Ives plc

The Forgiven

LAWRENCE OSBORNE

VINTAGE BOOKS
London

The Wet and the Dry
Bangkok Days
The Naked Tourist
The Accidental Connoisseur
American Normal
The Poisoned Embrace
Paris Dreambook
Ania Malina

For my mother, Kathleen Mary Grieve,
1933–2011

For my mother, Kathleen Mary Cross,
1935–2012

Many roads do not lead to the heart.
— Moroccan proverb

The Visitors at Azna

One

THEY DIDN'T SEE AFRICA UNTIL HALF past eleven. The mists broke apart and motorboats with European millionaires came swooping out of the blue with Sotogrande flags and a flash of tumblers. The migrants on the top deck began to shoulder their bags, revived by the idea of home, and the look of anxiety that hovered in their faces began to dispel. Perhaps it was just the sun. Their second-hand cars stored in the hull revved as their children scattered about with oranges in their hands, and an energy seemed to reach out from the edge of Africa to the Algeciras ferry, polarising it. The Europeans stiffened.

Sunbathing in their deck chairs, the British couple were surprised by the height of the land. On the tops of the mountains stood white antenna masts like lighthouses made of wire, and the mountains had a feltlike greenness that made you want to reach out and touch them. The Pillars of Hercules had stood near here, where the Atlantic rushes into the Mediterranean. There are places that are destined to seem like gates. One can't avoid the sensation of being sucked through a portal. The Englishman, a doctor of a certain age, shaded his eyes with a hand bristling with ginger hairs.

Even with the naked eye, they could make out the snaking outlines of roads that might have been there since Roman times. David Henniger thought: Perhaps it'll be easier than we think, this drive. Perhaps it'll be a pleasure after all. From a boom box near the flagpole came a few bars of *raï*, of Paris hip-hop. He watched his wife reading a Spanish paper, flicking the pages back and forth indifferently, then glanced down at his watch. People were waving from the approaching city, raising handkerchiefs and fingers, and Jo took off her shades for a moment to see where she was. He admired the frank confusion written all over her face. *L'Afrique.*

They went for a beer at the Hôtel d'Angleterre. It was not hot. The air was wet with recently broken mist. Con men and pretty 'guides' danced around them while the sun drenched the terrace with a smell of varnish and peppercorns and stale beer. A laughing mood dominated the seedy expats and their hangers-on nursing their plates of unshelled nuts and their cooled gins. We were once the most formidable bohemians, their faces said to the newcomers, and now we are delightful, playful shits because we have no choice.

The Hennigers had arranged for an agent to deal with the car rental, a man who would run back and forth with keys and contracts, and while they waited for him, they had a few beers with grenadine and some fried goat-cheese *cigares*. He waited to form an impression. The streets seemed massively solid with their French facades, and there was a gritty shade at their bottom. The girls were swift and insolent, with adultery in their eyes. It wasn't bad.

'I'm glad we aren't staying,' she said, biting her lip.

4

'We'll stay on the way back. It'll be interesting.'

He took off his tie. His eyes felt intensely alive somehow and he wondered if she ever noticed these slight alterations of mood, of intention. I like it, he thought. I like it better than she does. Maybe we'll stay a little after the weekend.

On the road to Chefchaouen, they didn't speak. The car rented from Avis Tangier was an old Camry, its brakes soft and its red leather torn. He drove it nervously in his perforated driving gloves, warily avoiding the women in ribboned straw hats who infested the hard shoulder, pushing mules ahead of them with sticks. The sun grew fierce; it was a long road bordered by stones and orange trees, and above it rose the hillside slums, the gimcrack apartment blocks, the antennae that decorate every middle-income city. One couldn't see the beginning or the end of it. There was just the taste of sea.

All was dust. He drove on doggedly, determined to get out of the city as fast as possible. The light all day had finally worn his eyes down; the road was reduced to a geometric glare alive with hostile movements: animals, children, trucks, broken-down thirty-year-old Mercedes.

The suburbs of Tangier were ruined, but the gardens were still there. And so were the crippled lemon trees and olives, the dogged disillusion and empty factories, the smell of seething young men.

The Hotel Salam in Chefchaouen looked over a river called the Oued el Kebir and a gorge; the road on which it stood, avenue Hassan II, was a steep lane of hotels, for the Marrakech and the Madrid were just next door, and along it the city walls loomed up, white and monkish. The tour buses were already there; the salon

5

was full of Dutch couples feeding upon mountains of turmeric eggs. The Hennigers were not sure whether to enter the hotel lounge and participate in this buffet orgy or stay aloof. The Dutch looked frantic and disturbed, as if they hadn't eaten in days. David wondered if they were given sandwiches on their immense buses. They were faintly disgusting, with their big red faces and their beefy adolescent ruminants grazing around the buffet tables. He was hungry himself.

'Let's eat straight away,' he said excitedly, 'but not here. Perhaps outside, away from the continental wildebeest? I wonder if one can get a drink that isn't Pellegrino Citrus?'

Fortunately the Salam had its own terrace and it was not too crowded. They took a table with views and ate their *tagine citron* with a bottle of cold Boullebemme. It was wine, at least, and he said a silent thank-you to it.

'Should you be drinking?' she asked quietly.

'Oh, it's just a glass. A glass of fly pee. This stuff is *fly pee*. Look at it.'

'It's not fly pee. It's fourteen per cent. You have to drive another five hours.'

She began to devour the salted olives at their table. David always took these sorts of remarks in his stride, and he settled down.

'It'll make it easier. I know it's the lame excuse of every alcoholic. But it will.'

'I shouldn't let you, Stumblebum.'

'I would anyway. The roads are empty.'

'What about the trees?'

There had been eleven years of this sort of contest; the exact, fastidious Jo crossing lances with the bad-tempered David, who always felt that women were out to suppress the peccadilloes that made life half worth living. Why did

6

they do this? Were they envious of life shimmering away with improvised masculine curiosities and pleasures without their consent? One had to ask the question. You could smile or not – it was up to you. Jo was ten years younger than him, a mere forty-one, but she acted like an ancient nanny. She enjoyed reproving him, pulling him back from tiny adventures that would have no consequences even if they were allowed to degenerate to their natural conclusions. I'd never hit a tree anyway, he thought. Never in a thousand years. Not even in my sleep.

She swallowed half a glass of the raw Moroccan wine and he raised an arch eyebrow. She wiped her mouth defiantly. The blood rushed into her brow, into the corners of her mouth.

'You always get what you want, David. It's our schema, isn't it? You always do what you bloody want.'

'I'm not putting your life in danger.' His voice was a little pleading. 'That's absurd.'

We'll see if it's absurd, she thought.

'Also,' he went on coolly, 'it's patently not true. I very rarely, as you put it, get to do what I want. Most of the time, I am following orders.'

At the bottom of the gorge stood white houses with jars of salted lemons on their roofs. Around them, dogs barked in the palm groves, and the waiters at the Salam seemed subtly ashamed of them. One of the Dutch beauties floated in the little terrace pool, rotating slowly under the first stars while gazing at her own toes. He watched her with meticulous curiosity. Her breasts nicely rounded, parting the waters. The dinner was short and efficient, because their minds were racing ahead to the journey instead of enjoying the present moment. Afterwards, he finished the remains of the Boullebemme

7

and cleaned his teeth with a pick from the centre of the table. Something in his voice was not quite right.

'I feel like going for a walk. Let's get coffee up at the *kasbah*, no? The waiters here are making me feel gloomy.'

Avenue Hassan II led straight into the Bab El Hammar and the *kasbah* by way of the lovely place El Makhzen. In the first hour of dimming, the menfolk were out in force on the long square filled with trees, eager for debate in crisply laundered *djellabas;* they stood around in circular groups holding hands, fingering rosaries behind their backs.

There was something shrill but paradoxically quiet about the masculine cleanliness, the speed of the children whistling about with shopping bags and peaches. The whitewash, the angular shadows. She gripped his hand, the marriage ring biting into his palm, and she held on to it as if it would provide long, consecutive moments of stability inside this flux. Did she need him more for a little while, just enough to get through this town? The petty disputes of the last few weeks melted away and in the end it was all just words and words, she thought, words that melt away easily as soon as you are in a strong enough sun and you are moving. They found a lopsided square with a fig tree where there was a Café du Miel with tables that all leaned to one side on the slope on cedarwood legs. It offered no drinks, but strong coffee with grains and a good smoke, and he felt at home at once. There was a saucer of cardamom seeds for the coffee and a plate of almond pastries. Small acts of delicacy. The streets were patriarchal, if you liked, but they possessed intimacy. The trees made delicate shadows on the underfoot stones. He stretched and dropped a cardamom pod into his coffee.

'I feel less tired now. I think this afternoon was the worst stretch. If we leave at seven, we can be there by midnight or so.'

'Do you think they'll wait up?'

'They'll wait up. We're a large percentage of their weekend, emotionally speaking. They'll be boozing long past midnight.'

Or all night, she thought hopefully.

'It's not a military timetable,' he said with more conciliation. 'If you want to stay here a night, I don't mind. I was thinking ... two nights of party might well be more than enough.'

She shook her head.

'I don't want to, I want to get to Richard's place.'

In a moment her eyes brimmed over, and she felt an irrational hatred of the whole situation. It was the usual things. The heat and the thick coffee and the stickiness in the air and the tone in his voice. That clipped and impatient twang seemed to go so perfectly with the way the men in the cafés stared at them with their eyes held back in some way, yet sharpened by their provincial curiosity and used like pointed sticks to pry. She had thought a trip through the desert would give her ideas for a new book, but such calculations rarely pan out. What kind of new book after all? Instead, she was beginning to feel boxed in by the schedule to which they had to stick, and the men in the street stared and stared and their hands played with rosaries on the surfaces of the tables. They stared so hard she felt her centre of gravity giving way. They stared with a blank hatred, but it was equally possible that it was not hatred but a sense of unconscious superiority that did not even need to be conscious in order to put the other in her place.

9

'It'll be all right,' he said tersely. 'We know they're repressed and enraged. They treat their woman like donkeys. For them, you are an escaped donkey.'

She looked away, and she was gripping her napkin.

'I hate it when you say that.'

'Why? It's true, isn't it?'

'It doesn't matter if it is.'

'I would say it mattered,' he countered. 'I would say it mattered if they disliked your presence because of your sex.'

'I'm sure it isn't that. And you have no idea how they treat their women – none.'

He laughed and picked up a cardamom with two fingers. She was being sophistic.

'Well, have it your way, Miss Feminist.'

Wanting to show off his French, he asked the owner of the Café du Miel seated at the next table how hot it was in the desert. The Moroccans went into the usual exaggerations.

'Vous allez souffrir, vous allez voir. Mais c'i beau, c'i très beau.'

On the walk back to the Salam, he took her hand. The dogs were so loud in the gorge that he couldn't relax; his mind began to turn with a pitiless inertia all its own. Had it been a good idea, he wondered, this extravagance, this sudden departing, this rush to amusement? All for the sake of fun and friendship and three days under a fiercer sun. He knew she hadn't wanted to come. But something in him enjoyed the coercion he was imposing upon her. He liked pissing people off when he thought their irritations sprang from their rigidity and hypocrisy, and hers certainly did. He thought of himself as a cleansing agent, a purifier of other people's prejudice. She would be better off for it in

10

the long run, he was certain, and as he thought this, a delicious pity crept into his calculations, a grim tenderness that had no actual purpose relative to his wife. It was like tending a pasture, clipping the edges with a sharp pair of shears. Keeping order with love and keeping the monsters at bay.

The Spanish Mosque was lit up, the water on the terrace pool flashing as the wind hit it. Two men walked arm in arm down Hassan II, whispering intently. No women on the streets now; it was the hour of men. Their eyes were upon the tall blonde in her worn cotton dress and red sandals, her jewellery and freckles. There was evidently a pleasure simply in tracking such a *gazelle* (that was the word they liked). Her gait that hoped to conceal itself from sexual curiosity, not quite a woman's sassy walk. They could easily guess that she was a writer, an intellectual, just as they could guess that he was a doctor and a bore.

David and Jo got into the car. He opened the Michelin map and struggled to find the fine red line that was the route they had to follow without fail. She kissed his cheek, and there was sand between her lips, just as there was sand on his face. It was already everywhere, and it irritated him. The granules itched inside his ears.

'I'd rather sleep than drive to nowhere,' he said.

He spat out a grain of sand to make her laugh. But still there was a needling reluctance in her voice, a physical disinclination of some kind. She didn't want to go. She always doubted him in moments of pressure, and when she doubted him, there was a tone in her voice that made him resist at once. So, naturally, they had to go.

'It's a bit mad to keep driving,' she tried.

'We're not staying in this dump. It's still light. There's still three hours of daylight left. It's a breeze. It's straight through.'

11

'But it's getting dark.'

'Not at all. It's getting less light, that's all.'

'We *could* stay.'

He turned the key in the ignition. 'Not a chance. The fleas would eat us.'

'Fleas?'

'Fleas. I noticed them at once.'

Oh, she thought disdainfully, it's a Moroccan hotel, so it must have fleas in it.

'I didn't see any fleas,' she said, pouting.

'You're not a doctor. They were everywhere. I even noticed them on the turmeric eggs. The Dutch will have a *very* bad night.'

At least they'll be in bed, she thought.

'It's one of those places,' he went on, 'that makes you want to move on. It's not just the hotels.'

Children stood by the road with their honey spools and fossilised shark teeth, holding up their treasures. They stopped at the long, spellbound lake of Aguelmane Sidi Ali. Ominous cedar forests clung to the mountainsides, and a few guides lounged at the edges of the oncoming night, watching them with a curious lack of interest. The sky was filled with dusk clouds, great shadows on the lake. Farther on, on the Col du Zad, it began to rain in spots, the fields of barren rocks hissing like frying pans being hit with cold oil. There was no one on the road, only a few army trucks. Gradually her mood grew more sombre. She glanced down at the Michelin map and it crossed her mind that one can follow maps too blindly; it was a tremendous gesture of trust. One had to believe that these childish squiggles corresponded to an entire country. So her eye followed the line of the headlights now carving flashing visions out of the dusk – white-washed barriers, spots of drinn grass, animals standing under the trees – and she did not quite believe it.

His hand reached down to the CD player and he pushed in a Lou Reed.

He said, 'It's the right road, isn't it?'

'There's only one road.'

He felt grimly satisfied.

'God, I hate Lou Reed. What a moron.'

'It's perfect road music.'

'That's what I mean. I also have Vivaldi. Almost as bad.'

Shaggy trees shot past in the side-mirror. Rocks painted with Arabic words and numerals, leafless thorned trees bent to one side. Men in sackcloth slept in ditches by the road, with pickaxes and chipped trilobite slabs laid next to them. They rolled into Midelt.

It was a pell-mell town of concrete and antennae. Its streets were filled with wild-eyed men in heavy woollen gowns exuding a ravenous, merry energy. There was a distant taste of quarries. Fossil country, with a long hill for a main street. The world capital of ammonites and crinoids. Desperate signs advertised *Fossiles en vente* and *Dents de requin.*

But in any case they drove straight through the town, after a quick espresso at the Hôtel Roi de la Bière. The car groaned as it pushed up a long incline and into the dark of new forests, and between the Atlas peaks the night sky suddenly came into definition, sharply illumined at its centre, a heartbreaking blue, but vague and treacherous as it reached down to the earth.

Close to midnight, they pulled over again. They were not sure how far they were from Errachidia, or from Midelt,

13

and the turn-off to Azna – tiny, by all accounts – lay closer to Errachidia. They would have to be extremely careful. 'We're going to miss it,' she wanted to say, but it was surely better not to. Instead, she walked down the middle of the road, letting something in her body go free, her hands flapping, and for the first time she drank in the sky and the hostility of the earth, which liberated rather than oppressed, at least for a few moments. Seeing this, he got out quickly and opened the torch on her. His voice was penetrating and hysterical, as if he understood perfectly that she had had a moment's freedom outside him.

'You'll get yourself killed like that. Are you nuts?'

She turned in a measured way and hovered just out of range. Her fists were clenched and she was not quite steady, not really erect.

'Get in,' he shouted. 'You're in the middle of the road.'

And suddenly, behind her, headlights approached. He grabbed her arm; she twisted away, but then scuttled round the car to her door.

'I'm not blind,' she hissed.

A large car swept towards them, a regal silver Mercedes convertible with the top down. They were both so surprised that they simply watched it roar past, its bumper polished like tableware, an anachronistic show of brutal luxury.

'Must be one of the guests,' David said, fumbling with the keys. 'We can follow them. A Mercedes!'

At this, she laughed outright.

'What if they're not guests?'

'We'll soon find out.'

'David, no. You're *not* to follow that car.'

He shot off, slamming the pedals, and his mouth was

grim and silly. She rolled down her window and decided to let this folly expend itself logically, because there was no way a worn-down Camry could keep up with a Mercedes. Its tail lights were already rapidly disappearing into the gloom ahead. She sat back and waited to see what her excitable husband would do, and how he would apologise in due course for his abominable language. His violent moods always exploded and dissolved almost in the same moment, and after them came the quiet of septic ponds and bombed cities. The rages of the modern husband, inexplicable, dense, obscure in origin. And there was something about the Mercedes that had infuriated him even further – its arrogant assurance. Were they Arabs?

He said, 'Did you see them?'

'Not a thing.'

'Strange they didn't stop. What if we had been broken down? They didn't even slow down.'

'Thank God they didn't stop.'

'I'm talking about the underlying attitude.'

What is the underlying attitude? she thought bitterly.

Soon they were alone again. Small white buildings floated by, long-abandoned ditches, destroyed gates, tracks running off into a vast palmery. She knew he was lost, and he knew that she knew. Insects began to crust the windscreen, a massacre of crane flies and moths.

As the road flattened out, the heat rose and touched the backs of her hands, the unprepared skin. Even above the hum of the engine, she fancied she could make out the slithering echoes of water wheels turning inside the oasis. Tracks spiralled off into the palmery, side-roads with villages listed in Arabic. But of course they could not read the names. Occasionally, places were also written in French, and these were the beacons of hope. But none of them was Azna.

He slowed the car under her insistence, and they stopped again to consult the ever more ambiguous map, on which Azna was not marked. He thought it must be on the way to the high village of Tafnet. There the road bifurcated, and both branches petered out. Perhaps the glamorous renovated *ksour* of Messieurs Richard and Dally was there, but they had said nothing about Tafnet in their directions. Nor were there any lights shining in the hills or inside the oasis. They had left too late, he knew, and his heart sank because in all likelihood it was his fault, and it couldn't be disguised. They would turn towards Tafnet and there would be an argument. He would drive for miles waiting to see if he had been right or wrong, and when he was wrong, she would tear him to pieces. Or he would be right.

'We should turn towards Tafnet,' he said calmly, folding the map. 'I don't see any other roads that might fit.'

'They didn't say anything about Tafnet.'

'I know, darling. But they may have assumed Azna would be marked along with Tafnet on the sign.'

'And what if it isn't?'

'Then we'll take a chance.'

'A *chance*, David?'

'Let's not have another scene. I'm as lost as you are.' His hand was shaking.

'It's the booze,' she said acidly.

'Get in. We'll get an inspiration. We'll find them.'

As he put on his seat belt, he said, 'It's not the booze, I can assure you. It's the worry. The booze never gets to me.'

A mile farther on, the headlights picked out a camel standing by the road picking leaves from an acacia.

Sand drifted over the road, and there were pieces of broken glass. The road turned round an outcrop of boulders covered with prickly pears and dropped a little, smoothing out.

Far ahead was a sign with several place names stacked on top of each other in Arabic and French. They made out the word *Tafnet*, and she said quietly, emphatically, 'No.'

'We have to turn,' he insisted.

She caught his arm and there was almost a tussle. They screamed at each other, and he missed the brake pedal, then found it. He didn't stop; he just wanted to clear the issue before they reached the sign. A gust of wind blew sand across the road and everything dimmed, and he said, 'Don't be so bloody stupid.' But her voice suddenly went calm.

'Turn on the main beam.'

The sand darkened the moon, and the outline of the road disappeared for a few moments. And then, as her eyes relaxed, she saw two men standing to the left side of the road. They were running towards the car, holding up their hands, and one of them also held up a cardboard sign that read *Fossiles*, with an exclamation mark. It seemed like such a ridiculous scam. 'Stop,' she said very calmly to her husband, but something in him seemed to have decided otherwise, and their dreamlike momentum continued. The sign flew into the air, and there was a crash of opposing wills. At least, that was how she thought of it. But in reality it was too quick for any thought to occur. The car's metal struck human bone, and the sound it made was like a single blow on a large, tautened drum – a *boom* that seemed to deafen and stun for a second, a sound she was sure she had heard before, but which was at the same time wholly new and fresh and derived from nothing previously known. It was a detonation of some kind that lasted for only a split second, but seemed to last for minutes, in the course of which her confidence in the future broke apart and died.

Two

IT WAS TEN O'CLOCK. SET WITHIN THE
ruined walls of the Azna *ksour*, the main mansion of
dark-brown pisé cast its square silhouette against the skies.
The old mud walls still stood, and the *ghorfas*, or granaries,
were four hundred years old, melted down with time and
connected by erratic adobe staircases. The *ksour* lay high
up on the hillside past Tafnet, and it had been abandoned
since independence in 1956. It was built close to a natural
spring that the Foreign Legion had dubbed *La Source des
Poissons*; its water was said to make sterile women pregnant. The river flowed around the cliffs where the houses
perched, half of them abandoned, and from them a flight
of steps plunged down to the pool where the women of
the Aït Atta floated in secret to recuperate their powers.

Then the foreigners came. *Les visiteurs*, as they were
called. Tall, golden men with bright eyes and fussy, incomprehensible tastes. They could have stepped off a ladder
dropped from the sky, for all the people of Azna knew.
The term *visitor* also implied that at some point in the
merciful future they would depart just as suddenly as they
had arrived. It was admitted that they were wealthy and
they spent their money in an exceedingly unwise and

profligate way, and that this was much to the advantage of the people. They hired many servants and staff and did not work them very hard. Once again, this was to the advantage of the people. But by the same token it could not be denied that there was something unquestionably demonic about them. It was not just their alcoholic habits, which were extreme even by the abject standards of Europeans. Nor was it just their distasteful sexual habits, though there was much to say about those. It was the way they sat at night on their roof with binoculars looking at stars, the way they sometimes slept all day until dusk, and the way they walked along the old trails at twilight with garlands of flowers and ice buckets. Moreover, they could not drink local water; they swam naked in their own swimming pool and sometimes, God forbid it, in the pools of the *Source des Poissons*, contaminating the source. '*Li jayin men lkharij gharab*' – foreigners are strange.

The few old people left in the habitable houses by the cliffs talked about the homosexuality of Dally Margolis and Richard Galloway with a dry, non-committal disgust. But secretly, despite their horror, they also admired the visitors' wealth and their cosmopolitan style. Oranges flown in from Spain! Butter from a single store in the 8th arrondissement in Paris! Drinking water shipped all the way from Meknes! They appreciated the influx of cash, the extravagant wages and the beautification of the *ksour* itself. It was said that Dally was the submissive one and Richard, with his slightly more austere tone, the dominant. They laughed. The jinns in the *ksar* and in the granaries, they whispered, were outraged by the presence of infidels in a place built expressly for Muslims, and at night everyone could hear the clash of pots and pans in the kitchens, victims of supernatural rages.

The jinns were right. There were scandalous goings-on in the main house, but no one ever saw inside it until the morning after. People said there were naked boys asleep on the floors — boys everywhere, and some of them Moroccans.

Earlier that day, as the sun dropped, the shadow cast eastwards by the crenellated walls, the lopsided rectangular towers and the half-melted *ghorfas* had formed a single menacing shape upon the shelves of rocks, an impression of decayed massivity. The yellow-throated tanagers went quiet and stood still on the roofs of the buildings, which were still hot from the sun, and from the river came a sound of aroused swallows. Rabbits could be seen waiting behind cacti, their ears completely erect. A shepherd walked languidly towards Tafnet a mile behind his near-invisible gaggle of goats, swinging a stick as if he wanted to decapitate someone. A swirl of dust rose from the far-off road that led eventually to the Tafilalet. The sound of chattering voices and a Natacha Atlas song coming from the *ksar* were not enough to make the old people sitting on the river wall turn their heads. They had heard it dozens of times before. There were always parties going on up at the house. 'Once,' they would say, 'we saw an infidel whore lying on her back in the *Source des Poissons*. Their men cannot get them pregnant!'

But when a Christian in a dinner suit stumbled down one starry night to say hello and admire the view, they smiled with mechanical courtesy. They raised their hands and cried '*Salaam aleikum*' and then '*La bess!*', 'No evil!'

The middle-aged American was walking along the ruined section of the *ksour* wall that had not yet been repaired.

He was in a Huntsman suit with a poppy and held a paper plate with some pieces of chocolate cherry cake, his shoes dusted from his walk. For the men of Azna, he was a sight. He was about forty-five, with Italian features, and no one knew who he was. Tom Day was a private investor in Dally's business, though he never asked questions about it and rarely showed his face at the latter's incessant 'happenings'. He was too old, he felt, and moreover he had already burned his candle at both ends, as ancient libertines are fond of admitting. The remaining piece of wax in the middle, he felt, was too precious to melt at parties, and his foremost interest was in merely making it last until the end without evaporating in the furnace of fun. No one knew how he made his money, and he never offered the information. It was beyond civilised discussion. He had retired at thirty-eight – that was all one needed to know. He lived alone in New York and kept a house in Ubud, in Bali. A few years earlier, his wife had run off with a hedge-fund manager. Nothing was known of her. Women run off and they fade mercifully from the mind.

The wall looked over the head of the valley, the road and, beyond that, the white edge of the Sahara. Day smoked a cigar, enjoying the puffery and swagger all around him and the way it was taking shape minute by minute, like some monstrous cartoon being drawn in front of his eyes. Something inflating. The staff were hanging fairy lights in tamarisk trees nearby. They made a fuss, cursing in Tamazight and making it clear that the boss had asked them to spell out specific designs with the lights. As they struggled, noisy cattle egrets chattered around them, as if humans and birds were at war for a moment, and the staff beat them off with sticks with many a *tsk-tsk*. The electricity was tried and failed. Allah was mentioned, but he did not intervene.

The generator was turned off and then on again, and the men in the topmost branches wove yet more bulbs around twigs. Who was it for? They were also hanging small tangerines with the stems wrapped in silver foil, which reminded him of the oranges hung on good-luck trees at Chinese New Year. A yapping of fennec foxes came over the little ravine where the old men sat smoking in the gloom. *La bess!*

He walked on top of the wall until he could see the main gate. It was hard not to feel disdain for the way they had done it up in lights and flowers. It was vulgar, but not vulgar enough. Cars roared up the dirt road, greeted at the entrance by extra hired hands in silly turbans and sashes, which the irrepressible Dally had designed himself. Out of them poured dozens of fab people, all of them laughing about the hardships of the Moroccan road. The women were already in their dresses and they had been drinking in the cars. It was like a ball in nineteenth-century Russia: the rushing up to the venue in carriages was part of the fun, part of the sex. He himself had driven a rental car from Meknes.

The floodlights were finally turned on and the lacework facade of the *ksar* became a brilliant image. A staff member came up to him with a tray held at the shoulder, and seemed to wonder what he was doing there all by himself when there were so many beautiful women to enjoy.

'*Vous désirez un cocktail, Monsieur? Un petit sandwich?*'

He walked through the *ksour* with his stub, sucking the last smoke out of it, and as he passed by the wall again, the tamarisk trees came alight and the staff applauded themselves. Allah was again mentioned, but this time even more emphatically. There was a pulsing celebration suddenly upon the air. He enjoyed the rushing and clapping and the way the servants sank their teeth into the oranges on the sly and caught his eye. Dally and Richard expected around forty people for the weekend, and the tiny houses were filling up. He almost admired it, this talent for weekends, which are usually forgettable – this talent, that is, for making them unforgettable. Dally, he thought, must be a man of meticulous inner workings, a man who is half clock, half ballerina, with a genius for orchestrations and appearances. He ran a number of e-commerce sites in the United States specializing in European fashion, one of the few areas of the economy to avoid the latest difficulties. What kind of name was Dally, anyway? A nickname someone had given him, an insult turned endearment?

He watched the guests spilling out of the main house's open doors into the courtyard, where trestle tables had been set up with bowls of fruit punch and iced rose water. There were plates of figs split down the middle and opened out. There was going to be a musical performance. A Gnawa group had arrived, hoisting their instruments. There was something a little urban about them, as if they had come from the city and not from the mountains, which was perhaps a sign of the times, and the tall European and American girls in their locally acquired pieces of ethnic clothing mingled among them with knowing looks of studied cool. One had to stop and watch that. The long, emaciated figures with their eyes ticking over like meters, taking in everything that 'world culture' threw their way. They were quite beautiful, but in a way that was far ahead of its time and which left him high and dry. Well, these are your people, he thought, and he didn't mean their shared race. They were the people of the megalopolises, and they were new. They moved like giraffes among the musicians, uttering friendly comments that were no doubt insolent to other ears. They made him remember that he was almost old, in that phase of preoldness that was curiously more alive that the preceding stages, but alive because it was ending. He clucked and rolled back on his expensive heels, which were already gathering white dust. What a figure you are, Old Day. Invited by accident to other people's fun and unwilling even to put a good face on it. You should stay at home.

The Gnawa put on a wild performance. It could easily have been music from the African hinterland, with its furious, hypnotic drums, but after all, it was already known from the CD floor of every Virgin Megastore, and half the people there had dutifully read their Paul Bowles. The hosts led the applause, standing before their guests for a few moments to express their gratitude that everyone had travelled so far. They spoke before their guests like a couple of Roman senators addressing the floor. They were dressed in matching dark-cream *djellabas*, and their hair was wet from a dip in the pool. There were a few ovations and obscene wisecracks. Dally, looking very bronzed and boyish, invited everyone to spoon into the bowls of Midelt honey — locally sourced, he pointed out — and the figs, explaining that they would start dinner at eleven. They were still waiting for a few guests who had not yet shown up. At this, the group dispersed and a few women got into swimsuits and headed for the pool. It was still over a hundred and four degrees an hour past sunset.

Day went over, too, hoping for a flirtation. It wasn't a bad vantage from which to survey the weekend's offerings. Around the palms that enclosed the pool there were others, all suffering slightly in the heat. An English accent here, an American there. They had all been drawn to a remote house in Morocco by the promise of adventure, of wealthy men. They didn't like to admit it, but that was how it worked. Some of them, however, had been driven there by their lovers, who wanted to show them off, and these 'jewels' had the busiest eyes of all. Their men were not unlike himself, but they were not really his sort of people, for all the communality with them he had admitted to himself a few minutes earlier. He had a sense that they would look down on him. Bored at last, he went into the house.

The *kasbah* was entered through spectacular hand-carved doors with iron studs. The vestibule was a bit like a Scottish castle, with Berber armour, swords and firearms slung along its stone walls and paintings of ponderous battle scenes posted between them. He spied *The Battle of the Three Kings*, a sixteenth-century battle loved by Moroccans because they were the winners and the king of Portugal was killed during it. The floors were brightly polished and embellished with menacing handmade nail heads. To one side lay the enormous dining room, where the tables were set and the AC units were already cooling the air. To the other lay a library and a games room. The dry British Richard had been at Christie's, fine-wines division; he had an eye for Islamic art.

As Day was murmuring 'total shit' to himself, he saw a large dog asleep on one of the horsehair sofas. It was a Great Dane, and it was flopped all over the cushions, its tongue hanging out as its chest heaved up and down. He went up to it and was about to pat it when he heard footsteps and Richard walked into the library distractedly, holding a painted paper lamp and a pair of electrical pliers. Startlingly, he had changed into a tuxedo, and he had been drinking pretty steadily. He didn't execute a straight line as he swept into the library as if looking for something. He saw the dog first, sighed and then realised it was Day standing there next to it. The English voice started up like a puff-puff train.

'So it's you. I didn't see you earlier.' The English face tensed as the mind behind it located his name and importance. 'Did Fatima get you a drink? You can't be in a library without a drink.'

'I didn't see Fatima.'

'I'll call her if you want.'

Day shook his head. He sat next to the shaggy dog. Was it snoring?

'Did you bring a girlfriend?' Richard asked, looking through one of his desks. He found a mobile phone and flipped it open.

'Not this time. The girls won't touch me.'

'Oh? Have you been a rascal? Dally tells me you have a thousand girlfriends and they all get on with each other.'

'I have three, and they all hate me.'

'Then you should get down to the pool. Did you see those Russians? *Oh là là.*'

Richard dialled his phone and waited. It rang, but no one answered. He left a message.

'Wondering where you are. Call me. We're eating at eleven. Drive safely.'

He shrugged and looked the American in the eye. There was something insolent about him.

'Who's that?'

'Two English friends. The man's an alcoholic, so I shouldn't have let them drive.'

They walked into the games room and then into a

gallery of small *mirhabs* painted black and white. Long windows showed the *ghorfas* lit up orange, and fruit trees in cherry-red boxes. Richard talked into his phone again.

'Fatima? Are the quails ready? The Santenay should be on ice. *Oui, sur glace.*'

'You have an impressive house,' Day said. 'I can't believe you don't live here.'

'We will live here. One has to get a little older before moving to the desert. One has to give up cities. Dally's not ready yet. I am, I must say. I'm staying on for a few weeks. The fourth tower has to be dealt with.'

'Do people ever get lost driving here?'

'All the time. We say it's part of the charm. The Moroccans leave them alone.'

'That's nice to know.'

'Shall we get some honey? The honey here is the best in the world. Dally and I eat it raw for breakfast with cannabis. It makes your day.'

'In that case, can I have it in bed tomorrow?'

'I'll see to it personally. With strong black coffee.'

'Insha'Allah.'

'I'm glad you're game, Tom. Some people aren't. We don't invite them back.'

The host looked glowing and lean as they walked out into the heat and the amber light of braziers. It was studiously retro, the whole thing, so that one couldn't quite relax. The swimsuited ones were now reborn in their long dresses and the punch was half finished. Moths danced around the stunned white faces and the lightly tanned limbs that moved near each other like particles swirling in water. The Gnawa were playing again. The players closed their eyes and swayed. At first it was grating, even annoying, and then eventually, through sheer dogged repetition, it got into the blood, into the nerves, and Day found himself swaying internally to it. One might as well give in.

Soon he was lost in it. He found a surly French girl and chatted her up as they stood not far from the gate, looking down from time to time at the white dust of the road crossed by tyre tracks. Her eyes were completely black, like a puppy's.

'I can't believe you're a friend of these idiots,' she said. 'I'm only here because of Mohammed Tarki. Do you know Mohammed? He's the coolest. He's only here to fund his film. He's making a film about nomads.'

'At least it isn't gypsies. Or mimes.'

'The nomads are going to save us,' she said gravely. 'They have the right environmental ideas.'

'Do they? Where is Mohammed?' he asked.

'He's over there. The beautiful boy.' She became coquettish. 'He says I look like a nomad, too. Pure.'

At five to eleven the bells were sounded and the guests were asked to seat themselves according to the name cards posted around the table. Tall Berber lamps of painted animal skin were lit around it and the sprays of lilies gave up an unctuous golden pollen that people tasted on their tongues; a pink-white glow bathed the tablecloth and the walls turned gold.

Castored ice bowls held the bottles of Santenay and Tempier rosé, and they were rolled around the room by the boys. The doors were closed against the heat, because the desert wind had risen and it tasted like an iron foundry. A man came in and began playing on an *oud*, bent over it as if these listeners did not exist.

This quiet, thoughtful music went unsavoured, Day thought, and it made him think of the paths that led out of Ubud, among rice paddies and terraces planted with palms so tall that only small children could climb them. A music like moving water because it was improvised, but also a music of great stillness and tenderness. People talked over it because their ears weren't used to it. The *kemia* were brought out – preserved lemon salads, marinated feta and fried beet greens flavoured with pepper accompanied by almond *breewats*. Richard hovered by the doors and looked at his watch repeatedly as the *kemia* were set down. He seemed to give up on his late arrivals and did not draw attention to them as he begged his guests to tuck in. Across from him, Day noticed the two place names that had not been claimed by the English couple. Some part of himself preferred, he had to admit, that the Hennigers had not arrived.

Plates of pigeon *pastilla* were brought in. Day found himself talking to an old Irishman in a filthy beret.

'I was driving along with Maisy when we saw a white couple by the road,' the Irishman said. 'They had obviously just had sex, so we left them alone. "Never interfere with people who've just had sex," I said to Maisy. They get violent.'

'Was that the English couple?' Day said.

'How would I know? I didn't stop. They might have been bandits dressed as English people. Or English bandits.'

The Irish couple laughed, throwing back their heads.

'Are you a homosexual, too?' the woman asked.

'That couple,' Day said, ignoring her. 'Were they having a row?'

'Obviously,' the Irishman snorted.

Rowing couples: they never turned up on time.

'We thought it best to let them get on with it.'

Day looked down the table, at the far end of which sat Dally, peeling eggs with his fingers. The appetizers had lit it with the wet colour of peppers and lemons, of salted olives and tomatoes. The man playing the *oud* stared back into their gazes with slightly shocked eyes, like someone who has seen a ghost. Day tried to hold his gaze. It was easy enough to see what he was thinking. These were unimaginable human beings, large, glossy and loud. They didn't eat with their fingers, and they didn't believe in God. They had descended from far-off lands with their leggy, terrifying girls, and here they were, entities to be reckoned with. They drank wine. Around the walls, the boys stood like caryatids, their hands folded in front of them, their eyes held quite still and expressionless. They were desert boys, Aït Atta or Glaoua, recruited in Errachidia or Taza and paid with food and lodging. They were paid not to react, but to look formidable in a frozen position.

As the meal progressed, a gold clock behind the table made its fussy European sounds marking the hours. The bottles emptied. Soon it was one o'clock. The *tagines* were served, then the pastries. Day talked to a secretive Dutch woman seated to his right, an archaeologist. She had been invited for her expertise and nothing else, and knew no one. Under her breath, she opined that the renovation of the *ksour* was 'a farce'.

'They are typical infidels,' she said seriously. 'They have no taste.'

He wanted to get to bed. Was no one else tired from the day's travels? The rose-water ice cream made his mouth tired. Dally made some toasts, drunk on his feet, his complexion burning with alcohol, and in this state he described, with some difficulties of speech, the long labours that had gone into the *ksour* to make it conform to what he called 'our vision of paradise'. A place in which to receive the people they loved.

'Richard and I never thought it would turn out so well. And we couldn't have done it without the help of our wonderful Moroccan friends.'

The Irishman leaned over to Day. 'Without their friends in the Ministry of the Interior, he means.'

'—I've always been sceptical about that phrase, the global village. But when you actually buy a village—'

As the laughter rose, Day noticed Richard rise and walk to the doors. He looked at his mobile phone, then shot a glance across the table at no one in particular. There was a Moroccan servant on the far side of the glass peering in with a noticeable anxiety. Richard quietly opened the door and slipped out. It was one o'clock or thereabouts and there was no sign of the party winding down. Another round of wine was wheeled out, and the desserts went into round two. Day looked over at the two empty place names. He had forgotten all about them.

Three

HAMID, THE SERVANT, WALKED NEXT TO Richard as they made their way along the flagged path to the main gate. He had been with them for almost seven years and had insinuated his way into their daily lives with a subtle intuition of the ways of rich foreigners. He had been a cook in a tourist hotel in Madrid before joining their household and from those distant Spanish days he retained an awareness of how to deal with men who had known little hardship. He was an encyclopaedia of indigenous proverbs, by which he steered the course of his modest life. Despite his anxiety now, he was controlled in his explanations of the late arrival of *les anglais*, and he resisted any temptation to overstate. He merely used the word *terrible*.

'They arrived five minutes ago, Monsieur. They are in a terrible state. There is something that is terrible in the extreme. There has been an accident down on the main road.'

I knew it, Richard thought darkly.

'When the car arrived at the gate, we saw at once that they had a wounded man in the back seat. Now we have verified, Monsieur. And it is a dead man. It is terrible.'

'Go on.'

'A Moroccan, Monsieur. The English hit him on the road. It is very unclear.'

There was nothing to say. They strode across the open space with the fairy lights in the trees spelling out the word 'Welcome' in Arabic, and Richard wondered what he would say to them. He asked Hamid quickly if he recognised the dead man.

'He's not from here, Monsieur. Who knows who he is?'

Richard knew the Hennigers from London. He had been at school with David. They were fun people. They were droll, rich, spirited, but they argued a lot. That was tiresome. And the doctor had a booze issue. At school (one couldn't remember much), he had been a witty, cruel little prick, but handsome and loyal. There was something crushed about him. He had always reminded Richard of the line from Plato that Dr Amos had drummed into them: 'Be kind, because everyone you meet is having a hard struggle.' But was David having a hard struggle? They kept up through the years; they liked each other, and Richard was always interested to see that big, bristling, angry shape of a man barging through a doorway. He enjoyed the crassly honest insults David shot at people at dinner parties and the way he got drunk – always winking at Richard as if he were putting it on. He was a buffoon, but there are useful buffoons and entertaining ones and even buffoons who make us wonder. The moneyed English buffoon is a particular species. It is much cruder than it lets on – it's a Viking with silverware. Richard smiled. That was Dr Henniger in a nutshell.

'Unclear?' he said to Hamid quietly. 'Why did you say it was unclear?'

'They say he was selling fossils by the road. He stepped out, and they struck him by accident. But it is night. The road there is deserted. There has never been a fossil seller on that road at night. Or in day. That is why it is unclear, Monsieur.' He drew himself up silently for the proverb muttered inside his own mind: 'Open your door to a good day and prepare yourself for a bad one.'

The Camry was parked just inside the gate, and the Hennigers had been taken to their house by the staff. The car was empty but for the body sprawled on the back seat. The servants crowded around with stricken looks, muttering quietly to themselves, three or four torches dancing around the spots of blood. When Richard came up, they drew back. He had a thunderous look on his face, though he was not aware of it, and he was thinking ahead with intensity and rational directness. He looked down and saw the hands of the body, chalk-white now, and noticed a diagonal white scar on the side of the left hand. It was an old scar.

'Does anyone recognise him?' he barked at the boys.

They shook their heads. He grabbed a torch and leaned into the back seat to look at the young, slightly bearded face that could have been peacefully sleeping. It was a boy of about twenty, slender and quite tall. A handsome boy, with a tattoo on his right hand.

'He is from the south,' Hamid said at his elbow.

'*Un chien sauvage,*' someone said.

They looked at his feet, with the sandals still attached to them though the bones had been broken, and at the robe torn in places and speckled with dried blood. The hands were white with dust. Blood had leaked all over the seat and the back of the front seats, too; a pool of it had formed on the car's floor. With no idea who to call, lost in a foreign country, the Hennigers had simply taken the victim with them and brought him here. It was the logical thing to have done. And yet it was incredibly awkward. He told the boys to take the body from the car and lay it out somewhere. Perhaps the garages, where none of the guests would wander.

'Shall we clean the car, Monsieur?'

'No. We have to call the police in Taza.'

Their faces fell and there was a moment's silence. It would take the police an hour to get there, if not more, so there was time for him to talk to the Hennigers. He took Hamid aside as the body was rolled out of the car and laid on a blanket. The hands flopped into the dust, and Richard and Hamid found themselves staring at them uncontrollably. Hamid seemed ashamed of something. He didn't want to be involved in this remarkable disaster.

'Hamid, did you believe their story?'

'But they are your guests. How am I not to believe them?'

'But did you, in fact, believe them?'

'I think they are very scared. They told the truth.'

Hamid's eyes turned away. There were times when discretion was not what Richard wanted from him, but the relation of employer to servant was impossible to surmount. The English were the master's guests. They must be respected. This attitude could not be penetrated.

'Go to the house and tell Monsieur Dally. Whisper in his ear and don't make a fuss. Tell him to meet me in the garage.'

'Yes, Monsieur.'

Richard went back to the car and looked it over. The massive dent on the left bumper was unmistakable enough. The headlight had been shattered and the bumper almost detached. So the boy had crossed the road from the left and been hit. They must have been going at a fair clip. He looked up at the moon and thought it a clear night. He walked through the gate onto the dirt road and looked down at the highway snaking round the bottom of the hill. One could see everything. One could see the formations of lignite on the mountains by the far side of the road, a distance of miles. The moon was full, and nothing escaped it. He'd be interested to hear what their story really was. He hadn't asked Hamid, because he wanted to hear it himself from their own lips. People change their stories rapidly. He opened the phone and lingered among the high roadside weeds for a few moments, wondering if he should explain anything to the police, and then decided not to think about it too much. Every minute of delay was incriminating.

'It is Richard Galloway here. At Ksour Azna.'

The voice at the other end was sluggish and slightly hostile, its French clogged with uncertainties.

'Good evening, Monsieur Galloway. Have you been burgled?'

They laughed. 'No, Yassine, I have an unfortunate situation. You will have to come over at once. A man has been hit by a car.'

'Is it one of your guests?'

'No, we don't know him. He might be local.'

'Is he dead?'

'He was dead when he came in.'

'Was the car belonging to a foreigner?'

'It was.'

'It is a shame.'

There was a dragging irritation in the voice.

37

'Monsieur Richard, keep everyone there, please. Put the body somewhere cool.'

'The kitchen?' he wanted to yell at Yassine.

'And, Monsieur Richard? Do not touch it.'

When Richard got back to the gate, he told the boys to send on a carafe of chilled water to the Hennigers' rooms. Soon Hamid came trotting up.

'Mr Dally, Monsieur, was very upset. One of the other boys must have told him. He has gone down to the garage.'

'I must see the Hennigers first. Is the party going okay?'

'They are all drunk and happy.'

'Perhaps,' Richard wondered aloud, 'I should calm the Hennigers down and get them into the dining room. There's nothing they can do about it now.'

'The others will be getting up from the dinner soon. Coffee and smoke.'

'What we don't want, Hamid, is a panic and a scene. They mustn't know that there's a body on the premises.'

'Naturally not, Monsieur!'

'Can you see to it?'

The paunchy Hamid stiffened. 'Count on me.' But to himself he thought, with disengaged fatalism: Piece by piece the camel enters the *couscous*.

Richard walked through the *ksour* to the little white-washed house where they had put the late arrivals. Most of the houses were still ruined, and they formed pictur-esque streets like those of a bombed city. Twenty were renovated and turned into guest rooms, each one subtly individual. Chalet 22 – they called them 'chalets' – was near the walls, with a small desert garden around it. The windows and door were wide open, and from the interior came the sound of a difficult argument, the voices force-fully lowered but hissing away vigorously. He hung back for a minute or two. Not because he wanted to hear what they were saying, but because he didn't want to embarrass them. Then the wife began to sob.

The husband let it flow for a while, and drifted to the open door. He lit a cigarette and said nothing. Cicadas purred in the rose bushes and around the hairy boles of the palms. The party could be heard easily. David was breathing heavily, confused, indignant. He was sure it wasn't his fault. He was certain of it, and he couldn't talk himself out of his own innocence, not even when he was truthful.

'I heard what happened,' Richard said as he walked out of the shadows and up to the door. Behind them, Jo lay curled on the brocaded tribal cushions of the bed. Richard closed the door behind them and went to put his arm round her. 'It's all right,' he said. There was a smell of sweat and dust in the room, of misery and disputes, and the bags had not yet been unpacked. It was a family scene, a scene of coupledom at its worst.

He had never quite understood how men and women could get on anyway. It seemed so unlikely that deep down he didn't believe in it. Women, he thought dourly, are born recriminators. Yet he had always liked Jo immensely. She was beautiful, spirited, a little mad, and she had that passive-aggressive, almost androgynous nobility that upper-middle-class British women often possessed, a hint of vast tenderness that could never arrive on your plate. She was a complete enigma, and he respected anyone resolute enough to be an enigma. She looked at his tuxedo with a hangdog trustingness. So people were dressed for dinner,

39

which meant that the world was still normal. She dried her eyes. This slender, dry gay man in his perfect tuxedo seemed more authoritative than her deflated husband still covered with dust and another man's blood.

'I think you should change, David. Both of you. I've heard it was an accident. There's nothing you can do. I think you should have showers and go down to dinner. The police will be here in an hour, but they'll want to see the body first, and it will take time. They know you're not going anywhere. And they'll know you've done nothing criminal. It'll be sorted out. The police officer told me to reassure you.'

'Did he?' she broke out.

'He did. I know him. It's all a formality. Perhaps Jo should shower first. You need to get out of those clothes.'

'I'd love a drink,' she said fiercely.

She went into the bathroom, and David changed in the main room. He couldn't stop shaking. Well, Richard thought, let him shake. He was dead sure this irresponsible bastard had had a drink on the road. Should he save him or let him hang? The Moroccan police would not be forgiving about a Breathalyzer test. Richard began as testily as he could.

'I have to ask you. How did it happen? I think you should tell me before you tell the *flics*. So we can iron anything out.'

'We were bowling along looking for the sign for Azna. There was a fossil seller standing by the road, like they always do. We'd seen hundreds of them since Chefchaouen. I couldn't see. There was a lot of sand blowing across the road. Then the guy just stepped in front of us. He wanted us to stop. We thought he would carjack us. We'd heard about the carjackings.'

'Carjackings?'

David threw up one hand. 'It's like he wanted to bluff us. Or commit suicide. It was like he didn't understand the speed of a car.'

Richard didn't know how to deal with an observation like that. A little dry irony?

'These are simple people, David. They don't always understand things like the speed of a car. Some of them don't even know what cars are. They've only seen them in films. Incredible, isn't it? In this day and age.'

'I'm surprised they've seen films.'

'It doesn't matter,' Jo said impatiently. 'The fact is, we hit him.'

Richard relented, and he merely watched David loosen his collar and sweat it out. The doctor didn't even feel the barb. 'These sorts of accidents happen. The main thing is to come clean, cooperate with the police and seem overwhelmingly contrite. Sometimes they will ask for a discreet bribe. We can do that, can't we?'

'If it's absolutely necessary.'

'It might be. We'll see. The guy there now isn't too bad. They'll probably ask you if you knew the kid. They always ask that.'

'How the hell could we have?'

'It's just their way of getting their suspicions out in the open. We have to go along with it.'

They were both English, so there was complicity. Us and them. The 'them' was especially Muslim officials who didn't drink. The question was, did the 'them' include the dead boy lying in the garage? They didn't even know his name. There was no ID on him, and it was highly unusual for a Moroccan not to be carrying ID. There was nothing in his pockets at all, not even a single *dirham* note. Normally, one would laugh.

41

David wondered if Richard was lying. There was something that made him think so. Not massively, but slightly. Lies are excusable, but it depends on what they are, and when he searched David's boxy, hypermasculine face, he found it half open like a box that hasn't been properly closed. The eyes were in eclipse.

Behind them, David crept about unsurely, trying to figure a way out of this mess, and prepared to bend things a little. His face sweated and wouldn't dry, and he rubbed his fingers frantically as if he wanted to get something off them, though he had obviously washed them thoroughly. He kicked off his expensive Oxfords in disgust and his face became petulantly enraged. Gradually he calmed down. Richard sat on the bed next to him while they listened to the woman showering in the next room. They had known each other for some time in London, but they had never seen each other elsewhere. Richard watched him gulp down the pitcher of water.

'It's so damn hot,' David moaned.

'Yes, it's the Sahara, old boy.'

'I know. But it's *so* hot.'

His teeth chattered.

'Have you told me everything, David? You might as well tell me everything, so I can help you.'

'I have.'

'Have you really?'

David tried to get up, then sat down again. 'I'm very sorry for the trouble. We both are. Incredibly sorry.'

'It's not something to apologise for. As long as I know you've remembered everything correctly.'

'I'm not sure I know what you mean.'

'You're okay to be grilled by this fat slob of a policeman? Do you speak any French?'

'Of course I speak French. And why would I not be okay?'

Richard got up and suddenly felt claustrophobic. A few stray thoughts rushed through his mind. The DJ from London, the people who wanted to arrive by helicopter – Lord Swann – the supply of dates and sugar from Errachidia, the pool party they were going to throw the following night. There was too much to remember. And the paparazzi they had turned away at the gates. It was all going awry and he was getting a headache.

The shower stopped and David began organising a fresh shirt. He dithered and his fingers struggled with buttons. 'Come down to dinner, both of you. No one will know anything. And if they do, what have you done wrong? You're as much victims as that poor kid.' Again, Richard's brisk tone to keep up morale.

David nodded, and tied up his shoes. He had nothing more to say and his shoulders slumped forward. He was like a Pinocchio with snipped wires, and it would take a miracle to get him rewired before the weekend was out. For the first time, Richard felt sorry for him. He leaned down and whispered, 'David, did you have a drink earlier?'

'Rubbish.'

Before Richard could ask again, Jo emerged. She was now noticeably less tense. Her skin had revived, and soon the three of them were upright, ready to roll. They sauntered back to the house in a chattering of egrets. By the opulently lit doors, the staff stood awkwardly, their nervousness written large on their faces, while bats wheeled close to their heads.

'Never mind the bats,' Richard drawled. 'They only live for twenty-four hours.'

There was a look of terror on Jo's face. It had suddenly dawned on her that this was a very elegant party and she didn't know anyone there. She faltered at the threshold as the sound of massed voices no longer in control of themselves swept through the opening doors and the candlelight burst on their eyes. She looked round at Richard and said, 'Aren't you coming in?'

'I have to go to the garage. That's where the boy is.'

'Couldn't you stay?'

'Not now. David will be next to you.'

She didn't seem very reassured.

'*Entrez*,' one of the staff said gently, holding open the door for her. The air-conditioning was a shock, and she hesitated.

'Go on,' Richard said. 'Be brave.'

But what did braveness have to do with it?

The boy had been laid out on one of the work tables in the garages — former stables that had been converted into a space for five cars. Between two jeeps, the mangled body lay in its stained *djellaba* with three oil lamps standing around it. Disturbed by the sight, the staff had turned off the overhead neon light and stood around the corpse, not knowing what to think. Dally was with them, pacing round the table without looking at it, and Hamid was there with him, observing him anxiously. Dally, he was thinking, was not a cool head. He overreacted to everything. He was not a commanding man. He cursed under his breath and kept asking Hamid when the police were arriving.

'They arrive when they arrive,' Hamid replied icily.

'It's a fucking disaster,' the American muttered.

The boy's hands were spread out on either side of him, and the eyes had been closed; the blood had come to a standstill. The staff whispered among themselves. Before them lay the considerable mystery of his identity.

Different tribes dealt in different fossils, and only black-market dealers crossed the lines. The Aït Atta, for example, dealt in crinoids. That much they knew. But was he Aït Atta? Some of the staff claimed that he might be from the north-facing mountains, those who called themselves 'the Atta of the shadow'. Some thought he might be Aït Iazzer or even Aït Merad. But they had no way of saying. They were merely speculating to dispel their unease.

Richard came in finally, at half past one. He was flustered and his face was damp, and when he saw the body, he went cold and officious.

'I want to know if we emptied his pockets thoroughly?'

'It was illegal,' Hamid whispered, 'but we did it anyway.'

'There was nothing in them,' Dally snapped. 'Which is not really possible. Where are the Hennigers?'

'They're at dinner. I think I calmed them down.'

'Was he drunk?'

'Not at all. I don't know what happened.'

'Not drunk *now*,' Dally sneered. 'He ran right over him. The kid wasn't just hit. Am I right, Hamid?'

They thought for a while. Richard stepped slowly round the table. The boy had cropped hair, dark-bronze skin with blue tattoos. A high, perfect, aristocratic nose and wide, sensual lips. It was a tragic waste of an exquisite boy, he thought airily.

Dally took his arm, going into a rapid English that would make their words private in front of the staff. He was visibly upset.

'What are we going to do, Richard? You've called the *flics*. So now it's going to be a circus.'

45

'What would you suggest?'

'I think we should get it settled tonight. We can pay them.'

'Settled? They have to find out who he is first. When they find that out, it might change.'

'Jesus, are you kidding?'

'I don't think we have anything to worry about. It's clear what happened.'

'Oh, is it? Is it clear that he has nothing on him? It's like he's been robbed. I don't think anything is clear at all. I think that Limey is hiding something. Any chance to fuck with us and they will.'

'They?' Richard opened his eyes wide.

'The Moroccans. They *will*, too. They will fuck with us.'

'He must have a family,' Richard said quietly, nodding at the body.

'That's what I mean. The family will show up – and then they'll fuck with us. They'll say the infidels killed their boy.'

'They might, yes. Which would be true.' Then he added, 'Dally, you really should calm down a bit. They're not going to fuck with us.'

Hamid looked at them intently, since he understood at least half of what they were saying, and his eyes seemed to pluck words out of the air and devour them. He understood that they were discussing fear of Moroccans. It was only natural. The rumours would spread like wildfire, and he wanted to touch them on the shoulder and tell them how little liked they were by the *indigènes*. Or rather, how little trusted they were. He was inclined to offer them some help, but he also enjoyed their sudden helplessness. It was interesting, to say the least. Truly, there was no queue of people waiting at the gate of Patience.

'What do you think, Hamid?'

'I think, Monsieur, we should tell the staff to not tell anyone in Tafnet.'

And he smiled, because it was impossible.

'Yes,' Richard said dutifully. 'Can you ask them?'

Suddenly there were tears in Dally's big brown eyes and a cow-look ruined his superbness.

'How?' he moaned.

The staff stirred, and they pulled out a chair for him. Richard asked them to close the doors to the garage and keep them shut. The guests' cars were all parked in the open, inside the *ksour* walls. It was childish, because of course they would find out, and it was not as if they would come storming down to the garage in a mob. It was more to calm Dally and help him retain his sanity.

'Get us some drinks from the house, will you?' Richard said to Hamid. 'Two Scotches. We'll take them outside.'

The weather had been stifling lately. The Chergui was blowing, with its saline taste and its withering scorn. Living things scattered before it.

They went outside to the gate, and the light of the stars cooled their minds by emptying them. The river echoed below, with its promise of cool, and gradually Dally stopped crying. 'That poor fucking kid,' he kept saying, as if he wanted to pound something with his fist. His brown silk shirt looked self-mocking now and faintly ridiculous.

The moon lit the rolling intermediate mountains the Moroccans called the *dir*, 'the belt', and which spanned the desert and the High Atlas. Hamid brought the drinks on a tray and set it on the low wall by the road. They were going to wait for Captain Yassine Benihadd here, apparently, though, in his opinion, it did not show good form in front of the local police. He could sense that they

47

were both panicking. Was their beautiful way of life, their partial exile, so detailed and meticulously planned, now in danger of being destroyed?

Two pairs of headlights shot up from the road below.

'Monsieur,' Hamid said gravely, 'it is the police. I will take away the drinks.'

Four

'WE WERE SAYING YOU MUST HAVE HAD an accident, but Mohammed said it was a flat tyre — they always get flats out in the desert — and we all felt sorry for you. A flat tyre, and in the dark! What a drag. Was it?'

'Don't ask them now,' Day said to the tiresome French girl. 'Can't you see they want to eat?'

'It's all right,' Jo said, her mouth trembling. 'We just need to recover.'

'People disappear here.' The girl laughed. 'They just vanish. Did the Arabs molest you?'

'I didn't catch your name,' David said stonily.

'Isabelle. I'm taking photographs of villages around here.'

'She's a nomad,' Day said. 'Her name's really Fatima Baba.'

'Je suis photographe.'

'She says she's a photograph.'

'Oh,' said David, not getting the joke.

The lamb and prune *tagine* appeared before the Hennigers. They didn't react, and then the beet salad and some warmed-up bread, and the room was so loud that soon they were almost forgotten, and Jo was relieved.

49

To be forgotten is dinner-party bliss. She ate too quickly and then the wine came, the cold, familiar Tempier that brought her back to memories of Europe, and she thought: I'll just get drunk, too, it's a way out. Gradually her nervousness dulled and her head cleared. The lilies suddenly caught her eye, and then the German crystal, the hard brightness that money buys and taste arranges, like waking up in a place in which you went to sleep but don't remember.

A few other guests called down the table. 'Welcome!' 'Sorry you had a hassle!' 'Remember us from Rome?' But she didn't recognise any of them. They were all remarkably dressed up for a desert dinner, with their buttonholes and linen suits and strapless dresses, and the man across from her, the American, was wearing a *poppy* in his lapel. He looked at her for long periods, unblinking, concentrating on her. She shot a look back at him and, for a second, their suspicions tangled, wrestling each other in mid-air.

'Did you pass Beni Mellal?' asked the Dutch lady whom Day had talked to earlier. David tried to be peppy.

'We came through Midelt. It's a different road, you see. Very scenic.'

'But that's a main road. Did you get lost, then?'

'We didn't get lost,' David said determinedly. 'It was just a long slog of a drive. It's through the high mountains.'

'It's the road most of us came on,' Day said.

'Yes, but we didn't know it.'

The room mellowed a little, and without anyone noticing, the *oud* player left the room with his instrument. Jo swung back her head to empty her glass. She didn't want to lie any more. She found the women down the table looking at her with humorous disbelief. A marital quarrel, they were thinking; a roadside row that must have looked funny to passers-by. The men looked at her with a different interest. Was she tellingly detached from her glowering husband?

'Yes,' David agreed, putting pieces of bread into his mouth like a small boy. 'But we're not used to the roads here. And it was dark. There was a sandstorm, too. We didn't know which turning it was.'

'So it wasn't a flat tyre?' Isabelle asked. 'You were just lost?'

'Exactly.'

'Not exactly,' Jo said coldly.

The table went quiet, and the mocking American put down his fork.

'Oh?' Day said.

'No, not exactly. On the way here we had an accident. We hit a Moroccan on the road and killed him.'

David turned to her, and his blush darkened. The party came to a standstill, and for some time the guests simply stared at the slightly bedraggled, beanpole English-woman who wrote children's books for a living and who was not really part of their game.

'Are you sure?' someone said.

Jo put her hand in front of her mouth and soon they understood that she was laughing, but that the laughter wasn't normal.

'It was an accident,' David said unnecessarily. 'He stepped in front of us.'

Jo ate while the room went quiet. She ate with her fingers. She no longer cared what they thought, and her body craved food. The *couscous* was sweetened with sugar and lines of melted cinnamon, and it warmed her, made the blood move inside her face. She peered round the room, at the gold frames of the paintings and the Egyptian glassware on the side-tables, and she felt the salty tang of pollen on her tongue. It was an incredible place, an Ali Baba palace. There was something Rudolph Valentino about it. You could imagine it in Whitley Heights in Los Angeles.

The lilies were opened up and their petals were beginning to ripen. The wine in the Riedel glasses was as dark as blood and you could see little peering faces reflected in them. The silver tureen in the centre of the table had lounging Titans for handles. A grotesque ladle leaned against it. Then she realised that she was spilling *couscous* grains all over the tablecloth and her lap. Her hand was not quite steady. Something stuck to her chin and her fingers were sticky. She was eating like a child.

The French girl looked at her archly and the others didn't know how to look at her. A few commiserations came in, and the hubbub returned. David licked his lips and looked away, his fist tightened around the stem of his glass, and far off in the depths of the house there was a tinkle of moving service trolleys and a sound of padding dogs, a comforting domesticity. How stupid it had been to come here. She felt tears rushing into her eyes, sticking to the lashes and hanging there like something poisonous and knowing.

'Was it an Arab?' Day said quietly.

The doors opened and Hamid was there, sallow and ruffled. He motioned to her and his lips mimed the word *Madame*. It was clear that the police were there.

'I think you're wanted,' Isabelle said.

* * *

The Hennigers walked behind Hamid as they made their way across the repaved paths towards the gate. The servant held up a metal lantern and turned to make sure they hadn't been abducted by evil spirits. His deepest superstitions were now aroused and he didn't want to be around these two cursed individuals who had taken the life of a Muslim on the road. They didn't seem remorseful. It is their way, Hamid thought with a bitterness of his own. They are like stones when it comes to us. They think we are flies.

As they walked past one of the braziers, sparks flew into his eyes and he picked up his pace. David was saying to Jo, 'I can't understand why you did it. Was it to humiliate me?'

'One can't keep pretending for ever. Why lie to them?'

Up ahead, lamps had been laid around their car. There were Moroccan policemen standing around it taking photographs of the bumpers and the wheels, kneeling close to the car's body. The gate floodlights had been turned off and the stars were as bright as the camera flashes.

'It would be madness to tell them there were two. We need to snuff this business out *now*. It wasn't our fault, was it?'

'I don't know why I agreed,' she whispered. 'I don't know why I went along with it.'

'They wanted the car. You seriously think I'm getting involved with this just because some carjacker wanted to shoot us in the head?'

'Carjacker?'

'You haven't been reading the papers. I have.'

He was drenched with sweat when they got to the open gate, where Benihadd and Richard were standing with a jug of iced lemonade. The Moroccan, he thought, looked him over with sceptical detachment before going to his wife, kissing her hand and saying *'Chère Madame'*. Benihadd wanted them to walk with him a little on the road outside, on which they had driven a few hours before, and he asked them in a courtly way, as if refusal would be all right with him, and soon they were strolling along the high edge of the road while the captain asked casual questions to put them at their ease. So David had a practice in Chelsea? That was a splendid *quartier*, wasn't it?

'And you, Madame. You write children's books?'

'Yes. Not very successful ones.'

'I am sure they are successful. May I have a title I can look up for my children?'

'My last one was *The Little House*.'

'Ah, but it is charming! Do you not find, Monsieur Galloway?'

'Charming,' Richard said.

Benihadd then made David go through the details of the accident.

'There was a sandstorm earlier,' the Englishman insisted, a little exasperated by the clarity of the moon now. He could see the other two were not convinced. 'It blew up suddenly, and we were lost.'

After he had finished, the captain looked down at David's boots.

'It was clear,' David added, 'that he was not interested in selling us fossils. How could he be? At midnight?'

'Monsieur Henniger, people here are sometimes desperate. It may seem surprising to you, but they will do almost anything to sell a single fossil. A trilobite, for example. For forty euros. It is a good sum for them.'

'I am aware of that. Of course. I know they are poor.' Nervously, David ran a hand through his hair. 'I am terribly sorry for all this, Captain. We are devastated. Devastated.'

Dévastés in French, but with the emphasis on the wrong syllable. The captain smiled and looked down at his nails.

'I am sure you are. But an accident is an accident. By the way, I was wondering. Are you sure there was only one man?'

'One.'

'Are you sure?'

'I couldn't be surer.'

Benihadd opened his arms as if to say, 'Well, there we are!'

They walked on. Could that really be it? she wondered incredulously. Corruption was marvellous sometimes. So easy, so quick, so essential. She didn't want to feel relieved, but she did, and as the load was lifted from her mind, her nostrils flared and picked up the aromas of the desert evening. There was a taste of smoke, and the wind rose and fell with sudden changes of direction. She hung behind them and her eye was drawn sideways to the tumbledown ravine with the palm grove at the bottom. There was also a faint scent of jasmine wafting up from it, and of animal manure. Beyond the river lay a series of jagged crests coloured like iron, upon which a few dun-coloured tents stood with long ropes mooring them to the ground. She had not noticed them before, and her curiosity was stirred. She felt intensely alone. She had little idea where she was. The desert, or its western edge. But what was the desert? And where did the river come from and where did it go? Didn't deserts and rivers contradict one another?

She heard her husband say to the policemen, 'We are very grateful, if there's anything we can do . . .' Her lungs filled with hot, clean air and her palms began to perspire in a quiet way, growing moister in ten-minute leaps. On the tops of the cliffs, goats stood in silence, peering down at the river as if contemplating suicide.

Richard turned, hung back and took her arm. He knew that she was covering something up, but he didn't say anything; he didn't hold it against her. It was a just a riddle that would not open yet.

'They're going to record it as an accidental death. I hope you can enjoy the rest of the weekend. After all this.'

'I want to sleep,' she said.

He wagged his finger, as if cancelling out this desire. 'But tomorrow we have the fire-eaters from Taza!'

As soon as the Hennigers left the room there was an uproar of gossip about them, and the dinner broke up with laughter and a rush for things to smoke. The doors leading to the central hall and the library were opened wide, and the guests began to drift out of the dining room.

They surged slowly into the library. More French windows opened onto a spacious patio that had been recently built, with abstract sculptures at the four corners. A bar had been set up here to concoct hot chocolate, Ovaltine and chamomile tea as bedtime elixirs; they were made up by an old man in ceremonial costume who worked by the light of a tall tubular oil lamp. There were orange trees in boxes here and taped Arab music.

The huddled, half-ruined buildings of the *ksour* shone like graphite under the moon. These fortified villages were built to repel the outside world. Next to the library, however, were yet more rooms that invited exploration. A 'tea room' with painted wood panels and an octagonal ceiling decorated with images of desert flamingos; a white 'reading room' with no books, just long Arab sofas and horsehair Indian Raj armchairs waxed to a colour of dark mustard. On the second floor there was another lounge, vast and cool, with antique telescopes and cartographic globes and rugs woven near Tinerhir. A flat-screen high-definition TV stood at one end, with a circular couch and various remote controls. The wide windows looked over the valley with military authority.

When David and Jo came back to the house, the air was filled with the smell of marijuana. The lounge was crammed with people, many of them lying on the floor and eating McVitie's crackers slathered with *majoun*, a mix of *kif*, dried fruits, nuts and sometimes fig jam. Some had fallen asleep where they fell, stuffed and stoned and exhausted. David and Jo recognised no one, and their determination to enjoy themselves a little after their ordeal began to ebb. They went back downstairs and wandered onto the baking patio, where sand was blowing about. David got them hot chocolates and they sat on the only bench, listening to the precarious voices babbling away on the first floor. They had no idea what to say to each other. The chocolate calmed them, however. They could hear animals walking around the perimeter wall, a pack of dogs, and the cooks playing guitars nearby. The Moroccan world was close and far off, concrete and abstract at the same time. The different modulation of the Moroccan voices made them carry far. There was something mocking in it, a fractious edge. Jo could sense them commenting privately on the absurd *gaouri*, the 'Romans', and their insolent women. Their food, their grotesque perfumes, their bad manners. She heard their bursts of laughter. 'It's directed at us,' she thought. 'They think of us as flies.' The cooks guffawed and the guitar fell silent for a few minutes.

David merely said, 'I don't like the sound of those bloody dogs. Don't they have a boy to drive them off?'

He had taken her hand, pressed it carefully. It was going to be all right now, except that it wasn't.

'I think they're wild camels,' she said. 'One of the staff said so.'

'They could still drive them off. Camels bite. No, they do. They like to bite people in the stomach. It's the leading cause of death among the Arabs. They should drive them off with water cannons.'

She began to laugh, or tried to.

'We should go to sleep, David. We must.'

'Why? I'm loosening up finally.'

'The sun'll be up in two hours, won't it? I want to sleep it off. I want to wake up again.'

He looked for the moon and didn't find it.

'You know, they won't come back, the police. It's over.'

There was something unintentionally nasty in the way he said it, something hasty and unseemly.

'I can't see how Richard did it,' she muttered. 'Did he bribe them? What the fuck did he do?'

'It wasn't that. Honestly, I think it's not for us to know. I think it's just a huge hassle for the police. There's too much paperwork involved. And, I hate to say it ...'

'Say it.'

'The kid is a nobody. He's dirt poor. He's from some village far away and no one knows who he is. There's nothing to be done.'

'What have we done, then?'

'I didn't mean it like that. I'm just stating the fact.'

He hugged her. The old gentleman fixing the hot chocolates snuffed the last candle, bowed and wished them goodnight. David thought about Benihadd's refusal to take the body away with him. 'We do not have a morgue at our post,' he had said. 'There will have to be arrangements tomorrow.' And he had added, without even a trace of irony, 'Here, even the garages are air-conditioned!'

They waited for him to close the doors behind him, a kind discretion. But they got up anyway and, once again, they didn't know what to say to each other. The facts were between them, stifling them. The dead boy was in the garage with the air-conditioning turned on, and a man sat next to him in vigil, praying next to a pot of mint tea. They were assassins.

They made their way back to the chalet without a servant.

'David, are you afraid at all?'

He said nothing, shaking his head. In the chalet, yellow leather *babouches* and hemmed towels had been laid out for them with a silver pot of sweetened tea. There was a note from Richard. 'Try and sleep. There's nothing to worry about.'

'I am not afraid,' David said in bed. 'Why should I be afraid?'

She lay awake, tormented, while he snored.

The wind quickened, and soon it was howling all down the valley. It spat sand from the deep desert all over the *ksour* of Azna like a hail of indescribable fineness. The casements and roofs hissed. The palm groves hissed, and the dogs scattered. The staff playing their guitars covered their heads with the hoods of their *burnouses* and in the garage the flames guttered and the man drinking tea suddenly looked up. Jo lay in the overblown and slightly Gothic four-poster waiting for the Ambien to kick in, a candle burning inside a lantern of coloured glass. She listened. Men were running through the dark. The great wooden slab of the door began to sweat.

As the night ended, the staff assembled by the garages out of their fanciful uniforms. They gathered by the doors in their workaday *burnouses* and smoked cigarettes together as the sand pitter-pattered around them. A grey light lit the half-ruined mud walls as the fairy lights were turned off. A tumultuous mood connected them, drew them together, though they said almost nothing. The ferocity of the wind was enough to restrain them. But rumours still flashed here and there. They pressed into the garages in small groups and paid their respects, looking down on the colourless corpse with a mixture of dread and determined fascination. Outside, someone muttered the word *roadkill.* By the gate, the cooks cowered from the wind, looking out at the brownish miasma that smothered the road and the cliffs. What they had seen in the garage made them vaguely mutinous, though they wouldn't mutiny against a cushy job. There were motivated by a rage that was not clear even to themselves. Deep down, they did not and could not accept the idea of an accident. A Muslim had been killed by a Christian. The mind could not accept it entirely, except on the flimsy level of reason.

'I have heard,' one of them said, 'that his legs were pulped. They ran over him, maybe more than once.'

'My uncle is right. They think of us as flies. They cannot help themselves. And they are not mindful.'

'They must have reversed over him. It defies belief.'

'It was fate, then.'

'But they did not hesitate. They reversed over him.'

They winced in the wind and considered the word *reversed.* It was typical. Of course the infidels reversed. They didn't want a witness to their blundering, their crime. They covered their tracks. It was unsurprising, and it was probably unconscious on the part of the foreigners. That was the most incredible thing about it. Just as you would swat a fly.

'The police have done nothing,' one of them commented, rubbing his index finger against his thumb.

'What do you expect them to do?'

Money: that was the issue. The foreigners always had it.

Five

_____

WHEN THE SCAR ON THE DEAD BOY'S LEFT hand was mentioned, some of them, thinking back with care, remembered a tall boy with a subtle distraction written across his face, an anger that they recognised, but which in him was more prolonged, more deepened by events that were not disclosed. Perhaps, they thought, that was him. A loping, tense boy who worked in the prepping yards in Erfoud and who had a scar on his left hand from an accident with a lathe. It was him, they thought.

His name was Driss. He had emigrated to France some time back. When he returned, he had gone to work at the Mirzan quarry at the same wage he had enjoyed a year earlier. He lodged in Erfoud. Ismael, the younger boy who had stood with him that night by the road as the Hennigers drove up drunk and wild-eyed, sometimes saw him prepping outside near the telecommunications tower in the centre of the town. His head covered with sacking to keep the sun off him and chipping away with his meticulous technique at Tridents he obtained on the black market. He had prepped all his life, like Ismael. It was what he knew, and for that reason he hated it.

Ismael watched. Driss seemed badly dressed and irritable, as if his French adventure had failed, and he smoked a lot of *kif* in the evenings with the boys from Alnif who worked in the prepping yards. He looked thinner and more anguished, and he talked without the loose charm that had once made him a favourite with the girls. Such transformations, Ismael reasoned, happened among the unbelievers.

Ismael saw him at the Green Coconut and the Hotel Tafilalet talking loudly at the ammonite bar, boasting about the money he made from tourists at the five-star *ksour* hotels on the outskirts of town. Soon they were hanging out. Driss came to the quarry on off-days, and he was there before first light, squatting by the entrance with his teapot and his harmonica waiting for the little girls to come down and give him pieces of bread from the foreman. They worked in the intolerable afternoons chiselling out a great ancient fish that a customer from Spain had commissioned for a private bar. They stayed till after dark, making fires on the top of the cliff and looking down at the walls studded with ammonites and crinoids that remained half emergent, their demonic provenance so obvious that it did not merit attention. Nightmare forms that no human, and certainly no reasonable God, could have dreamed up. They were demons that had fallen long ago from the skies and lain for thousands of years among humans, not part of God's created world. They came from another dimension, from the malevolent spirit world. Their faces were supernatural, it could not be denied. They caused nightmares to appear among the believers, they were hostile to love and peace. Violence was their fruit.

Is was then that the flies dispersed at last and Ismael and Driss lay under the honey moons with their pipes and Driss talked about his time abroad. It was as if he had never talked about it with anyone. It was because Ismael had known him when they were kids. They were always together in those days and they had started at the quarry together.

'The problem with you,' Driss said as they lay watching the sunset after the quarry workers had left for town, 'is that you stayed a kid. You never left the *bled*. It's too bad.'

'I'll leave one day.'

'Yeah, but you never left until now. What counts is what you did, not what you're gonna do. You understand that, *mec*?'

Ismael could only nod dejectedly. True, he had done nothing, nothing at all, and he never would do anything.

Driss rolled a joint of fresh sweet green weed and they shared it as a way of sealing themselves off from the heat.

'Once you cross the sea,' he went on, 'everything in your head changes. Everything falls apart. You look at everything differently. Some French broad said to me, "Travel broadens the mind."'

'What?'

'Ah, never mind. French broads are always talking. It just stayed with me, that one.'

He smiled at the younger boy's naïveté, because Ismael could only take his word for everything.

'The French broads,' the latter said. 'Do they go with us?'

'The scabby ones do.'

But the others? Ismael thought.

'As for the fine ones, forget it.'

A shame, the younger boy thought.

They lay still, smoking.

'When you have some dough,' Driss said, 'they will consider it.'

'How much?'

'Two hands' full.'

'*Ah, les salopes.*'

'*Leurs salopes sont comme les nôtres.*'

'I knew it, by God.'

The lit joint flared up and showed Driss's face tautened by pessimistic pride, but not by the disdain suggested by his phrases. He was never obvious. Even his toughness was not obvious; it was not like the toughness of other boys. You would never guess he was barely twenty-one. He could lie on bare stone without moving for hours, unmoved, consumed by thoughts that seemed to come and go inside him like wild animals, and nothing showed on his face but the vibrations of those 'animals'. He had learned to not show anything, and to Ismael he revealed only his experiences, not his emotions.

Sometimes Driss slept in the quarry, in the geometrical trenches, wrapped in a piece of tarpaulin. It didn't seem to affect him. He came and went and no one knew anything about him. He wore a *chech* wound tightly around his head and his eyes darted out with their gentle ferocity and you were left guessing by their mildness and coldness. He was eager to talk after the sun had gone down and the stars brought out his volubility.

They made a fire when the nights were chilly, and Driss talked about the arguments with his father, that narrow-minded bumpkin, and how he had hitched a ride to Midelt and then Azrou and then down to Fez, a city like no other, a city he would have stayed in if there had been any work other than in the stinking tanneries.

He asked Ismael if he had ever been farther than Midelt, and the boy shook his head.

'You're all the same,' Driss snorted. 'You never go anywhere.'

'It's the money. How can one live?'

'If one wants to live, one finds a way. The world is made for living in. Why are you so scared of it?'

'One never knows.'

'Ismael, you have no instinct. That's why you're always afraid of the unknown. I thought to myself, All men are the same everywhere. They can be used, exploited, befriended.'

Ismael crouched on the rock and looked into the fire. They were roasting goat from the Erfoud market; the bread lay in the open under a stone. Down in the road, the lamps of the fossil diggers on their bikes floated slowly past in the clouds of moonlit sand, edging their way back to the perimeters of the town where pale lights stood guard and the trees had not yet died. He couldn't imagine them, let alone Spaniards and Frenchmen. The world, when he considered it, was not a place where instinct could carve out a safe passage.

'Still,' he muttered defensively, 'you need a bit of cash for the road.'

'I left with nothing. My father refused to give me a single *dirham*. He couldn't have cared less and he said that if I went to France, I would die there.'

'*Ah, le salaud.*'

'They are beaten-down slaves. I told him so to his face.'

Well, Ismael thought, I am only eighteen. When I am Driss's age, I will have gone beyond Midelt. I will have done something.

And he promised himself without uttering a word.

'He laughed,' Driss went on bitterly. 'He said I'd end up as a janitor if I was lucky.'

'It is what fathers say to keep us safe.'

'He is jealous of me, like all fathers. That's all.'

Insulting their fathers made Ismael nervous, and he said nothing. He scratched his ear and waited for the conversation to move on, and he felt the coiled tension inside the older boy.

'But you came back,' he said at length.

Driss admitted that it was inevitable.

'I didn't like the food over there. Unbelievers are unbelievers.'

Yes, so much was unpleasantly undeniable, and Ismael said so.

'But still,' he added, 'we have to make money here.'

'I have a plan,' Driss said. 'Don't you worry about making money. There's money everywhere here. Look around you.'

But it's not for us, Ismael thought. It's for Norway.

Driss lay on his back and stared up at the constellations, none of which he knew.

'I know what you think, Ismael. You are not bold.'

'I think too . . .'

'You think that you don't want to spend the rest of your life hammering at fossils in a trench. But you are vague. You do not have a plan.'

'No,' the other conceded.

When they were a little stoned, Ismael asked him about France. Did he remember the pictures of Sweden that Driss's father so treasured that he stuck to the walls of his house? A land green and wet, with wonderful, fearsome pornography and hotels with fireplaces. A land protected by clouds. A land blessed by someone else's god.

'It is not green,' Driss corrected him. 'The clouds make it grey.'

They laughed.

'Truly,' Ismael said.

'I wouldn't exchange it for my desert. The tar of my country is better than the honey of others.' It was a good proverb.

'You would exchange it.'

'I was there, you fool. Everything there deceived me. It is not what you think, what you all think. You have it all wrong, you suckers. There is nothing there for us.'

'Nothing at all?'

Driss shook his head.

'Nothing at all. Even the sex is not for us.'

'It's a shame.'

'Perhaps, perhaps not.'

Driss reached over and opened the can of Red Bull they had brought for the morning. Ismael's burning curiosity irritated him, and yet it was an audience at least. His nightmares had been coming back, and when he slept out at Mirzan, he had visions. The foreman's little children used to throw stones at him until their father intervened. He let them torment him – it probably did them good. It was a favour the foreman would return later. That night, he would dream of the motorway from Málaga to the French border, which he had traversed on the back of a vegetable truck driven by a *maghrébin*. An endless road worthy of a nightmare.

Ismael lit his second joint and they braced themselves against the wind blowing up from the road, where nothing could be seen.

'But tell me,' he said. 'How did you get to Spain? And you with no money and no papers. How did you do it?'

'It's a long story, and the truth is, I made it up as I went along. I had no real plans.'

'You went to Spain on an illegal boat, the preppers say.'

'True. I landed on the other side, but it was not as you all think. There was no trouble. I landed next to a luxury marina and swam in.'

'God be thanked.'

'It wasn't even luck. The traffickers waited until the coastguards were away. It made me laugh.'

So that's how it was, Ismael thought. Anyone could do the same.

'You paid them,' he said to Driss.

The older boy began to talk. He didn't care if Ismael was even there; he only wanted to talk about himself.

'It was July,' he said, 'and the heat had come. I walked through the marina at three in the morning, the marina called Sotogrande. No one even noticed me. I had nothing, not even a bag. Not even a watch. Nothing stopped me.'

Six

AN HOUR PAST DAWN A FEW GUESTS WERE
seen wandering about the *ksour* in evening clothes, asking
directions and in some instances demanding breakfast. It
had been prepared. In the dining room, tables were already
set, freshened by pots of lilacs. The coffee was being brewed;
croissants and pastries baked in the ovens. The whole
building smelled of hot butter and coffee and the sugar of
the sweating lilacs. The windows had been closed against
the inclement weather and the overhead fans switched on.
A single man sat at a table, a German journalist who had
managed to procure a day-old newspaper. The staff on duty
in the room watched him swat the flies that buzzed around
his head. On the insides of the windows, hundreds of these
same grey flies seemed to have collected. They were sheltering from the scalding Chergui, which had pushed the
thermometers up to a hundred and fifteen degrees overnight. It was a sign of bad weather indeed when the flies
came inside to escape. The servants had been ordered to
kill them with aerosol insecticides.

Hamid was in charge of the younger boys. After a
brief sleep, he walked up to the gate and dispersed them
to their duties. The sun came up, dimmed by dust and

sand, and the early-morning types among the guests became more numerous. They walked about in their dressing gowns and *babouches*, cheerful and yawning, and exchanged notes with other guests. Hamid wondered if they were discussing the accident of the night before. But there was no apprehension in their faces. It was the sand, the wind, that was disturbing them most. Sand had got into the yogurt; it was in their hair, in their teeth. They were not prepared for the sand, not by a long shot. Overnight, it had turned into a formidable enemy. An enemy that was so small, so insidious that they could not fight it. Nothing is more enraging than an unfair fight. The women complained; the men gritted their teeth and asked the staff for assistance. 'With the sand?' the staff asked incredulously.

'Don't you have screens? Masks?'

Hamid dashed about. Apart from an unsatisfactory nap he hadn't slept in twenty-four hours, but there was so much to do. The champagne in the cellars had to be counted and calculated for both lunch and the evening party. The *couscous* deliveries from the local villages had to be coordinated; a consignment of dates and fresh mint was arriving shortly. His head buzzed. The masters were sleeping it off in the top bedroom in Tower 1, as they called it, and they could not be disturbed. The daily running of the operations was up to him. Truly, the world had not promised anything to anyone and no man ever lived the way he wished.

In the garage, the dead boy seemed to be sleeping as well. His skin had turned a tint of blue, and his lips were black. Those keeping vigil began to wonder what would happen next. Under Islamic law, a body must be buried with haste, but no one had yet claimed him. They hoped that the invisible gossip wires of the desert would send this news far into the interior. That someone would come. The police had said they would wait until sundown.

But Hamid was disturbed by this arrangement. He was not sure that it was lawful, that it followed custom. Discreetly, therefore, he prepared a bicycle to transport the body to the local graveyard if it became necessary. He went to the gate and peered down the road, checking his watch. His heart was beating irregularly, very irregularly indeed. He had the feeling that he was being watched, that his heartbeats were actually being counted.

Seven

JO WAS RUNNING IN HER DREAM, BUT
suddenly her eyes opened: a butterfly hovered against
the glass, a twist of black velvet and lemon, and the
casement was filled with sunlight. The sand had fallen
still. In the dream she was running downhill towards
a glade of poplar trees where there was a well
surrounded by crows pecking at grains in the loose earth
round about. She knew it from somewhere. The lid of
the well had been discarded, and she felt that someone
had got there before her, someone who was hidden
somewhere. But she came down anyway among the
trees, and for a few moments the dream and the insect
pressed against the glass in real life merged confusingly.
In the dream the sun was hot as it slanted through the
poplars and she came to the edge of the well and peered
in. Just as the dream was breaking apart, she knew that
she had been running through it all night. She peered
down and saw the flash of a black reflection, a point
of darkness and the motion of a bucket slapping against
the walls of the well. The rope attached to it hung wet
by her ear and it was moving. She reached out and
stilled it. She pulled and the bucket moved upwards,

swaying and slopping. Far down in that claustrophobic darkness she could sense something coiled inside the cup of animal skin, a small animal of some kind, a piglet or a young goat, and as she pulled the rope, the liquid black of its eyes suddenly appeared, staring up at her, and there was someone behind her in the poplar shadows, and she knew he carried an axe.

She lay for some time collecting her thoughts, with the blueness of the sky reflected all over the room, slowly realising that she was alone in the chalet. David had gone out. Then, element by element, she went over the previous night so that she knew it was real. A lizard on the white wall stared down at her, swivelling its head at an impossible angle. The eyes had pieces of dark-orange rind in them, concentrated within a knowing brilliance. So it was all true. She hadn't dreamed it.

Her long, athletic limbs filled the bed, which was sprinkled with sand. It was nearly midday. Light, percussive laughter floated over from the main house. She turned on her back and filled her lungs to bursting. The black despair of the night was not as strong as she had feared it would be. For one thing, she was no longer physically exhausted, and for another, she was thinking about it alone without David's constant harassment.

She showered lazily. The water from the roof was scalding. Her introspection was perfect. If only she could be alone for the next twenty-four hours. If only David wouldn't come back and the guests would ride off into the desert, never to return. It was disarming the way Richard and Dally had Fortnum & Mason toiletries in all the rooms. She washed her hair, turned off the air-conditioning, and put on her bathrobe.

Outside, the air was bright but savagely hot. The paths

were piled with sand, and the mountains beyond the walls had the colour of cool ash. Azna was of the same colour, like something that has burned overnight and settled into a pile. She winced in the heat. As if summoned purely by her thoughts, a boy was walking towards her, his white robe billowing around him and his *babouches* slapping the path.

'*Café?*'

'You're a godsend! Can I have some hot milk?'

She took it on the porch in her sunglasses with some toast and strawberry jam. Crickets ricocheted around her, and a gay splashing echoed from the pool area, where the girls laughed as if they were alone in the world. In the shadow of the house a few tables were set up with napkins. The wind had died down completely and palms stood motionless against a blank sky. She folded the toast slices and stuffed them into her mouth. Idly, she thought about her books. She hadn't written one in eight years, but stories and ideas were constantly suggesting themselves. She stretched her shins into the sun and let them burn a little. Punishment, she thought. The boy returned with oranges that had obviously been stored in a fridge, a small silver knife laid next to them. He had forgotten the honey.

'Where is my husband?' she asked.

He shrugged. 'I didn't see him.'

The boy was *haratin*, with black features. He nodded and looked away. She had a sudden desire to engage him, to ask him all kinds of insolent questions. There was just a chance that he would tell the truth. Am I beautiful? Is my husband mad? Am I mad? But he responded slothfully, reluctantly, when she asked again if he knew anything about the dead boy. She wanted to know if they were angry.

75

She went over to the house in her big yellow summer dress, which she had bought in a Chelsea antique store. It was patched up and precarious, and she knew that she was far too old for it, but it was okay for Morocco and a party where no one knew her or even cared. In a house full of buxom young women, she didn't have to be careful about her appearance. She was free. She breezed up to the house and for a moment admired the elaborate surfaces that adorned its sides. A riot of filigree screens and lacelike carvings made the four-sided structure look like an incredibly detailed sculpture made out of milk chocolate. A whole wall was covered with all sorts of lozenges, diamond-shaped motifs, and tiny lathed columns. She heard the music, the chatter coming from inside, the voice of Dally, and then, thinking better of her planned entry, she skirted round the house and wandered into the small maze of lanes and houses that sloped gently from it to the south wall. A space had been cleared among them and turned into a piazza with marble tiles. She walked across it, feeling the heat burst through the soles of her leather slippers, and snapped her fingers at her sides. Horse riding? He *was* mad. He wanted to escape from her and clear his head, but he had gone about it eccentrically.

The lanes shimmered with tall flowering weeds pestered by bees. Those houses that were still empty breathed a smell of moss and decayed timber and dried flowers. Some corroded steps led up to the top of the wall and she climbed them, breathing hard in the heat. A dense smell of dry herbs and smoke rose from the hillsides below, and people walked on the road in wide straw hats, beating skanky donkeys with sticks and hollering upwards towards the *ksour*. The echoes of these voices were clipped; they rang out clear across the empty spaces.

There was a surprising normality to everything, no sense of crisis or anguish. She ran her hand along the hot baked mud of the wall and let her chin burn a little under the rim of her baseball cap. Like Hamid's, her heart was not behaving regularly. Her fair, freckled skin recoiled from the light, and the thought of David riding blithely across the mountain infuriated her. So often he took things into his own hands and took off, oblivious, neither enjoying himself nor doing anything especially useful. He had left on a whim, because he couldn't face the horror that the morning would bring, and yet it had to be faced because everything has to be faced, and if he didn't face it, she would have to. She could sense that nothing had been concluded. The crisis would roll on, and it would drag them downwards into some plot over which they would have no influence.

Farther along the same wall, she spotted the American from the dinner taking photographs, kneeling behind the parapet and taking his time with each shot. He was so wrapped up in his task that he didn't notice her until she was a few feet away. He appeared very pleased. There was a quick 'Hiya' and he got off his knees, doffing his straw pork-pie hat. He flipped it and said, 'I got it in Casablanca. Made in China.' He put it back on and nudged his aviator glasses. She liked him, she decided on the spot. There was something affable and solid about him, a good-sport aura, and he was one of those who watch and take notes, who never take their eyes off you. Perhaps they were the only two sane people there, it occurred to her.

* * *

77

For the first time, she looked around herself. She hadn't been able to notice anything the night before. She'd had no cognisance as to where she was. Now she saw the menacing slopes of tawny rock dotted with date palms, the valley sweeping down to plains that seemed white, like flats of dried salt. Above Azna, lumpen peaks reared up, made of great round boulders piled on top of each other like a children's game. This kind of stone seemed to shine in the light, as if its surfaces had been polished with wax. There were hardly any trees, only outcrops of prickly pears and tufts of yellow flowers like wild mustard. The *ksour* was made of dried mud, and so it appeared to rise spontaneously out of the earth itself, like something that had been spat up by a subterranean eruption. The courageous folly of choosing such a location for a holiday home was immediately obvious, and one had to admire it. Day pointed to a neighbouring *ksour* on the far side of the road, a rectangular shape clinging to the side of an identically inhospitable mountainside. It was owned by a German couple, he said. They, too, had festive weekends.

'It's a wild sort of place,' she murmured.

'I wouldn't live here. They're living out some sort of fantasy, I imagine.' He wasn't interested in the hosts at that moment, however. He came forward, ready to console. 'Are you all right?'

She seemed startled that anyone should ask her that. 'All right? No, I'm lost. It's like going through the Looking Glass. And I haven't seen Richard today.'

'I think it's all been settled. You'll have to fill out some forms and I expect that'll be the end of it.'

She sank her face into her hands for a moment and rested against the wall. Settled? But nothing was settled.

'This morning I thought it was a dream. For a moment I was happy again. How could we have been so stupid?'

Day touched her arm.

'Shall we go down and get some lunch? There's little point in blaming yourself.'

Her eyes began to drip. But her body was still, fixed to the wall. He waited it out. She was a woman of high but discreet internal tension, with her tall, loopy frame, her exaggerated freckles and her patient, exact voice. Everything about her was compressed, internalised, and yet when she looked at you without forethought, the blueness in her eyes opened up suddenly and you found yourself entering them and, as you entered, a door closed behind you and you couldn't leave.

'Everyone speeds,' he said firmly. 'It's not the issue.'

'But it is the issue, you know. We killed that boy because we were going too fast. And because we were having an argument.'

He waited patiently. The calm exhaustion after emotion is what one waits for. Her skin had a wonderful melancholy about it, a dusky ripeness. From the house came the sound of live jazz, a band playing in the tent that had just been erected, a tinny jumble of trombones and cymbals and bassoons. The music was romping away, badly played but saucy. As soon as she heard it, she smiled.

'So you like jazz?' he said gaily.

'I loathe it. But it always makes me hungry.'

In reality, she was scanning the hills, the ravines, rather than thinking about jazz. There was a puff of dust in the distance. Her eyes narrowed and she frowned. Horses, perhaps. She was never jealous of David, but it was remarkable that she remembered this fact only now. She never thought of what he was doing while he was away from her; she felt his absence as a vacuum that couldn't last very long. She wasn't ever jealous; she was annoyed only by his occasional failure to tell her where he was. It was informational insecurity.

'My husband went riding this morning,' she said distractedly. 'Who did he go riding with, though?'

Day licked his chapped lips. 'There was a group of Eurotrash, girls in riding boots, that sort of thing. I think I saw him. I would have thought it was far too hot for that sort of thing. Don't horses get heatstroke?'

'It wasn't very nice of him,' she said, pouting. 'Aren't there lawyers and policemen waiting to torture us?'

He turned and skipped down the adobe staircase to the bottom of the wall, darting with a gasp into the shadow and grinning up at her. He was trim, boyish and not too American after all.

'I doubt it. Dally and Dick are the feudal lords here. Everyone kisses their arse. You should get out of that sun before you start bleeding.'

'I don't bleed very easily.'

They went slowly back to the house. Her dress, yellow and ripe-looking like some huge, floppy flower with crinkled petals and blood-stained hems, swished against his legs. It seemed as if she wanted to be amused. There are women like that, he thought to himself: permanently half interested in life, waiting for a sudden attack, a sudden onset of charm. He thought of them as the Waiting Fruit. You could always tickle them with a bit of bawdy, letting them know that you were a gentle, caring cad. They would hesitate, pretend to disapprove, and then the sexual elastic inside them would distend, grow taut, then relax. At that moment, they could be picked. It didn't matter at all if they were married. He described how he had spent the night in Casablanca before driving out here. He had gone to one of the beach clubs in the suburb of Aïn Diab and played ping-pong with a hooker at the Tahiti.

'You didn't!' she cried.

'I did. Desperate hookers find me irresistible. I have a smell of decaying money about me. It's one of the best things about money. That smell.'

'Did you sleep with her?'

'Oh, come on.'

'You did.'

He made her laugh, and that was something, to her mind. It was quite surprising. What was she laughing at? He had even teeth. It was as if his dentist had filed them all down so that they formed a symmetrical row.

'I wouldn't tell a lady,' he groaned. 'Not even my mother.'

'Your mother would be fascinated.'

She liked her dress rubbing his legs. It was her way of feeling his legs without doing anything.

On another note, he asked, 'Have you been here before?'

She shook her head and frowned again. 'We rarely get away on holiday. David works all the time. His patients are all rich old bags who harass him mercilessly round the clock. We are ruled by his pager.'

'So he's a doctor, then?'

'I'm sorry . . . I didn't even say.'

'Well, I like it here. It seems like a country where a useless man could be happy. Maybe I'll move.'

Meanwhile her eyes had dried. No more crying, she thought, but it occurred to her that she should ask Richard to see the body. She had to see it and say something to it. A prayer at least, even if it was not in the right language, or from the right book.

* * *

As they went through the enormous Berber tent where the jazz was playing, she looked for him everywhere. A small crowd picked at the buffet and drank from an elegant bar draped in white cloth. Powerful electric fans did their best to keep it cool. The ground was covered with brown and gold Atta carpets with lozenge designs that looked like eyes, and there were low sofas with brocaded peach-coloured cushions. Day suddenly took her hand for a moment, to pull her through a knot of people, and she was not startled enough to snatch it back. So he pulled her through. They went to the bar and got a drink. At the same time people came up to her and asked her if she was all right. They were talking about the accident, but discreetly, under their breath, and when they saw her, they felt they ought to say something. They cradled her shoulder with their hands and said, 'How horrible!' To which there was nothing she could say.

She was soon lost, bewildered, irritated. Where was David? She hung onto the kind American and begged him to take her out again. They borrowed some parasols from the staff and walked towards the pool, which was planted all about with cypress trees and offered shade. The whole scene seemed pointless to her now, with the Paris dresses and the tinkly jazz that was out of place. The idea of champagne made her sick; the sight of the *mezze* laid out in the tent struck her as needlessly provocative to the staff, who looked on with noticeably greater coolness. The American seemed nice – but who was he? What did he want? By the gates there was a small crowd of Berbers who seemed to be waiting for something, and as Day and Jo approached them, the group shifted on their feet, muttering, pulling back a little, but staring violently. Day gripped her hand and said, close to her ear, 'They seem put out by you. Hang onto me. I look violent.'

Hamid was arguing with some of them, clearly asking them to step back through the gates. Reluctantly, they agreed, and the courtyard cleared out as the gates were closed and bolted. Seeing Jo, Hamid came up with a flurry of tight-lipped apologies.

'The horses are back, Madame. Your husband is taking a shower. I think it was a bad idea to go out on horses.'

'Why, what happened?'

'Your husband can tell you. It is all foolish.'

'Where is Monsieur Richard?'

'He has gone to Tazat to talk to the police.'

She would have gone on with more insistent questions, but the sun was too strong and she was beginning to waver. Hamid was becoming more blank towards them, more testy, and she felt that he didn't like her. She wasn't sure what to do. Bluntly, she asked if she could see the body, which she knew was in the garage. For a moment he appeared stunned. Then he shook his head emphatically and glowered. No, Madame, that was out of the question. Monsieur Richard would never forgive him if he permitted that. It was not a sight for a woman, especially not one of the parties involved.

'I'll ask Monsieur Richard,' she said icily.

'As you like, Madame.'

Before she turned to go, she said, 'What were those men doing inside the gate?'

'They are locals,' Hamid replied. 'They are upset by the events of last night.'

'What do you mean, upset?'

'They were rowdy at first, but we calmed them down.'

'Rowdy?'

83

Her tone must have been aggressive, because he returned her stare with even greater force. She felt the American hand pulling her away.

'What were they rowdy about?'

It was a queer English word Hamid had learned from Richard, and he wondered if he had misused it.

'They were noisy and offended, Madame.'

'By me?' she gasped.

Day whispered in her ear.

'Now, now. Don't bait him.'

With the gates bolted, the staff went back to the tent. Jo and Day threaded their way through the maze of houses towards her chalet, and halfway there he stopped. The sun was now full, at its height, and they stood starkly isolated by it.

'You should talk this over with your husband alone.'

'I should. Shall we meet later?'

She thanked him quickly and walked off, turning once to shoot him a smile. She shouted over, 'Are you going to the pool this afternoon?'

He nodded. 'It's better than horse riding.'

Already from the pool came a sound of ice cubes and laughter, making it clear that the guests were not thinking too much about her problems or the accident. At least such thinking was compatible with getting on with their weekend. She walked like someone on their way to a shop, thrusting her legs too quickly, flapping her arms. She didn't forget the man watching her go, or the interest in his eyes, because there were indisputable things that didn't need to be thought about. She knew he was an unserious womaniser. But in London no one ever looked twice at her; she was sure that David's friends all felt sorry for him when, as they said, 'he could have had anyone'. The American was a nice compensation.

At the street corner nearest the chalet, she looked up and saw buzzards circling the *ksour*, as if mating. The houses shot razor-sharp shadows across the paving. Only now did she notice the flower boxes hanging on all the doors, and the brass hands of Fatima on the doors, positioned superstitiously upside down. The parts of the fantasy village that were restored were so well done that one had to concentrate to notice the discrepancies, the cracks. The walls were so perfectly surfaced. The doors were all new, varnished, and made to look old. Even the hands of Fatima were imposters. They made for a strange contradistinction with the ruined dwellings all around them.

David was on the bed, nursing his face with a towel, through which a spot of blood had permeated. He sat up and there was a look of bruised astonishment on his face. As she rushed over to the bed, he let the towel drop to reveal a small gash on the side of his forehead. 'You fell off your horse,' she cried, but he shook his head impatiently and snatched the towel back from her as she dabbed the cut.

'Why would I fall off a bloody horse? I learned to ride, didn't I? And why were you walking back with that idiotic American?'

'Well, if you didn't fall . . .'

'Bloody Moroccan threw a stone at me.'

'What?'

'We were riding up on the hill. There was a pack of them waiting for us. Towel-heads.'

She settled beside him and took back the towel. Her little 'oh!' of shock at the word went unnoticed. But she went dark inside for a moment.

'You're the towel-head now. That could've been nasty.'

'It *was* nasty. Little cunt aimed it well.'

'Why were you riding at all?' she asked impatiently. 'That was pure folly.'

He looked childishly surprised.

'Why? They were going riding, so I joined. You were fast asleep.'

'It just seems like folly. And I am right.'

'They were lying in wait behind the rocks at the top of the hill. We couldn't have known that.'

'I find that hard to believe.'

But she thought of the angry men by the gate.

'It doesn't matter what you believe,' he said waspishly. 'I was with two French girls. They didn't throw stones at *them*.'

The cut was nothing much and it had been tended by Richard's local doctor, who was staying at the house for the weekend. But the shock had been great. David was shaken and his whole body twitched nervously. He clutched neurotically at the towel, dabbing the cut though it was dry, and the repetition of this movement calmed him bit by bit.

'The little bastards,' he growled futilely.

They were riding across open country, he explained. The two French girls were slightly behind him. What he didn't tell his wife was that they were succulent in their way and he was in a flirty mood with them. They had spent time in London and spoke English well.

They rode for three or four miles along the trail that led past Tafnet, in single file, exchanging little jokes along the way. He had thought it would be a pleasant diversion from all the hassle and horror. They were all bad riders, and it took a while to reach the top of the hill, where the stream tumbled between high, gold-coloured rocks.

He was feeling recovered after his long sleep. Where the path curved as it rose towards the next peak, there

86

was a wooden shack, and there the miscreants were hiding. He didn't see them; he just heard a stone ricochet against the ground. It made the horse jump, and as he turned it round, another stone hit him square in the face.

He dismounted and ran towards the shack, but the girls called him back. Five or six Arab boys ran backwards and taunted him from afar, running up another slope and laughing at the horsed *gaouri*. He didn't know what they called him. It sounded like *hassi*. But he saw the ragged hate in their faces. More stones rained down on them, hitting the horses and causing the girls to wheel about. The superficial gash bled profusely.

'We came back at once. They followed us, still throwing stones. I always said they were an irrational people. So now they think I am responsible.'

'Perhaps we should just leave,' she said quietly.

'It's so incredibly primitive,' he ploughed on, ignoring her. 'They think of it as an eye for an eye. It's like Sicily a hundred years ago. It's like *The Godfather*. So word got out. There was a crowd when we got back to the gates. The locals were out in force. What a bunch! Half of them with no eyes or teeth. They didn't seem to like seeing me on a horse. They thought I was enjoying myself.'

'And weren't you?'

'That's not really the point. Is it against the law to unwind a bit after a traumatic event?'

She got up coldly and poured him a glass of lemonade from the jug that was always on the sideboard, and always replenished without them knowing how.

'It was just inconsiderate. You must have known they wouldn't be thrilled by it.'

'So now I have to think about what they are, and are not, *thrilled* by? Thrilled?'

'You know what I mean.'

'Hamid said it was some kids from the other side of the valley. Everyone has heard about it. They're insatiable gossips, apparently.'

'Here, drink this.'

'Yak-yak-yak. It's a function of being illiterate.'

He was getting delirious. She pushed him back into the pillows and made fun of him.

'What a nice little fascist you've become since being hit by a stone. Is that all it takes?'

'It could have blinded me. It could have disfigured me.'

She made the fan turn faster, and when it was running at breakneck speed, she got up and closed the shutters with their rusted hooks. It was the sunlight itself that made them angrier and less controlled. She put a cold facecloth on his brow and lay with him for a while. They wouldn't sleep, but they could surely slow themselves down. He babbled a bit more, then gave up.

She opened a magazine and read for a while as he fell into a long, grumpy doze. Months of low-level disagreement and tension between them were finding a new surface. His practice was going badly. She couldn't exactly figure out why. Was there a dearth of people with skin cancers in modern London? Last year, he was sued by a patient. He hadn't talked about it, but he had lost. It wasn't written about in the papers, and in conversation he quickly brushed the subject aside. 'It's my life,' his attitude seemed to be. 'If it goes wrong, I'd rather it went wrong in private.'

So she gave up trying to talk about it. The months went by when she wrote nothing, imagined nothing and cared even less. A person can come to a point in their career when the magic formulas that worked before no longer work. Perhaps most people get to that point. It's an interesting junction in life, but not an easy one to actually live through. The crackling anger in his voice as he poured scorn on the Arabs was a function of his private failures. On the other hand, they had thrown a stone at him. The look in Hamid's eyes was not easy to dismiss, either.

She closed the magazine and put her arms half-heartedly around him. She had to remember that he was a man of dismissive judgements that were often right. He was a bit of an animal. He smelled things out, and he was rarely off the mark. It was what had always compelled her about him. But the downside to David's enviable trait was a brittle vulnerability before things that didn't exist inside his admirably supple world. He was supple with things he did know and brittle with things he didn't, and the latter broke him. So he could be flipped easily, and then he became less intelligent, less penetrating; it was then that he needed protection from himself.

She leaned down and brushed the tip of his sunburned nose with her lips.

'You look like a pirate. Like Blackbeard after a sword fight.'

'Be glad I don't have a sword.'

'Beast. No more wisecracks about Moroccans.'

'It depends on how many stones they throw at me. One wisecrack per stone. I think that's fair. Sticks and stones, and all that. It's between us. There's no one listening. I need to get it off my chest. It's an injustice, that's all.'

But the boy is dead, she thought.

89

'Sometimes things aren't fair,' she said. 'One gets blamed for things one hasn't done.'

'Not me.'

'Especially you.'

Eight

ALONG THE MUD WALLS, THE LIZARDS scattered lethargically. They darted into crevices, leaving the pale-red surfaces clean and hot. The cactus spines shone like polished steel, and the dust on the road gradually settled with the gravitational grace of a mass of feathers descending from a burst pillow. In the *Source des Poissons* a single girl with delicate coffee-coloured tattoos on her hands floated on her back. She looked up at the clusters of unripe dates on the undersides of the palms that were reflected in the water, then spread her hands through the cold water and thought of a certain boy, who at that very moment was driving goats into the shade of a tree. A dragonfly skimmed the water. The cicadas died off and the girl closed her eyes. When the dragonflies mated an inch above the water, they looked as if they were strangling each other to death. She watched them dance across the black surface, their wings making a quietly desperate, vicious sound that was pleasing to the ear.

The trees went silent and from afar she could hear the hum of the generators inside the foreigners' *ksour*. The old men sitting on the wall under the tamarisks lit their cheap cigarettes. For three hours no one would do anything.

It was like night. In the garage, the air-conditioners hummed and Richard stood alone with the body, anxiously glancing at his watch. His skin prickled with the heat that penetrated even into this secluded place. His back was wet and he marvelled at how dry the dead boy's skin was. It was like writing paper.

By the gate, meanwhile, a man stood with his hand on the bolt, listening carefully. The small crowd had finally dispersed, driven off by the seasonable temperatures, and its members now lay under trees, on lice-ridden mattresses, on pieces of palm bark. They lay awake waiting for the sun to decline. All it needed was a certain eager patience. The guests inside the *ksour* did much the same. Some lay on floating mattresses in the pool, half asleep; others made love in their rooms, taking care not to make too much noise. A few read books with an iced orange juice at their side. They had tracked their position on maps, some of them, and on GPS devices, but their sense of place was not yet firm. Their minds drifted easily. They ironed their lips with lip balm and evened the tanning oil on their noses, wondering what they were going to do next. There was a fancy-dress ball in the evening – costumes provided – but would they be expected to dance? Would they be expected to be themselves or to impersonate people they were not? Would it be fun or the reverse of fun, whatever that was?

In the highest room of the house, a private drawing room painted with apple-green geometrical tile designs where Dally and Richard spent hours alone reading and tipping bottles of Laphroaig before sunset, the two men stood by the great plate-glass window watching a swirl of dust rising from the distant road.

'Looks like a car,' Dally said hopefully.

'It isn't the police. They said they were dealing with a morgue, but I haven't heard from them.'

Richard wondered if he should call Hamid. The afternoon was winding down and the trees were spreading their shadows around the cliffs. They had been sleeping for two hours and the nightmares had not completely blown off. But what would Hamid do? He decided to wait and see. When the body was finally taken away, the cloud hanging over them would presumably be lifted at a stroke. All they had to do was remove it circumspectly, without desecration of custom.

'It's definitely a car, Dick.'

'The mint suppliers?'

'They came this morning. Maybe someone from the morgue.'

'But which morgue?'

Dally shrugged. He had no idea what morgues there were in the neighbourhood of Azna. He didn't know if they had morgues at all. Didn't they just throw the body into a pit or something?

Richard had to handle Dally carefully sometimes. He was liable to go off, if arrangements carefully made suddenly came unstuck.

'There's a morgue in Errachidia. Might be a pick-up from them.'

Dally did go off. 'I wish you hadn't invited those English people. What a bore they are. And what a mess they've made.'

'Are they a bore?'

'They're a horrible bore. And did you see Mr Limey's shoes?'

Richard nodded. 'It's a type, Dally. He's a public-school doctor. What do you expect?'

'I guarantee that tonight they're the only ones who don't dress up. They'll claim they have post-traumatic stress disorder.'

'I'm sure it's what they have.'

'I saw him grab a drink at the breakfast buffet. He was guzzling it. His hand was shaking. He's pathetic. Never again with those two, I swear.'

Probably wise, Richard thought dourly.

'We should have invited the Bainbridges. They're genuinely wacko at least. And they don't kill people on the way up.'

'There's always next time.'

They laughed, complicit again. The swirls of dust had reached the cliffs where the tents stood, baking mud-brown in a lengthening sun. Dally poured himself a Scotch. Slowly, Richard got dressed. He loved the desert at this hour. A wild camel nosed its way along the black ribbon of the road, and far off at the opening of the valley a menacing orange light gathered. The fig trees in the garden shuddered as if beaten with sticks, but there was little wind during those moments. The hour of dusk could be tasted, but not seen.

The cattle egrets and African finches came back to settle in their ruined nooks, and an old man in a tattered coffee-coloured *djellaba* rolled out of the Toyota jeep that had pulled up in front of the main gates, and bared his six gold teeth in a grimace of extreme discomfort. The car that Dally and Richard had seen had savaged number plates and panels patched up with cheap epoxy; its wipers were bent back and the radio antenna had collapsed. The other occupants remained inside, huddled together in their ragged *chechs*. But at length, as the old man approached the door and took off his cloth cap, they also got out and stretched their legs. 'A cold place,' they muttered, keeping their expressions tense. Their clothes were caked with grit and sand, and as they unbent themselves, a small cloud rose from them. They beat their sleeves and *chechs* gently, stretched their mouths and looked warily around them. A dark-orange powder caked the car, clogging the grille and the side-mirrors, and on the back seat lay a large sack of uncooked rice. The men of Azna could tell there were weapons in the car, though none could see them. There was a smell of weapons. A smell of bullets and goat grease.

The old man walked up to the closed gate and slowly, orchestrating creaky knees, knelt down in the dust. He settled in, holding his hands together across his chest. His eyes were completely expressionless. Almost under his breath at first, then louder, he said the following words: 'I am Abdellah Taheri of the Aït Kebbash from Tafal'aalt. I am here to collect my son. Will you hear me? Will you open your gate?'

He said it again and again, while his companions watched him impassively. They were middle-aged men with grizzled half-beards and large, blunted hands. They were thin desert men of the far south, with bird-beak noses and stony eyes set close together, their teeth half silver. Their faces were covered; their clothes were white and indigo. Their hands were scarred. They spoke Tamazight.

Hamid heard the voice at once. He crept to the gate and put his ear against it. It was the thing he had been expecting all along. The old man raised his voice and he repeated his demand until even the guests could hear it. His voice carried far on the shrieking wind. It was a level, grave voice with no trace of hysteria or emotional exaggeration. Like a repeated hammer blow, it struck

95

home until it produced movement, reaction. Voices can open doors. Richard came down quickly to the gate.

'The father?' he hissed at Hamid.

The servant nodded.

'Well, open up, then. Are you going to keep them there?'

'Are you sure, Monsieur? They are Aït Kebbash.'

Richard smirked. 'So?'

'Very well, Monsieur. But they will try and extort money from you. May you be warned!'

Richard ignored him. He heard the word *Tafal'aalt*. Was it a village somewhere? He asked Hamid if he had ever heard of it; the latter shook his head.

'Where do the Aït Kebbash live?'

Hamid shrugged. 'Far, far out.'

And he made a grim gesture with one hand.

'They must have driven all night,' Richard said.

'All day and all night. Many nights.'

'Open the gates, then.'

'They will blackmail you, Monsieur. They are blackmailers.'

It was Richard who slid open the huge bolt.

'Keep the guests away from here. We don't want them nosing around while this is going on.'

'Do not step out, Richard. Let the other step in. We will see how he is.'

'You mean, enraged?'

When the gate opened, the old man just as slowly stood up. He brushed off his knees and put his cap back on his head, and the men by the car didn't move as the gates swung open and the staff called out, beckoning him forward. There were summary greetings, exchanges, and Hamid courteously asked where they had driven from.

Tafal'aalt was a village of one hundred souls on the far side of the Tafilalet, far out where the edge of the oasis was drying out and the desert plain was advancing. It was beyond the remote fossil town of Alnif. It was on the farthest edge of human habitation, close to the Algerian border and the lonely mountain of Issomour, where fine trilobites and aquifers were quarried. Jbel Issomour was where they made their living, in the quarries that circled the mountain. Nearby, they explained, was Hmor Lagdad, the mountain called the Red-Cheeked One, which could be seen from a great distance off and which they all knew because it could be seen faintly from the quarries just outside Erfoud. Hamid said that he was deeply sorry about his son. What was the boy's name?

'Driss, my only son.'

'May Allah have mercy.'

'Allah has made it so.'

Hamid was suddenly moved. At last, the corpse had a name and an identity, and he was relieved. To die on the road in the middle of the night was a dog's death.

'We have kept him here, if it please you,' Hamid said, ushering the old man towards the garage doors. 'We have kept vigil every hour.'

He regretted maligning the men from Tafal'aalt as blackmailers, though he knew that they were exactly that. A man can be both a blackmailer by culture and a bereaved father, can he not? Abdellah was frail and stringy, and he must have had a son late in life. His clothes were wretched. Hamid wondered what fossils the Aït Kebbash specialised in. They made no money either way. They were people surviving at a subsistence level, unimaginable even to the poorest peasants in greener parts. They had the Toyota, and probably little else of value. He felt

97

for them. Could anyone really imagine their lives? One look at them was enough to confirm that they made their living as fossil diggers and preppers. That they eked out a miserable existence trading second-rate trilobites in the tourist shops of Erfoud and Rissani. One saw types like that all over the place, shabby desperadoes wandering from table to table at the hotels, offering trays of their wares, quietly hustling Westerners on the side, swearing their trilobites were the rarest of the Sahara, but going home empty-handed to their shacks on the edge of the desert. The oases were dying because of a tree infection called Bayoud disease, and all that was left to them, it was popularly observed, was a trickling trade in fossilised fish. So he was polite to the Aït Kebbash, good Muslims from the scorched corners of the earth, who had nothing and who gave nothing either.

The desert men came in warily, holding their bodies delicately apart from their surroundings as if they were long used to doing so. They looked around themselves at the Cherokee jeeps with their state-of-the-art CD players, and their eyes went heavy and calculating. They had never been inside the house of a foreigner before. They could not imagine how it could be inhabited. The infidels had no comforts, no delicacy. They had no sense of order or cleanliness or properness.

'It is like a stables,' one of them quipped.

'Truly,' Abdellah said with great seriousness.

At once, however, their thoughts were swept up by the dead boy laid out in the centre of the room, and the father was allowed to step out alone to approach his dead son. The staff gathered to watch this as well, because it was a drama that they both dreaded and were compelled by. At its heart was an injustice. A young life had been cut short, a Muslim father propelled into unimaginable grief, and the guilty ones had not even appeared before the people to explain their actions or to offer their heartfelt apologies. They had been let off by the police without so much as a light reprimand; indeed, the police had probably *apologised* to the detestable visitors, for money speaks to the impure of heart, and those who possess it can do as they wish, even among the pure of heart. The onlookers therefore watched the old man totter towards his son and their eyes filled with tears. A quiet, communicable rage spread among them and they clenched their fists out of view. The old man, meanwhile, conducted himself with considerable restraint. His stupefaction was written all over him, but his lips did not move; he did not blink. He did not give way to that same stupefaction. He merely approached the terrifying object and drank it in with his eyes. It did not seem to move him outwardly. It merely sucked him into its supernatural spell. The son that was living had gone through a metamorphosis that he could not comprehend or accept; gaiety and love had turned into pure materiality. It was as if his son's beauty was only now revealed to him and he was stunned by it, so much so that his motor reflexes could not respond to this emergency. His hands dangled limply at his sides and he absorbed and absorbed until he could absorb no longer, and when his capacity to absorb was exhausted he found himself not full with grief, but emptied with it, and at that moment his mind went away, and his heart with it, and he was left standing like something hanging by a filthy little string, a small animal that has been strung up by a primitive trap and is about to die.

At length, however, his lips did begin to move. They pronounced nothing, but they moved. A cool dread spread around him, so that the onlookers were ruffled yet again by a restless mood. They felt themselves growing dark and suspicious. Abdellah lost all consciousness of them as his grief came upon him. His mind whirled and all was indistinct at its edges. Where was he? He felt the words of the Prophet simmering at its deepest part and the words of his own father murmuring behind them, and he looked up at the ceiling and the stalactites of cobwebs looked like dusty daggers pointed down at his heart. The killers. Where were the killers?

It was a question that also occurred to the stiffly over-dressed boys as they laid the napkins around that evening's dinner table, whose theme was Bandits and Corsairs. They laid out the heavy French forks with agile and hostile minds, stifled by their bow ties, crimped by the cufflinks they had to sport, thinking to themselves with quiet fever about the whereabouts of *les anglais*, whom no one had seen all afternoon.

They didn't speak among themselves except to ask one another questions about the utensils. Another generation of flies, exterminated with the aerosols, had to be swept away from under the windows, and they did this with solemn brooms, performing long, graceful strokes. Later, they were going to have to dress as either bandits or corsairs, and some of them would even wear swords. With appre-hension, they listened to the Ella Fitzgerald purring away in the library and the clink of glasses that went perfectly with glissando female laughter. It was a sound texture that embodied things they both desired and detested. The sound of women and whisky glasses could be counted as belonging to the desirable or the undesirable side according to tempera-ment, but that of clacking billiard balls was unambiguously positive. They would have crept into the house at night and played the table if there were any way of muffling the sound. They could hear the men from London and New York talking in bold voices about their wives. The sandwich services rolled from room to room and there was a padding of spoiled Irish greyhounds, and the village boys dreamed of castles and luxury villas and orgies with Jaguars waiting outside. These weird, faithless men, they thought, were reprehensible in many ways, but they had nevertheless succeeded at purely material things. They had a grudging envy of them on that account, but the envy never quite became respect. But who can say that the two things are not sometimes identical?

As they swept up the dead flies and laid out the large Talavera plates upon which Rif cuisine and seafood would be served later in the evening, they scanned the doors for scenes that might be revealed beyond them, pricking their ears to detect morsels of scandal. As Moroccans, they were expert linguists, adept in several tongues: French, English, Spanish, Arabic, Berber dialects and, in the case of one or two from the deep south, Hassaniya. Their ears were subtly attuned to the slipping between these various languages. They were born observers and critics, because that's the way history had made them.

Hamid swept into the dining room and seemed pleased. He clapped his hands impatiently and shooed them into the corridor.

'The bowls of nuts are running low in the library. The dogs haven't been fed. The wine is still warm. The fans are at the wrong speed. Must I do everything myself?' And under his breath, he added, 'Dogs.'

Then he went up to the second floor, where Monsieur Richard was alone on the telephone with a look of vexation. 'I can't help it,' he was saying quietly, straining his neck muscles. 'One doesn't plan these things.' Hamid hung by the door with the worried expression that he knew annoyed Monsieur, but which also goaded him into action. Richard looked up quickly and cupped a hand over the mobile telephone.

'What is it, Hamid?'

Hamid stepped carefully into the room. Richard was in a smoking jacket, which was so old it must have belonged to a grandfather. He looked a little shabby with the desert behind him fading out into darkness. There was a smell of whisky in the room, of male sex. The hand that cupped the phone was wet from the olives in the bowl by the sofa.

'The father,' Hamid began, 'says the English must pay him.'

Nine

AS THEY SAT IN THE QUARRY THAT DAY,
Driss continued his story to Ismael. The younger boy
listened with a spooked attentiveness, his eyes unblinking
as they stared as far into Driss's eyes as they could.
Ismael wanted to know if he was telling the truth, if
the story of his emigration was not a little exaggerated,
as such stories almost always were. The man coming
back from France was always a little Marco Polo. He
could make up what he wanted. He could weave a
thousand tales and no one could contradict him about
any details, because those who had also been there also
had a vested interest in the exaggerations.

'As I was saying,' Driss said, a little portentously, 'I
jumped ship and swam ashore a mile south of the marina
of Sotogrande.'

He waded ashore onto a small dirty beach next to a
cannery, where the sand shelved steeply. It was a starless
night and there was no one there. Just a road bordered
by high umbels and weeds, wooden stakes, the edges of
tattered vineyards. He walked into Sotogrande along the
shore, undisturbed, without witness. He crept through
the arcades of the marina, which was a few miles north

of Algeciras, and as he did so, he felt light in his wet sandals, subtly justified and in his element.

The land smelled like Morocco. Cypresses, resin, lemons and dry dust. The breeze had forest in it and parched hillsides and the smell of algae drying on stones. He had been on the boat all night long and his limbs shook as he went unnoticed past the terraced fish restaurants and the tapas bars where the yachters revelled with their wives. He heard nothing as he went past the closed shops and made his way out to the small road that ran past the marina's outer gates. The cicadas shrilled along this road, which wound through darkness towards a village called San Martín. His feet left wet prints behind him on the dusted tarmac, the trail of a dripping thief.

How could it be so easy? Like a dream, he said to Ismael, a dream where you get everything you want.

An hour through the gentle night, to the petrol station in San Martín. High trees sheltered the last stretch of the road, poplars with tapered tips and birds still singing higher up where eucalyptus stood. Its peacefulness astounded him. So this was Spain. Encouraged, he sat down in the verge and collected his energy. There were no cops about, and no cars either, and the hills around him were as dark as the Rif, and maybe even darker. For the first time in his life he was about to do something truly illegal.

The petrol station was a self-service with credit-card pumps lit up all night. Its roof murmured with hundreds of moths. Underneath, picked out by the excessive lights, an old woman stood fuelling her car. She was white, maybe not even Spanish, in slacks and open-toed sandals and a coquettish headscarf and, by God, she was not attractive to the eyes. He watched her for some time as she filled her tank and until he was sure that she was entirely alone. He could not know why she was filling her car at four in the morning. Perhaps she had insomnia or she preferred the cooler hours. It didn't much matter. Finally reassured, he dusted himself down and walked slowly up to the station, his sandals scraping the road alerting her to his presence and causing her to wheel around with the pump still in her hand. He did not walk up to her, but hesitated by the closed-up station shop, where he feigned surprise (as if he had wanted to buy something, though he had nothing in the way of cash) and then sat down on the kerb and said to her in Spanish, 'Buenos días', the only thing he had learned in that language.

She said nothing back, and he noticed the small things: her finger releasing the trigger of the pump, the shifty look to the darkness to be assured that the Muslim was alone and not part of a gang. He knew at once that she, too, was a foreigner. One can always tell. So they were two foreigners in a petrol station at four in the morning and they had nothing to say. All she thought was: This man knows I have a credit card.

By God, Driss said, I was dripping all over that petrol station. I looked as if I had just emerged from the sea like a monster, and this old woman simply stared at me and waited for me to say something. I was astonished, and all I could do was walk towards her with my hands held up.

'Ah,' Ismael said, 'that must have been funny. She must have feared for her life.'

She did, Driss said. He was sure of it.

He walked towards her and she let go of the pump. But then, surprisingly, she calmly took out her credit card, stepped to the machine and swiped it. She waited for her receipt, folded it and pocketed it. She then looked up and said something to him in Spanish.

'*Vous ne comprenez pas?*' she went on when he shook his head, and he could tell at once that she was English.

They spoke in French then.

'You look awfully wet,' she said kindly, and then asked him if he had eaten anything in the last twenty-four hours, and in fact he had not.

'How dreadful,' she said in her funny accent.

'I ate two nights ago.'

'Over there?'

He nodded.

'I see. And how did you come over?'

The explanation sounded like the truth to her.

'How marvellously brave of you,' she said gravely.

'It was what it was.'

'Well, I am Angela. My husband, Roger, and I have a bed and breakfast on the hill up there outside the village.'

They both looked up at nothing, at the outline of the hill that was somehow visible. First light, he thought.

'Where are you going to stay?' she asked. 'You can't sit around in a petrol station.'

He had had no idea. *Stay?*

'I was going to hitch a ride.'

'So that's why you came to a petrol station. Hitch a ride to where?'

'Paris.'

'You're just a boy. That's quite unreasonable. You'll never get there dressed like that.'

She walked round the little cheap car, the kind of car Moroccans would have, and she seemed irritated by the impracticality of his plan. There was an old 'Nukes? No thanks' sticker on the rear bumper.

'And what are you going to do in Paris?'

'Get a job as a janitor.'

She laughed, and in her face was the phrase 'What a people you are.'

'Get in,' she said. 'You may as well come up and have some soup before you die of hunger. If you don't have papers, they'll pick you up on the road.'

If? he thought with dry amusement.

'You are very kind,' he muttered as he slipped into the passenger seat and then sat very still, waiting. He could have robbed her right there and then, and he could have driven away in her car all the way to Paris and no one would have known. He knew how far it was. A day's drive, and nothing more, and all on expensive roads. He could have done it easily.

He watched her fumble with the keys, her foot depressing the pedals, small feet in espadrilles like an ancient hippie. She could have been his grandmother, and yet she was dressed like a free young spirit, with bangles on her wrists and a floral dress that was, to his taste, borderline impertinent.

By either side of the road at the top of the hill stood commercial greenhouses covered with plastic sheeting. The Bloodworths had bought a walled farmhouse at the summit and from its high windows the valley could be seen, and the greenhouses sprawled around it. Sunflowers pressed against the outer walls, thousands of them, and beyond them were walnut trees, pale lemon trees, sloped fields of white grapes.

She led him through a handsome house with Spanish *baúls* and dressers and polished tables and whitewashed walls, and on the far side of the kitchen lay a pool within three walls and gardens of snapdragons. It was lit from below. The husband was asleep, and in the morning, she said, she would explain everything to him. Meanwhile, eat some gazpacho.

She turned off the light and left the oil lamp on the table. He ate savagely. She had dry clothes for him, and flip-flops, pillows, sheets, a small room under the rafters in the guest wing, where no one was staying at that moment. Why was she doing it? Because of his youth, because of his hopelessness? Or for other reasons.

He ate alone at the table downstairs, with damselflies whirling around him, and salted the bread from a silver cellar shaped like a chess bishop. Angela locked up the house. She gave him a key to his room and told him not to go out on the road by himself until she had discussed things with her husband. Roger always had good ideas.

Impulsively, he kissed her hand and she drew it back abruptly.

'No, no,' she said. 'It's our pleasure to do it. Don't be silly now.'

He slept deeply in the attic. His nightmares were novel. He woke on the floor surrounded by the cast-off pillows, and there was a sound of cuckoos coming from deep inside the landscape as if they and only they belonged there. He thought: It's a trap. Now Driss is doomed among the unbelievers. He is in their attic naked and alone.

At noon the Bloodworths were waiting for him downstairs by the pool, an elderly English couple in wicker chairs reading the British papers with their coffee and a jug of iced orange juice, pale as ghosts in the Spanish heat amid the ageing colour of their subtropical gardens. The husband was a retired chemical engineer. He was about seventy, thin and piercing in his way, and when Driss appeared in his borrowed clothes, he got up cheerily and shook his hand and invited him to eat some brioches, which, by God, he was sure were poisoned. But, as it happened, and as God willed, they were not poisoned, and the unbelievers were not evil of heart. They were merely simpletons. Allah had written it thus.

'Angela here says you are on the run from the Spanish police,' Roger said in English. 'Just for being an immigrant. Well, we think that's rotten, don't we, Angela? How would you like to work for us for a while as our gardener? Board and lodging and three hundred euros a month?'

When this was translated, Driss had to quell his confusion, and he said yes, that he would, though something in his heart told him not to.

'It will be easy,' the Englishman went on. 'We'll give you time to settle down and learn some Spanish and, whenever you want, you can move on more safely. How does that sound to you?'

That was how it began, he told Ismael. He had no choice but to go along with it, and soon he was gardening every day under the old man's supervision, for the infidel was an expert gardener and he knew the name and habits of every flower and plant that grew in that land. He knew all about sunflowers and how to make saxifrage grow on rocks and how to rear sage and thyme among his beds of petunias. And Driss had never seen a valley like that, a place so blindingly green and coloured with flowers that it made you feel you had been excluded hitherto from something sweet and nameless, a place where there were water echoes and smoke from hunting guns and a sound of distant dogs, and cypresses dark as green ink with a shade he had never seen cast by trees.

Lemons and almonds on the near slopes, and the musky smell of tomatoes ripening in the greenhouses. Yes, Driss said, as if agreeing himself and turning a regrettable memory inside himself like something being rotated on a spit: it was a vision of paradise to me at that time.

Ten

RICHARD LIT A CIGARETTE AND COLLAPSED on his sofa. He was already exhausted and dying for the charade of a weekend to be over. It was a total failure. Things carried on, but there was a feeling of deceit and unease hanging over everything. The old man in the garage, the gang waiting by the gates and the muttering, superstitious staff suddenly turning against him. David was the bringer of jinxes and bad luck, and Richard's sympathy for him was diminishing by the hour. Pay? He would now have to have a mad scene with David about this. The doctor would throw a fit; Richard would play devil's advocate while actually believing the advocacy. 'Pay him,' he would say, 'and make him go away.' And when David was actually in the room half an hour later, that was exactly what he said.

'Never,' David insisted, shaking his head like a pissed-off schoolboy. 'You don't pay someone because of an accident.'

Richard made sure the doors were closed and he also made sure Hamid kept everyone else away. David was sweating again, and he adamantly refused to put on a costume.

'I'm not putting on a costume until we have this sorted.'

'Fair enough. Let's sort it, then.'

'I'm not paying him.'

'Did you meet him?'

David shook his head.

'You should meet him. He's a grieving father, for God's sake. I called Benihadd. He says it's the custom here. You don't have to do it, but if you don't, it could make things so much more awkward.'

David looked at him coldly. So it was a set-up, he thought wildly. It felt to him that moving walls were closing in on him, squeezing him tighter and tighter. The Arabs just wanted money out of you. It was a squeeze. Their grief and annoyance were always exaggerated.

'I don't even know how much he wants,' Richard admitted, walking around the room in his slippers. 'It might just be a thousand euros or something.'

'Or a fuck of a lot more.'

'We could just ask him, couldn't we?'

'It's blackmail,' David said. 'It's blackmail pure and simple.'

Richard was gentle with him, because he agreed with it. But so what if it was? So what if it was blackmail? What was the word for *blackmail* in their language – did they even have one?

'You seem very equanimous about it,' David remarked, his face suddenly twitching. 'What if it was a thousand euros? It's not nothing. Anyway, it's the principle of the thing, *plus* a thousand euros.'

'If it was a thousand, it wouldn't be very much.'

'What are they going to do otherwise?' David sneered. 'Lynch me? They do have an army here, don't they?'

'I wasn't thinking about them lynching you. I was thinking about them *not going away*.'

'Oh, your precious weekend, of course! We mustn't forget that. So we'll have a nice weekend in the country while they screw me out of a thousand euros?'

'I think it's better than the alternative, don't you?'

The heat between them had quickly risen and Richard felt his face go hot and red. David looked like a plump, sullen toad on his leather chair, his legs wide apart, his Thomas Pink shirt wrecked by the heat and perspiration. He stared around him with an alert, knowing desperation. Squeezed, he was being squeezed, and there was no one to defend him but himself. He hated the way white people gave in to blackmail in places like this. The Muslims had the upper hand and they used it mercilessly, but the cowardly whites beaten down by decades of guilt and political correctness couldn't admit how ruthlessly they were being dealt with. What did they think, that villagers in the Sahara living in shit thought like themselves? It beggared belief.

There was deep inside David a core of the officer class, the colonial officer class to which his grandfathers on both sides had belonged. There were many more men like him than one assumed, largely because they were so careful to conceal their opinions in moments of stress. But when he felt threatened, he lost his reserve and his disguise. He became supercilious and defiant, and he relished the breaking of the contemporary taboos, which in any case had never seemed to him convincing. He thought political correctness was an invention of spineless Americans wallowing in their racial hellhole. It was just that the British had adopted it with an even sillier intensity. It was guilt for its own sake, and it changed nothing. And now Richard.

He sat back with seething sarcasm.

'And what are the alternatives, Dicky? Do they practice castration out here? Or do the police come and screw you as well? Have we thought of contacting the consulate in Casablanca? What about your contacts in the Ministry of the Interior?'

'My contacts? I've no idea what you're talking about. The consulate won't help you. They think of this place as the far side of the moon. We do want to cut down on the red tape. You could be far worse off going that route.'

David looked at his nails, as people do when they are on the passive offensive. 'I could take that risk. You see, you feel guilty and threatened because you live here. I feel nothing of the sort. I don't owe Moroccans anything. I'm not French.'

'David, I dare say you aren't really thinking about your own interests. Or Jo's. If we call the consulate, there would have to be a thorough, I mean *thorough*, look at this whole thing. It would be under the microscope. I don't think you'd want that.'

'I . . .'

'No, no, David, I don't think you would.'

Richard went to the drinks cabinet and snapped it open angrily. Give the toad a stiff drink and force him round. He had a few ancestors in the East India Company as well. Most of them were into watercolours, archaeology and Eastern religion. It didn't necessarily make you into a hard-arse.

He didn't bother asking what David wanted. He just made up a hugely alcoholic gin and tonic, no ice. He rattled it about to mix it and controlled the outburst of rage that was fast approaching. Suddenly he remembered an incident from school thirty-five years earlier. It was a funny incident, but it seemed less funny now. One Parents' Day at Ardingly College, one of the boys started throwing mice off a rooftop at the parents and masters assembled below. Each mouse was equipped with a little parachute decorated with a swastika. Naturally, the parachutes didn't work. The mice hurtled to their deaths and were squashed against the flagstones with the swastika parachutes draped over them. The rumour was, it was David Henniger. He was caned for it, wasn't he? Richard tried to remember. But was David announcing his love of swastikas or − much more likely − vilifying the masters and parents as swastika types? Richard turned and offered the toad his booze.

The toad's greedy eyes mellowed at once.

'Cheers, guv'nor,' he growled and grabbed the glass gratefully. He took a swig straight away.

Richard walked to the windows. There was a puzzle before them. How would they unlock it? It was a puzzle of diplomacy, of tact. He had made his point about David's not wanting a real investigation. So he *was* hiding something. The father of Driss could not know that, however. Or did he know it? 'The men of the desert know everything,' Hamid said once, like a quote out of *Lawrence of Arabia*. But they didn't, really. They were just efficient pessimists, and therefore astute readers of human nature. They always assumed the worst, and that made them correct nine times out of ten. Their pessimism, however, was not like David's. David was someone who believed that the past was superior to the present, and that was a different sort of pessimist. It was not the entire past that was superior, of course; it was mostly just the British nineteenth to the mid-twentieth century.

The Moroccans, on the other hand, believed as Hamid did when he quoted the famous proverb 'The past is gone, what is hoped for is absent and there is only the hour in which you are.' Richard sat down next to him and clacked his glass.

'Slàinte,' he murmured, offering the Celtic toast.

'Bums up.'

They drank morosely. Candles were being lit one by one in the grounds of the *ksour*, like a sky coming alight at night. David looked at his watch. He was thinking about his wife.

'I think,' Richard said more conspiratorially, 'that we should go down and talk to the old crow. Perhaps we can work something out. I've been here for a while, let me tell you, and that's how one works things out here. No rages and fits. No self-righteous finger-wagging. It doesn't work. It's always best to listen to what they want. Usually they just want something and they'll tell you. When you give it to them, you can forget everything.'

David continued drinking with surly swigs.

'Once they sense how weak we are, they'll go for broke. Since they've got nothing.'

'It doesn't always work like that. I'm glad you've agreed, then,' Richard concluded tersely. 'We might be both pleasantly surprised.'

'Pleasantly?' David said as he tipped his glass empty.

Richard wanted to berate him, to get it off his chest. If he had been honest all along, they could have called the consulate and left it at that. But the arrogant shit had lied and kept something to himself, and consequently Abdellah, the mourning father, had the upper hand. One is the author of one's own misfortunes, he wanted to say loudly. But David wouldn't listen.

'I mean,' Richard corrected himself, 'that it might not be as bad as we think.'

I know when I'm being robbed, David thought.

You're not being robbed, Richard would have replied. You're being spared.

David stared at the ice cube at the bottom of his glass. He knew it was his fault and he kept his silence. If only he could be transported back to Putney by a devious machine of the future, with a single flick of a switch.

They went down into the party together. Dancing had broken out with horrifying sincerity in the library. Richard had given orders about this, but the French contingent was drunk and they didn't see why not. They had some Joe Dassin on the turntable and were doing the twist to 'BipBip'. Half the guests were in costume, sashed and hatted, and the gin fizz at the outside bar had run dry. Champagne and orange juice was being mustered, and the small triangular mint sandwiches over which he and Dally had pored for a day were making their appearance alongside bowls of beet-leaf salad. The fire-eaters from Taza had arrived and were sitting glumly by themselves with their apparatus, waiting for instructions. Richard went up to them and shook their hands with the smattering of Berber words he had learned. They bowed and touched their chests. The outdoor sofas that night were draped with goatskins and piled with sequinned cushions, and large mono-chrome tribal carpets connected them. David walked over their geometrical eyes carefully, as if squishing them underfoot. He hoped it was taboo, that the jinns would get pissed off. He hated all this ethnic pretence and affectation. One could treat people decently without aping them, without rolling out their carpets every-where. He himself treated all races at St Ann's, and the Hippocratic oath made multiculturalism come alive, for once. But there were no grounds for aesthetic surrender. When we saw Western knick-knacks in their houses, we laughed at them, didn't we? Dismal kitsch, we said to ourselves. This was no different.

Yet Richard seemed at ease with it. He was a bit of an orientalist snob, obviously, even if you conceded that most of it came from his insufferable boyfriend, who, they said, liked the servants on the side. But then gays always came to North Africa. It was an Edwardian tradition. David's own grandfather Edwin had done so, to great scandal. Had they all followed Oscar Wilde to Algiers? Because they could, he thought. Because they had the power. The braziers licked against dark air, which somehow was not at all dark. A boy staggered past with a crate of ice piled with apricots, with stiff leaves still attached to the fruit. One always looked up, searching for the moon.

As they walked side by side, David wondered if Richard despised him, because it certainly seemed that way. He was used to it. People nearly always thought David was something he wasn't. A man driven by rage and curmudgeonly emotion. But then England was now a country dominated, he felt, by childish propaganda and feel-good campaigns designed to facilitate a harmony that never arrived in quite the form that the engineers hoped. There was little room for people who just thought what they thought, and said so, even if what they thought could not be summarised in slogans or even in books. Many of his colleagues were Muslims. Internally, his dialogue with them was comical and rich and largely tolerant. It was not murderous except when he felt them siding with their *ummah* after an outrage committed by their own, for a bomb on a train did not make him any closer to them, but he saw no reason to feel apologetic for that and they did not reproach him. There was decency between them of a sort. A decency that was mutually enjoyable on odd occasions, as when he congratulated Dr Mutaba on a perfectly performed ear operation on one of his old ladies. As for his own image as the roly-poly Tory with his boozy red nose, it was a stock figure to which he was not attached and, moreover, one was in good company and it didn't really matter. It wasn't bad to have a streak of the late Evelyn Waugh in one's veins. It was a facade, a diversion, and an excuse for others not to look closer. No human being is that simple or that repulsive. A man sets himself up as a cartoon, but it is always for a reason that will become apparent down the road. As he walked through the heat, he felt as if he were distancing himself from what might happen to him shortly. He would now be free to drink himself to death, at least. His image as a curmudgeon might actually be useful if the Arabs got unpleasant, and, besides, it was just what liberals liked to think about others. Dogmatic as always. But then liberals never understood anything about anything deep down, because they didn't really understand cruelty and power except through being in opposition to them. Their body language revealed them. It was easy to oppose those things when you yourself didn't have to use them. But when you did . . . the tables turned with the speed of a knife being tossed into the air, and being disgusted and opposed and indignant didn't cut it any more. Any fool could feel those things.

They weren't wise enough, he thought smugly as they sweated between the restored houses, alone with the sound of their sandals crunching white-hot dirt. They thought everything in the world was like them, driven by ideas. How stupid can you get? Power in the racial sense was merely *how many of you there are.* That was simple enough, no? Everyone on earth seemed to understand that except white liberals. It wasn't a simple or coarse rejection of others. Because he didn't hate others; he was just indifferent to them or regarded them as rivals. There was a vast difference between those two emotions. And they *were* rivals. Human beings are always rivals. He remembered a comment made by the Mexican writer Carlos Fuentes about Hispanic illegal immigration into the United States. It was, the great man had observed mildly and approvingly, 'chromosomatic imperialism'. So there you had it in black and white.

He patted the cold sweat on his face as they walked outside. He hated the heat. He hated the sand in the air, the smell of earth and cooking fat. He hated the fucking turbans they wore at night.

Richard turned to him. 'This won't take a minute. We'll see the fire-eaters from Taza later on. They are really alarming.'

'Oh, great.'

They went past an open space with people dancing. David watched them as if he were deaf, as if the music didn't exist, which made it a horrible sight. People jigging about like epileptics. He loved only the smell of the expensive perfume on the women's bodies, sweated off and floating free. Why hadn't they gone to Rome instead? This very moment they could be sitting down at

Ristorante 59 on Via Angelo Brunetti and ordering a nice cold bottle of Greco di Tufa. What a mistake he had made in coming here. But he had made it for Jo, and he was sure it would 'mend her,' as he so often put it to himself. Everyone can be a fool.

She needed a break, a real break. She hadn't written anything in years. She was bitterly unhappy, and maybe it was mostly because of him, but there it was − one should never deviate from what one really likes. The whole idea of 'exploring' as an earnest moral project is pitifully ridiculous, and it always leads to failure, if not acute suffering. What a fool he'd been. There was no need to travel at all, really, except to go somewhere *more beautiful,* which for David meant an Italian or a French city with a better way of life than London or New York. Places with better food, calmer dynamics, better architecture. You went there and recharged your batteries. You drank and ate unreasonably, with no thought to what you would look like next week with fatter love-handles, and that was good. Life was better for a while, so you got your money's worth. Most of the rest of the world, on the other hand, was just hassle. Perhaps he just didn't understand it.

'I admit all that,' he thought, looking at his dusted shoes, which no longer responded to polish. 'So I'm not exactly a chauvinist, am I? I'm a perfectionist. I just think some Muslims treat their people like donkeys. I'm sorry, but they do. They manifestly do treat their people like donkeys. It's not our fault, never was. It's their right if they want to.'

By the gates, the Toyota stood in semi-darkness, its back hatch open, and around it a few villagers stood as if waiting for some dramatic relief to the tedium of the day, which was just like the tedium of every other day. They listened to the Seventies disco music coming from inside the *ksour* with their usual indifference, no longer bothering to imagine that anything decadent was going on. They were more interested in the solitary policeman lounging on the wall and eating a sandwich, and in the prospect of the swaddled body of Driss appearing through the gate. The sun had dropped out of sight behind the distant horizons, and the air above the sunken springs had turned grey and moist. The dragonflies had quietened down. Among the ruined houses along the Tafnet road, the wild flowers stood unwilted in morose bunches, their heads made of deep-gold petals that broke the dark. The men smoked their long clay pipes, holding the bowls in their left hand, and they had nothing to say. Gossip had exhausted itself.

As Richard and David came to the garage, the men from Tafal'aalt were there drinking mint tea and squatting at the base of the wall. They looked up with a soft, withdrawn curiosity. It was Richard who was nervous, for he felt nervous around Moroccans when Hamid could not be found immediately. And now Hamid was not around, drawn elsewhere, no doubt, by his innumerable duties. Richard therefore hesitated at the door of the garage. He sensed at once that the men from Tafal'aalt were unlike anyone he had encountered in this country. They were bone-dry and minimal in some way, like pieces of driftwood that have been whittled down to their essential shapes. They moved very slowly but with that purposefulness that makes even humble people seem formidable and relentless and aristocratic. Their poverty only accentuated this dangerous, fluid nobility. The intense darkness of their skin was like something acquired by effort, like carbuncles or scars. They talked in a subdued, gracious manner, as if nothing was worth shouting for or could be obtained in this way anyway. One couldn't say what they were ever thinking, or calculating, because it was possible that they did neither. They were mouldy and dusty, arthritic and dried-out, and when they spoke, the eyes suddenly came alive, their hands moved like paddles flapping up and down and one didn't know what to think about them.

'Where is the father?' he said to them in his blunt, rusting Arabic, and they made a gesture that said 'Where do you think? Inside.'

He waited for Hamid, who soon appeared, huffing and puffing, though quite splendid in a ceremonial *djellaba*. The guests were complaining about the cucumber canapés, and Hamid had had to have a whole set remade at the last moment. Can cucumbers, he'd been thinking for the last hour, really go off?

'Monsieur,' he gasped, holding his sides, 'I have been running all this time. I am sorry.'

'It's all right, Hamid. Catch your breath.'

Richard took a quick look at David, who was pale and ice-cold.

'Are you ready for this, David?'

David nodded disdainfully and took his own steps towards the garage door, which was open and somewhat thronged. Richard ordered the bystanders back and took Hamid and David with him into the garage.

The lights were all on. The father stood by the body, shaken by his own expressionless tears, and Richard saw at once that there was nothing calculating about him. That was unfortunate, and his heart sank a little. The old man simply stared at them, his hands clenched by his sides. David was unable to stop himself staring openly at the body of Driss, which he had never really looked at during the night. He couldn't find within himself the appropriate emotion, but at least he could look sincerely grave, astounded. He was not invited to shake the man's hand, and he knew intuitively that such a gesture had to wait. He waited, and he allowed his heart rate to rise, then fall again. Gradually, his sweat cooled. He lost his fear and he began to calculate the probable financial damage.

It was Hamid who had to speak, and in broken Tamazight.

'This,' he said solemnly, indicating David, 'is the man who was driving last night. He declares his innocence, before God.'

But his tone indicated to the Aït Kebbash that Hamid, too, had his doubts, and they were not doubts that could be easily tamed.

Abdellah looked at David with a childish clarity, his eyes wide open and questioning and yet somehow refusing to pose any question at all. For a moment David thought that they were remarkably free of acrimony. How could it be? The old man seemed to be simply examining him as one would a stone or a locust hanging in a tree. He looked right through him, too, as if the internal organs were visible and could be judged. He looked through him and there was no expression on his face.

The air conditioners hummed loudly in the confined space and the old man was actually shivering slightly, his *burnouse* gathered tightly around his head.

It was Hamid who said, 'Are you taking the body home now?'

'We are, God willing.'

Richard strained to understand these odd words in Tamazight, but failed. He shot David a worried look.

'Do you want to talk to the Englishman?' Hamid went on, bending solicitously towards the old man.

Abdellah turned to face David more fully.

'You may speak to him,' Hamid said quietly, 'and I will translate.'

'No, I will speak to you,' the father responded.

Hamid stepped over to Richard for a moment. 'He says he will speak to me. Perhaps it is because you are not believers.'

David shrugged. 'Here we go.'

'It's fine,' Richard reassured him. 'Go ahead.'

Abdellah spoke with his eyes fixed on Hamid's round, pleasant face, with its waxy, comfortable complexion. His voice was gently coaxing in some way, but also hard, and either way, it never lost its exquisite sense of measurement. He talked as if he had prepared his speech over many hours, as if every word had already been worked out and fitted into an irresistible argument. There was no visible effort in what he now said to Hamid, so that as he listened, the latter simply nodded and thought to himself: It's the most reasonable thing imaginable. The old man occasionally emphasised a point with a jab of his index finger. He spoke more intensely now, and Hamid leaned forward even farther. The two Europeans were excluded completely. Richard rested his chin in his hand, cocking his head to one side and trying to disguise his befuddlement. He knew enough about locals to realise that the old man was

125

proposing something quite complicated and that Hamid was going along with it. At length, the talking between them subsided, the old man turned away and Hamid stepped over to the Europeans, subtly changing his demeanour as he did so. A little abashed but also foxy, he protected himself with some obsequious apologies before reporting that the father had made a rather unusual suggestion, though Richard was not sure that *suggestion* was the most appropriate word. *Insistence* might be more like it. Abdellah, Hamid said, wanted David to return with them to Tafal'aalt to bury Driss. He thought it only right and proper that the man responsible for his death should do this, and he was certain that David would agree to it, being a man of honour as he most obviously was. Indeed, how could he not agree to it? It was a father's request to the killer of his son, but it was made with respect, with reserve, with a deep sense of propriety. It was customary in these parts, Hamid went on uncertainly, and his voice betrayed the extent of that uncertainty. Richard squinted, and he felt the question posed by Abdellah's demand widening and deepening in some new dimension that could not be framed and resisted by the usual objections.

'Is it?' he whispered in disbelief.

'Well, Monsieur, I cannot quite say. It is the deep desert. These are not people I know, in all honesty. They say it is their custom, and I will have to believe them.'

Richard reflected. Nothing about the old man inspired suspicion. Nothing whatsoever. He was, after all, the aggrieved party, the victim, so to speak. But he couldn't believe it was just a matter of David paying his respects to the grieving family. There had to be something else, and he said so.

'Perhaps,' Hamid prevaricated, 'the family might appreciate a sign of Monsieur David's remorse.'

'Is that what he said?'

'Not at all. But it will be understood. We do not *say* such things.'

'But David has to know what is going on. He has to know the amount.'

Hamid shrugged ineffably.

'I cannot ask him, Monsieur. It would be gross. Monsieur David just has to take a certain amount with him.'

'But Monsieur David,' David said, 'has not agreed to this absurd plan. Go back with them to their unknown village? Are you crazy?'

Hamid turned to him with a steely, harsh courtesy.

'Monsieur David, I hate to say it, but it may be that you have no choice. They are not entirely asking you. They are being polite. I think they will insist.'

There was stupefaction in David's mind for a few minutes, but in truth he had been expecting something of this kind all along. Of course they wouldn't just take a handout. They'd extract as much out of him as they could. They'd hold him in some village until he agreed. It was pathetically predictable, with their bandit mentality and their extort-the-infidel ethic. He knew it would be useless to keep arguing against it, because Richard would insist, and would argue that, all in all, going back to the village for a night and paying his respects would be a damn sight easier than doing anything else. A handout would be easily affordable for a man of David's income. And all of that was true. He felt immensely tired by the whole thing, almost worn out, and he already knew that he would give in. The idea in some way offered him relief. Since everyone seemed to

127

tacitly think that he was guilty anyway, it would actually be a relief to be forgiven in some way. And nobody could forgive him except this shabby, stony old man in his dark brown *burnouse*. If this implacable father didn't forgive him, no one could. Being forgiven and being exonerated by the authorities were two very different things, and it was because the people themselves felt that difference that he was forced into doing as Abdellah asked. It was a way out, and it was the only way out.

Unforgiven, he thought, I'll be a marked man.

Richard read his face accurately enough, and the host felt a quick relief that David understood what he had to do.

'I was expecting worse,' Richard whispered into his ear. 'You could make a trip out of it. You'll be back in a couple of days.'

David twitched, and remained dignified, but Hamid caught his quick, disgusted nod.

'So you will agree?' he urged.

'I suppose I do.'

'It is an excellent decision, if I may say.'

'We'll see about that. How much money shall I take with me?'

Hamid looked slyly over at the father. 'Take everything you have. Then give it all and say it is what you have. They will accept it. They are poor people, poorer than you can imagine.'

Poor makes greedy, David wanted to add.

'It's not ideal,' Richard said, with an unavoidable sense of relief, 'but it's not so bad. It'll be interesting.'

'Has it occurred to you, Richard, that they are planning something a lot nastier than you anticipate? I mean, it's just a thought, old boy. There wouldn't be much stopping them once they've fleeced all the cash off me. They might have rather unwelcoming feelings towards me, since, you know, I bumped off their boy and all that. Did we think about that?' He glared at Hamid.

'Well, Hamid? Do you have any thoughts along those lines?'

'Monsieur, you are exaggerating.'

'Am I? Am I really?'

'Yes,' Richard intervened, 'you are. That's the last thing they're going to do. God, David. Are you paranoid *all* the time?'

'Jo will take it badly.'

'She'll understand. I'll talk to her if you want.'

David raised an abrupt but unconvincing hand. 'No, no more interventions, please. I'll do it myself. Well, what a jolly weekend.' He beamed horribly at the old man. 'I say, Mr Deep Villager, when do we leave?'

Outraged, Hamid provided him with the real name, but David couldn't get his tongue round it.

'Just say Monsieur Taheri,' Richard snapped finally, letting all his accumulated irritation burst out at last. 'Or just Monsieur.'

'*Monsieur*,' David said to the old man, who did not even look at him. '*Quand voulez-vous partir?*'

'*Tout de suite,*' the old man replied without missing a beat.

David felt the condensation of his own glands growing cold all over his body, the sticky coolness of a thousand bumps of sweat. He steadied the sudden giddiness that overcame him and he did this by using his closed fists as ballast. This made the overhead light, which had been swinging wildly, become still again. He blinked.

129

Richard wanted to disengage, to leave it at that. He was being cut off, abandoned. It was damage control. It's your circus, *old boy*, Richard was thinking. Go dance in it.

'I have to talk to my wife,' David said to Abdellah, as Hamid translated. 'She'll be extremely unhappy.'

'She might be,' Richard agreed sadly.

'A gazelle is a gazelle,' the old man said, as if this needed no further explanation, and Hamid smiled, and if it had been polite, he would have laughed. *'Ghanchoufou achno mkhebilina ghedda,'* he murmured — we'll see what tomorrow brings.

Jo waited for him on the porch of their chalet. As the light faded, the staff came by to light tall mosquito tapers, though she had the impression that the air was so scorching that even mosquitoes couldn't survive in it. They brought with them painted plates of melon and Italian prosciutto, stemmed glasses with a pricked peach in each one submerged in champagne. It was the German cocktail *Kullerpfirsich*, the peaches rolling as the bubbles entered the fork grooves and made the fruit turn. The Moroccan boys were highly startled by this invention, which might have seemed to them like a sleight of witchcraft, and they set down her drink as if they were dying to be rid of it. They wore *tarbouches* that night, and she felt for them.

'Why do the peaches turn?' they asked with big eyes.

'Because Monsieur Richard made them,' she replied.

Out of nowhere, a firework rocket shot up into the sky, narrowly missing the moon. Silver sparks floated back down, and by their light, she saw the edges of the outdoor disco and its seething mass of heads and arms.

They had set up fake silver palm trees around it ribboned with rose-coloured lights, and between them were narrow silk tents with high-pitched roofs, inside which there were probably refreshments or dope. Richard and Dally made a point of making naughty stuff available to their guests in insouciant ways that obviously gave them a good laugh. There were plates of *majoun* crackers in the library at all hours, reefers expertly made up stacked in cedarwood boxes on the hallway tables. You'd see some elderly *roué* pause as he swept by on his way to dinner, sniff the goods and pick one up with a mincing elegance. The idea was to get them all stoned all the time, and it had worked because they were all stoned now, she was sure, all except for David and her. A collective mood had come upon them. A couple staggered by trailing fallen olives and cocktail sticks, very young, the girl incredibly glamorous and the boy soaking wet. They cast a quick look at her and the girl said 'Coming?' Their faces were like young wolves. The girl looked like Isadora Duncan just before the strangulation. Jo shook her head and raised her spinning peach. See, no need for anything else.

'It was what I was saying about the Americans in Iraq . . .'

The girl's voice trailed off, and she lost her balance, falling to one side, but held up. Another rocket zoomed up and expired in a shower of special effects. She looked at her watch. Where was David? A large plastic beach ball appeared over the heads of the dancers, kept aloft by successive pokes and slaps, rolling around just like her peach. A wave of laughter. Her anxiety would not relent, however. It was an exhausting guilt that had no issue, no resolution. Who could she beg to be forgiven? There was not a soul to beg, if not the old man at the gates, and David was dealing with him. And she hadn't begged anything from anyone her whole life. How did you do it?

She felt herself losing distinctness. Though her body remained still, her mind whirled round and round on an increasingly unstable axis. The body can turn to sand, dissolving at its extremities and mixing with its surroundings, gradually disappearing, merging into other things. The moon rose, thank God. And then the familiar form came hunkering down the strange repaved paths that criss-crossed Dally and Richard's fantasia like so many black snakes. She tensed. David was grim, as always.

She sometimes wondered if she really hated him. You know, she'd say to herself, that jittery hatred that is a perfect counterfeit for an exhausted, dissolving love. You can hate a man simply because you *let him in,* and then he didn't do what he was supposed to do. It was insulted feminine egotism in some ways, but other than that, she thought primly, the sacrilege was all his. He blustered and bullied. His pride was insurmountable. Men are the sinners, not us. She believed she had minor faults, not sins.

She gulped down the whole glass of fizzy and then took a wet bite out of the alcoholic peach.

'They're dancing like babies,' he said coldly as he came up, searching at once for a towel with which to wipe his hands. 'I'm so glad I can't dance.'

He slumped down next to her, and his face was grainily damp and sickly-looking. The resignation in his voice now was startling, and she waited to see what it might be. One never knew with him. Disasters broke over him like dust storms and were gone before you knew it, leaving behind them his rugged, obstinate form that reminded her of a great pile of boulders.

He sat back, and his bitterness made no bones about itself.

'Dicky and the Arab servant have cooked up a perfectly wonderful plan for me. I'm to go back with the old crone to his village in the middle of nowhere and do some atonement. I have no idea what they have in mind. I have to take all the cash. Dicky says he'll lend you whatever you need here, which is nothing. I agreed to go. Everyone seems to think it's the only thing to do. The nomads might get nasty.'

'They're not nomads, darling.'

'Well, whatever they are. I am being hauled back to a place I can't pronounce. Still, at least there'll be no dancing.'

'That's what *you* think.'

He groaned, and they managed a moment of black humour.

'When are you leaving?'

'Right now. He wants to leave in an hour. The body . . .'

'I am coming, too,' she announced after a dead silence.

'Out of the question. *Pas de gazelles,* the old geezer said. No women, which means no you. You are staying. You would be an insufferable complication.'

She tried to make a faint argument out of it, but it was like rolling a ball uphill, and soon enough the struggle fizzled out. She didn't want to go, after all, and no amount of rhetoric could hide the fact. She felt a sadistic triumph. It was right that he went, and somehow she didn't think it was dangerous at all, merely worrying.

For the following few minutes she packed a shaving bag for him, taking care to do it well. She stowed away his toiletries and toothbrush, his aftershave and razors, his vitamin pills and his cotton balls. She folded a few clothes into his sports bag and zipped both bags up. It was like packing a kid off to school. Her mind raced ahead. It never occurred to her that they might harm him. But for a moment, she stuffed a knuckle into her mouth and felt the tears surge. They weren't for him. They were for their past, which had suddenly disappeared. When she came back outside, he was drinking heavily, staring fixedly at the gold outline of the house and its filigree windows.

'You shouldn't,' was all she said.

'I don't care about offending them. I am an infidel. I am *allowed* to drink.'

'But you shouldn't . . . for yourself.'

She cupped his neck in her hand, leaned down and kissed the wet forehead.

'That's precisely the reason I drink,' he murmured.

She didn't know what to say to him. Come back safe? Don't mortgage the house?

'Have you seen the place on a map?' was what she did say.

He shook his head. He said he didn't much care where it was.

'I'm sure Richard wouldn't let you go if there was a risk. It's not that big a country.'

He took her hand for a while, and in some sick way he was also quite relieved to be going. One wanted to cross the bridge and have done with a lot of things. He stared glumly down at the two ice cubes at the bottom of his glass swimming about in a diluted Johnny Walker, and his mind clouded. It's all my fault, he wanted to say, so it's for the best. Stay and have fun.

'I order you to have a good time.' He smiled. 'I'll be fine. *Tutto bene.* Think of it as a jaunt in the desert. Tea in the Sahara. The whole thing will be silly and I'll probably enjoy myself in the end.' He almost snarled. 'I think they just want closure. A gesture of solidarity. They want me to say I'm sorry. That's what people always want. It's like being on *Oprah.*'

'And will you say sorry?'

'I'll say sorry, yes. I *am* sorry.'

'That's a relief to hear. For a while I thought you weren't sorry.'

He rolled his eyes, and her fingers went through his heat-coarsened hair, springy with salt-and-pepper curls. He was sulking, feeling like a victim. His hand trembled as it gripped the drink that was gradually poisoning him. They were playing Lucio Dalla in the disco, pop of the Italian Seventies. He wouldn't miss that, would he? He turned to her, caressing the knuckles of her hand as it pressed against his shoulder, and there was the unspeakable thing passing between them, the dribs and drabs of the old complicity. Laugh at the world together. Enjoy the same wine. Remember the little hotel in Rome? But the bag was packed in the other room, and up at the gate the men of the Aït Kebbash were waiting for him. Their mood was not grim, but they were anxious to perform a legitimate burial. When they got there, the car was already running; the body had been scrupulously wrapped like a mummy and had been loaded into the back of the jeep, its awkward length bent in the middle slightly. Abdellah waited impatiently for the murderer of his son to appear with his travelling bags. His mood

135

was indescribable, even to himself. But, then, he would never have tried to describe it to himself.

His soul was in darkness, just as his mind was. He licked his lips and cast a dry, scornful look at the pitiful *Source des Poissons*. But deep down, he was envious of it, bitterly covetous.

Eleven

IT WAS AUGUST NOW, DRISS SAID, AND Roger
made him coffee every morning in the outbuilding when
there were guests in the rooms, and he would see human
visions in slippers and gowns come down to the pool with
bowls of strawberries and half-hearted cigarettes like delicate animals coming down to a watering hole. The European
guests. French couples and families from London and
Dublin. Some of them kept yachts at Sotogrande for the
summer. Roger kept him away from them, closing the door
of the outbuilding while he sipped his coffee and making
sure no one saw him until he was dressed up in his straw
hat and gardening jacket, an anonymous scarecrow they
would not ask questions about. Then, disguised, he ventured
out into the sunlight with his pruning shears and pail.

Roger showed him the gardens he and Angela had
built since they had moved to Spain eleven years earlier.
They were English gardens by inspiration, but given
'new blood' by a better climate. Driss had to learn every
shrub and petal. He had to learn to trowel and seed and
trim as carefully as you would trim your nails.

'Well,' Roger would say as they walked slowly through
the gardens in the mornings, 'I would like it if you could

teach me some Arabic. I might as well take advantage of you.'

The infidels were always telling jokes. But were their jokes really jokes? They were always jolly and sweet, those two, but was it really jolliness and sweetness? A dark screw turned in his heart, since he knew that unbelievers were as devious as they come, and sought in the end only the undoing of believers. It was their nature, about which they could do nothing.

Within the parameters of this doubt, however, he felt affection for the Bloodworths. In the main house, whose shutters could be closed against spying by the guests, he played chess with Roger while strangely soothing music came from the sound system and Angela made them dinner in painted dishes that were not unlike Moroccan dishes. He could not beat the old man at chess and it vaguely annoyed him, but in the centre of the table there were bowls of apricots and dusty figs and they ate them with a knife while the cicadas sang close to the windows. The old infidels had such a calmness about them, such a contentedness, that he wondered where such a quality came from. He had not encountered such old people before, but then he had not lived with old people at all, apart from his own father. Were they Christians or were they godless? It was a question that vexed him as he lay awake at night.

But at dinner they asked him gentle questions. Where was he from? What had he done as a living?

He said, 'I am a fossil prepper. That is my trade.'

'So you are a skilled man?' Angela asked.

'I am skilled in that. But in France I am going to be a janitor.'

'But you could stay with us,' Roger said to him one night. 'Isn't gardening better than being a janitor?'

But being a janitor, Driss thought, you have the keys to all the apartments.

They made careful plans for his time in San Martín. He was not allowed to walk down to the gate or wander along the road or go down to San Martín itself. He might be seen, they said, and the local police were always looking out for illegals working in the farms and greenhouses. He was to stay at the property, lying low and working on the grounds. He could telephone his family from the house if he wished, but the idea of phoning to Issomour made him smile. The idea of his father picking up a phone and saying 'Hello?' So he worked for weeks in this way, hidden by a straw hat, pruning fruit trees and hedges and living from the table of the Bloodworths. The infidels gave him wine, which he politely refused.

It was not, he said to Ismael, that he hated them. He loved them. It was their pity he hated. They seemed not to be aware that he, Driss, could destroy them at any moment he chose. Destroy them and loot the little safe in their office, where Roger kept all their earnings from the bed and breakfast. They were not even aware of the compassion he was showing them. They looked right past his manhood and ignored it, as if it didn't exist and he was just a child who needed a bowl of milk every day.

'He's lying,' Ismael suddenly thought. 'He never went to France at all. He was in Spain. He stayed at the house of the old ones.'

Driss sucked on his joint and he knew what the other was thinking, but his concentration was elsewhere: the past, which he never thought about, that considerable landscape haunted by ruined factories, poisoned rivers and battle sites.

'I was just biding my time, Ismael. I was wondering what to do. Depart for Paris or wait and see what the English people would do for me? I was making more money than I had in my life. Three hundred euros a month.'

By October he had a thousand saved up. But he knew that the office held thousands of euros more, maybe tens of thousands. The old ones kept as much as they could in cash to avoid paying taxes. So they were sly in their way, too, like everyone else. He noticed the sheaves of banknotes the Englishman tied up every night with rubber bands, oblivious to his presence, and the way he ordered them inside the safe in the neatest way imaginable. But however much he quietly observed the combinations Roger used to close the safe door, he could not memorise them. Nevertheless, he began to think about them. He was sure that eventually he would memorise the numbers and, when he did, he would have to think carefully about what to do. One might call it theft, but he would have called it something else. He would have called it necessity and law-of-life.

He knew his duties well, and the routines expected of him. He went to bed in the attic room late, so the guests would not run into him. He went up with an oil lamp after all the doors had been closed for the night, and he went down the long corridor at the top of the house listening to the faint sounds coming from the far side of the doors. A man of the desert, he would think gleefully, a man of Tafal'aalt, alone in the house of the unbelievers with an oil lamp and a piece of chewing gum, going to his bed with a kitchen knife on his person. His meekness and obedience amused him. He was playing along, of course, while he figured out the vast *gaouri* world and how it ticked, and while he did so, he permitted himself an unnatural humility that would prove useful to him if he was patient. He lay low.

He read into the night in his room – magazines that Roger gave him, *Paris Match* and *Der Stern* – and entered the wider world he had never seen through their photographs. When he turned off the lamp, he thought about his years at Issomour – truly stupid, wasted years.

Only now did he think of his father getting him up at five in the morning to climb the cliff faces with his hammers and chisels, beating him when he was surly and reluctant and telling him he was a lazy nonentity who would come to nothing and was no use to his father or his mother. A boy like him, disobedient and work-shy, would bring them all down if he didn't take his work seriously. At age ten, he was working the face of the cliff for ten hours a day, from dawn till the beginning of dusk and sometimes longer, alone at the end of a secured rope tied round his middle, dancing from hole to hole and tapping at the shells of trilobites with his chisel until they came away from the rock. Sometimes he would lie down in the caves from exhaustion and look out over the desert, over the huddled cement houses and the graveyard and the parched line of the *oued* and its diseased oasis and the gardens soaked in sand. Already he felt a hatred for this place, which was his home, and his eyes strained to the horizon to see what there might be beyond it.

They said the desert was once a vast sea, but if only it were now. There was the road that went up to Alnif, but it was not a road, just a scar on the land's surface. Along it came the jeeps carrying off the trilobites, and the men walking with their flocks as if lost. On the roof of Issomour, where they sometimes climbed to escape the rites of work, the trenches were filled with aquifers.

In November the rains came and the tourists dried up. Part of the house was boarded up, and the Bloodworths retreated to their winter routines, living in the heated ground floor of the house. The gardens became dewy and misted, and he wandered through them with a growing impatience. He began to think about Paris. The afternoons became shorter and the sound of hunting guns louder and closer. 'By God,' he admitted to Ismael, 'I did not have the courage to think of anything but Paris.'

He thought about it incessantly, and he began to ask Roger about the roads that led there. They were wide roads that swept through the mountains into France, and they cost a fortune to use. But he knew that the Moroccans drove on them all the way from Algeciras, and he might hitch a ride with some of them. The English seemed dismayed when he announced to them this scatterbrained plan, and they tried to talk him out of it. It was curious, he thought, how bored and lonely they seemed when the summer had passed, as if they dreaded the winter alone with each other in their chilly house on top of the hill. They wanted him to stay, and not because they needed help in the gardens, not because they couldn't clean the swimming pool by themselves. One night he heard them arguing in the main house, the man shrieking like a girl. Something broke, a dish perhaps, or a ceramic cup, and a door was slammed shut. Small disturbances in a small teacup. About what could an old couple argue with such force? Some nights they told him about their past, their hippie days wandering Asia with knapsacks and going to the famous Tangerine Dream concert in Reims Cathedral with Nico. They had always wanted to get out of England either way, and nothing had been able to hold them back. Yes, they said humorously, they understood all about the urges of migrants! One is born to wander the earth, Angela said, on one's own two feet, with no barriers or walls. The persecution of migrants was an injury against basic human nature. But Driss, for his part, had no idea what they were talking about. He wanted to get to Paris without the police knowing, and that was all. Human nature?

Sometimes he wanted to climb the wall and walk down to San Martín just to see the girls sitting in the cafés, but there was no way to do it. The English made it clear that if he did so, he would be compromising not just himself but themselves as well. But at night he could see the village's lights at the bottom of the valley, and the Bloodworths went there every night for a glass of *fino* and a chat. He began to feel imprisoned, and in need of opening the doors. He just lacked money, enough money to live in Paris for a winter. There was a simple solution.

'But,' said Ismael, 'they were now your friends.'

Driss extinguished his joint and turned on his side to look down at the road, from where he seemed to expect some small miracle. It was on this road that his dope arrived, or his payments for black-market fossils.

'We have no friends when we are making our way upwards. Wasn't I just their house slave? What was the point of it all?'

'They were lonely.'

'Yes, but is it my fault? Am I a dog? They could buy a pet if they wanted one.'

'By God, it is true.'

'They were unbelievers, and they took me in for their own reasons. Did I owe them obedience?'

143

'You did not.'

'Well, then. I took stock of the situation.'

'I can understand,' Ismael concurred.

'Am I beholden to them? I had no agreement with them. God only knew what was in their hearts. The pictures they hung in their rooms – I am telling you – they were demonic. Things I have never seen before. Pictures of their prophet with blood coming out of his mouth. Well, and pictures of naked women painted by Italians. I owed them only the food they gave me, and, it's true, they took me in.' Perhaps, he thought to himself, they thought of me as a son. But sons are not pet dogs. They are unpredictable and strong and they go their own way.

He thought wistfully of the bed they had given him, the thick mattress, the head-enveloping pillows, and the night table with the carved ashwood lamp and the antique Cinzano ashtray and the books in German. The slippers left out for him, the bottle of water and the dried lavender in the vase on the sill, the shutters pinned with hooks and the sage suspended in a cloth packet from the rafter beams. The crucifix pinned to the white space above the bed. A meticulous cleanliness with a tint of lavender and a smell of laundry powder. It was a room made by the delicate, lovely Angela, who herself was like a piece of ancient paper shaped into a human form. It had all her precision and softness of touch and, as he thought of it, he felt a forlorn amazement and regret at its passing, for he had never found a room like that since then and most probably never would. It was that softness and cleanliness and crispness that he would never find again. Their guests, after all, paid a hundred and thirty euros a night to stay in such rooms.

All the same, he reflected, such things did not accord

with the kind of man he wanted to be. He wanted to be dry, hard, adamant, decisive and ruthless, without stain and without undue obligation. A desert man is a desert man; he is not seduced by pillows, of all things. He is not seduced by anything that men or women can fabricate. He is isolated and cruel, without being petty or mean-spirited. He takes what he can take because God has given him permission to take from those who deny Him. Was it not perfectly simple? No one could dispute the logic.

What he could not understand about the Bloodworths was that they had helped someone who was not one of them. It was the thing that troubled him most about them, the thing that most baffled and enraged him, because he himself would never have helped an unbeliever over a believer or at least, before doing so, he would have to have a great powwow with himself and explain it to himself. But they had seemed to do it spontaneously, out of the goodness of their hearts. It checkmated him, and he didn't want to be checkmated by two old English hotel-keepers. It was he who should be checkmating them, not the other way round.

He began to prowl about at night, not taking the oil lamp, but allowing the darkness to conceal him, skirting the house so that he could see into the lighted windows. This, at least, suddenly gave him power over his benefactors.

He saw Roger in his tiny study with his fox skulls and his maps and his bookcases, bowed over some enormous book by the light of a lamp with a rectangular green shade. He saw the pen move and the cup of coffee steam and the faint music percolating out of the windows. At one, the light went off and the old man padded his way to their sleeping quarters, and Driss was alone between the tall cypresses, abandoned in a way, waiting for the last sound to come from the old ones and then creeping to the kitchen door to see if he could force it. It was always locked.

A voice inside him whispered, 'You weakling, you coward, you have no force, no determination. You want to go back to sleeping on a roof in Erfoud and being mocked for the black eyes your father gives you? Do you really want to fail?'

But he had not been able to remember the combinations, and so he had to use guile, patience, a ruse of some kind. If the world is war for the weak, then ruses are the latter's weapons of choice. One had to be patient until the moment came when one's ruse could work.

He observed everything more attentively throughout the house, and there came a weekend when Roger had to go back to England to attend to his business affairs. They told him merrily at breakfast, and Roger leaned over and said to him, very seriously, that he would have to 'look after' Angela while he was away and, when he returned, they would talk about his plan to go to Paris. Maybe they could help.

'Thank you,' Driss said, with tears in his eyes, because he felt he had been very patient with his issue and that finally his patience had received some recognition. He had tended that garden faithfully every day for four months.

'Though, I must say,' Roger went on, 'I cannot see how we could ever find anyone to replace you. You have saved our business.'

What he had meant when he referred to Paris was putting Driss's papers in order. But Driss had not understood this at all. Driss thought, 'He'll buy me a train ticket to Paris!' If Roger did this, however, it would only solve a quarter of his problems.

'So did he buy the ticket?' Ismael asked.

'It would not have mattered. I needed more money than that. This is the way life is.'

Twelve

TWO BOYS IN TARBOUCHES STOOD ON either side of Richard with incongruous glasses of minted iced lemonade, lit like Egyptian statues in the heightened light created by the gate lamps, which had all been turned on as if to expose any possible subterfuge. It was a curious parting gesture on the part of an embarrassed host who took his duties seriously. A gesture of inadequate regret. A third boy carried David's two bags. The wind picked up now, scattering dust over all present. The Englishman looked once again like a kid being packed off to some distant, unpleasant boarding school from which he might not return entirely intact. Jo, Richard thought, looked surprisingly energetic.

'We're giving you a sleeping bag, too,' he said in a chatty way as David and Jo drank their lemonades. 'Stone floors and all that.'

'Sleeping bag?'

The look of horror on David's face was more than comical.

'They might not have a bed out there. They don't always sleep on beds.'

'What?'

Richard laughed and clapped his arm.

'Don't look so terrified. It's like camping. It'll do your spine good.'

'My spine's perfectly fine.'

A final gloom came over David's face and he gritted his teeth in a very demonstrative way, so that everyone knew he was gritting them and why. Jo took his hand, then swung herself against him and gave him a long kiss. As if slighted by this show of affection, the Aït Kebbash turned away towards their battered vehicle, and this was the sign that the discussions and delays were over and that it was time to attend to more serious things. A body must be buried with all haste, and every delay is a breach of contract with the holy texts. A kiss is nothing, marital affection a gust of wind.

On one side of the jeep David now saw that there was a crude yellow painting of a trilobite. The floor was littered with prepping tools and rolls of old newspapers. A tall man wearing a lime-green sweater in the suffocating heat came up quickly to open the front passenger door for him, skipping round him with a spurt of agility. David watched his hand yank open the door; it was practically black, the nails clogged with oil. The Aït Kebbash uttered some curt farewells and piled into the car with the force of a rugby scrum, squeezing themselves into the available spaces with a few ominously angry words. Jo and Richard came to the window, which was broken but half down. The servants were already filing back inside, and the disco music had grown louder, booming against the silence of the desert. One by one, the mental strings that bound David to the knowable world began to snap apart, and he drifted away, gripping the window glass and frowning.

'Look after her, Dicky.'

'I expect one of them will give you a ride back afterwards,' Richard said affably, putting his arm round Jo and pulling her a little towards him. 'If not, call us on your mobile and we'll figure something out.'

'Will it work out there?'

'Of course it will. We use ours all the time.'

It was the father who got in to drive. He didn't care that the *gaouri* were talking among themselves: he started the engine with a gruff motion.

'Call as often as you can anyway,' Jo pleaded.

There was still a trace of orange flare in the eastern sky as the car began to roll down to the long road that connected Tafnet to the main highway to Errachidia. The owner of Azna and a few others watched it approach the first bend, its tail lights flickering on and off, and it was only there that its headlight came on and the prickly pears appeared on the edges of the cliffs. Poor sod, Richard thought, and then he said it, only louder than he had thought it.

'Poor sod. It'll be a difficult couple of days. I somehow suspect that David has never slept on a stone floor before.'

'Never,' Jo said.

'It'll be a learning experience. Shall we go in and get a drink? We'll call him in a couple of hours and make sure they haven't raped him. No, darling, I'm just kidding. He was looking rather cute with those bags, though. Like a Boy Scout on his way to Auschwitz.'

'David is *anything* but a Boy Scout.'

She couldn't help smiling at this remark, and the distortion of her face lasted all the way to the first of the open-air bars that had been set up round the dance floor, where the glare of the metal palm trees and the sudden

150

onset of loud music drowned out her misery, but also her natural cautiousness and reserve. Richard's chirpiness, his jauntiness, reassured her because one was never jaunty when things were serious, or when people might get hurt. And Richard knew the desert far better than either she or David. She relaxed much more quickly than she might have thought possible, and as they threaded their way into the crowd, and Richard slickly procured her a double gin and tonic with a sliver of shaved cucumber, she let herself give in at last to the spirit of a long, confused party. He thrust the cold glass between her hands and gave her a quick asexual hug, a kiss on the side of her face.

'Come on, bunny. Relax. I am *not* going to let you mope in your room popping pills. Why don't you meet some people? We invite only the best people, you know. Some of them are quite amusing.'

'I must look like shit.'

'It's a hundred degrees at nine o'clock. Everyone looks like shit, my darling. And besides, you don't look like shit at all. *Tout au contraire.* You look splendiferous.'

'I usually don't drink things as big as this, Richard.'

She looked down at the enormous gin and tonic with its curl of cucumber, and he raised her hands so that the brim of the glass touched her lower lip.

'Doctor's orders. Drink it all down. It's mostly ice anyway. It'll just make you cold.'

His eyes went piggy and funny and she couldn't help it – she laughed and did as she was told. The ice cubes slammed against her lips as the incredibly strong dose of gin slipped inside her. Trojan horse, she thought for some reason, and then leaned back on her heels, felt the sweat emerging on her neck and watched the mass of dancing bodies.

The whole area was dark apart from the strings of lights shaped like rose hips that swathed the metal trees. The outdoor bar was covered with thick white linen, with the staff done up as corsairs with toy swords, and among the guests she noticed great balloon-shaped turbans, naked chests and eye patches, wigs and knee-high boots. The music had switched to Sly and the Family Stone, and inside the thicket of limbs she spotted the American, Day, dancing with a very pretty girl.

Richard stood by her until he was sure she was drinking heartily.

'You can dance,' he said quietly. 'It's not a crime. David's all right. As we speak, he's probably having a joint with the Aït Kebbash. They're enormous potheads, you know. Incorrigible. He'll be stoned the whole time.'

She said nothing, speaking instead to herself.

'I think I'll wait till I calm down. Maybe another drink or two.'

'Look, there's Lord Swann. He came on a helicopter last night that landed at Rich. No, luvvy, that's a town in these parts, believe it or not. It's been called Rich for centuries. Perhaps it means *poor* in Berber.'

And there was the lord, who looked like a seventy-year-old plumber, turning on his heels to something funkadelic. Richard clapped his hands, delighted.

'He always shows up for the girls. He has an incredible collection of Sahara fossil aquifers at home. He'll probably tell you about them when he chats you up later on.'

'I never know what to say to lords. I feel like they've run out of things to say.'

'But let's not hate them. I find them very tolerant. They are potheads, too, like the Aït Kebbash. I've always been meaning to introduce these two groups. I have a feeling they'd get on.'

It seemed like an hour later that she was wandering through the brightly lit house, where the carved wooden screen smelled of patchouli oil and the floors exuded a warm, earthy scent of pine needles. It was, in the end, a house that imposed itself as a personality in its own right, a character with history and emotions, and the stairwells breathed like lungs, with soft, momentary breezes that came and went without noise, with a shuffle of tassels and curtain hems. She found a quiet corner where some antique lances hung on a wall and flipped open her mobile phone. The steel blades shone above her and her nostrils filled with a scent of damp but exotic domesticity. Smoked tea and varnish and carpet dust. She dialled David's number and heard it ring: a small miracle. She waited impatiently, the phone pressed too tight to her ear, but he didn't pick up. It was possible, of course, that he had moved out of their reception area, just as it was possible that he would soon move back into it. Richard had warned her there was spotty coverage in the desert. But the futility of the call depressed her. Perhaps he *was* smoking a joint in the car. Finally she gave up and pocketed the phone. She was a little tipsy as she tottered through the galleries and halls, her hands held out to grip things and steady herself. She slipped through a maze of lustrous objects whose specificity she couldn't quite determine, because she wasn't paying attention and she didn't care where she was. There was a large, colourful bird in a cage hanging by a piano, its claws wrapped round a brass swing, and brass lanterns with green glass suspended above her from chains, and pieces of antique weaponry, and skin lamps pierced with hundred-year-old multicoloured glass. She walked through the rooms as if she were blind, letting the gin carry her. When she heard voices, she backed away, seeking more pools of isolation.

She was sitting alone on one of the Raj horsehairs in the library when Hamid came to look for her. It was about an hour before midnight, and for some reason the dozen caged birds scattered throughout the house had started singing in five different mutually exclusive keys. She looked up to see Hamid in a cherry sash peering down at her with a cup of coffee in one hand, a spoon balanced on the saucer with a square of wrapped chocolate, as in a restaurant. 'Monsieur Richard,' he said, 'thought you might want this.' The fire-eaters of Taza were about to perform, and he wanted her to come outside and enjoy it. A coffee would revive her.

'How did he know I was in here?' she asked incredulously.

'Monsieur Richard knows everything, Madame.'

She took the cup and placed it on the arm of the sofa.

'I will wait to take you outside, Madame.'

She really wished he wouldn't, but now that he had his orders, it would be pointless to try to talk him out of it. She gulped down the coffee and then the sliver of chocolate. The molten black eyes took her in easily. She was shaking very slightly. David didn't call; the unknown had swallowed him up, and it might as well swallow her up as well. But for her, the unknown was just a rich man's party.

Hamid seemed to be putting her under surveillance. She stood up when her cup was emptied and asked him to lead the way. He always bowed when asked to do something, but his bows were never entirely compliant. They were reminders that he knew the score and you didn't.

They went through the dining room, where the table

was magnificently set for another late-night gastronomic orgy. There was a galleon made of pink sugar in the middle of it.

In the gardens, the disco had been interrupted, and rows of sofas were set up with rugs and furs thrown over them. Water pipes were serviced by the staff, who went from sofa to sofa with tongs grasping tiny morsels of fruit-flavoured charcoal.

Hamid led her to a chair where a table had been set up with a pitcher of lemon water, and next to it sat Richard and Dally nestled in each other's arms. On a sand stage surrounded on all sides by the guests stood the men from Taza in their outlandish costumes, drummers to one side, their tools dripping with petrol. The noise of the drumming had risen to block out everything else, and the faces around them were already altered by it, shiny, fixed, tuned out from subtler feelings, the eyes concentrated but not able to think, and they gave you only the option of joining in this coordinated mood, not of standing apart from it and watching from a distance. But Richard, sensing that this was not her type of entertainment, shot her a comforting look and Dally held out his hand for her.

'It's all too awful,' he shouted — a thing that should have been said quietly. She nodded and just sat back, unable to do anything else. She hated this sort of thing, but it couldn't be avoided now.

The fire-eaters went into their routine. They were stripped to the waist, their chests oiled, and they dipped their inflammable rods in the buckets of petrol and whipped them into the air above their heads, their feet moving in small motions to the pace of the drumming. Cocking back their heads, they held the flaming spears with two hands and brought the fire down towards their mouths, which would miraculously extinguish them. A low gasp went up from the audience, the gasp of unsurprised but chilled children at a fair. She was not interested, but her own revulsion was interesting enough. She felt a momentary blackout shut her down, and she reached out to grip the pitcher of water. A great arc of flame – of fiery saliva – shot across the stage, and the faces went orange for a second and then seemed to disappear.

'I don't know why it is,' Lord Swann was saying, 'but the *kif* here is stronger than the stuff in Tunisia. Maribel says it makes her hallucinate. Dicky, I think you have a man up in the hills who grows it for you.'

'I'm not saying anything.'

The lord made a swooning expression, and the girls with him, who were one-third his age, all giggled and reached for their cigarette lighters.

'See, girls? He's such a scallywag. Dicky and I have been playing ping-pong for years at the Athenaeum. He scalps me.'

They sat in a ring on the far side of the house, on square tribal cushions, with metal cups of tangerine sorbet and biscotti. The fire-eaters had dispersed to eat with the staff, and the party had become amorphous and loose, which was the way Richard liked it. He kept an eye on its progress, but he rarely intervened directly. He lay back and looked at the intense stars. They seemed to be approaching the earth rather than receding from it. He thought coolly about Jo and her mental state. Was she coping? He couldn't find her anywhere. And David was driving, driving through the desert, and Richard had lied to him about everything, but it had been necessary. The fool wouldn't have gone without a few euphemisms.

'I heard there was an accident last night,' the over-bearing Swann cried. 'Someone was hurt. Am I off?'

Richard explained.

'Ah,' the lord said, sucking in his *kif* smoke on his back. His Chelsea boots stuck up like little black gravestones. 'Mad dog's an Englishman who goes out on a moonlit night.'

'It's never happened before,' Richard said pointlessly.

His parties were written up on blogs across Europe, in garish magazines and sometimes in the *New York Times*, and he didn't want a bad reputation to descend upon them.

'Where's the dolt?' the lord demanded.

'We sent him into the desert to die.'

A lord's chuckle. 'Good. Quite right.'

'It's one of those things,' Richard said neutrally, digging into his sorbet. 'He probably mistook the accelerator for the brake pedal.'

'I had a chauffeur like that once. I had him killed, too.'

A plump, slothful girl in huge tribal earrings turned on her hip and brushed a mound of whitish hair out of her eyes.

'I can see these huge reptiles everywhere,' she purred.

'Maribel, stop smoking at once.'

'*You're* a huge reptile, Daddy.'

The lord laughed.

'She's such a prize, this one. She hallucinates every time. Even with rum and Coke.'

'I can see penguins,' Dally said. 'They're marching towards the granaries.'

'Personally,' Richard drawled, 'this stuff just makes me unfaithful. I don't see anything. Perhaps I have a mediocre mind.'

The lord sighed and crossed his gravestones.

'Are you unfaithful, Maribel?'

'Not when there's so many reptiles around.'

He winked at Richard. 'See? What's the bloody point of bringing them?'

Richard smoked more slowly than the others, with that measured self-restraint that he had learned from his Moroccan lovers. He had fewer than Dally, but he chose men who could teach him things. They had taught him how to sleep properly, how to lie on one's side, how to eat with one hand, how to be in repose, how to smoke without becoming excited. How to be *slow*.

He didn't become stoned; he merely allowed himself to slow to the speed of treacle dripping off a spoon. The girls laughed and rolled. The lord lit up with impotent desires that sparkled inside him and went up in smoke. This was how newcomers to the land were. They couldn't quite adjust. Richard, on the other hand, knew how to smell the wind coming off the valley, how to appreciate the taste of the local lemons. He was rarely excited nowadays, or thrown off-balance, because this, after all, was the life he wanted, and he consumed it drop by drop, like a liqueur. He frequently felt that he was the only white man of his acquaintance who was able to do this. Even Dally had not mastered it. His busy American nature obstructed the way, clouding his spontaneity with all kinds of wooden preconceptions that made him hesitant and flat. He couldn't quite get it.

Richard looked over at him now, taking in his full Mick Jaggery lips and his pointed *babouches* dangling on the ends of his long white feet. He was like a mechanical toy dog watching butterflies fly past its nose. That's life, the toy dog would think in perplexity, raising a little metal paw to try and catch it, but what is it?

Some time after midnight, Jo found the pool empty. She was drunk enough to take off her clothes and wander to one of the corner ladders and stand there in the moonlight naked. The moon danced as a dinner-plate-sized counter-image on the water's surface, not even undulating, intensifying by its presence the depth of the shadows lurking around the pool. She hoped someone was looking. She turned herself this way and that and laughed and let it come on if it wanted. So much the better. The heat had come down. The skies were so clear that the whole hillside was shocked into visibility. Cacti beyond the walls shone like tin; the rock formations offered a thousand ancient details. The air was warm, soothing, still, and the palms murmured as a breeze sifted through them, then stilled themselves in preparation for the next murmur. A Martini glass stood on the edge of the pool, an olive still stuck inside it, and sticky forks lay on abandoned china plates set down by the feet of deck chairs, their prongs caked with crumbs of carrot cake and melted icing. Towels lay about in what had once been pools of water. From the ditches on the far side of the wall came the shrill of the frogs the hosts might well have placed there for effect. Who knew what here was artificial and what was indig-enous? She lowered herself into the water, which was so warm it was almost distasteful.

The tiles were cornflower blue, with a Roman-style whale depicted on the bottom. When you swam over it, you saw that the whale was entwined with a boy. She glided over this kitsch mosaic scene and flipped onto her back, letting her breasts break water. First the silence of underwater, then the open sounds of the night and the relaxation of the optic nerves. A cicada started up from a hole in the wall and there were echoes coming over the stone slopes. Reverberations of hooves and falling stones, ghosts about, and the party and its hum. She counted her heartbeats for a minute. At the centre of the pool she rotated slowly. A cluster of stars – Aquila? – glowed down on her and she thought of her abandoned work, her books long dead, in the process of being forgotten by the world's feckless children. Every career has a few moments of visibility followed by a long, painful subsidence into total anonymity. The strange thing was that, on some level, she didn't mind as much as she had expected to mind. In her writing, she couldn't think of anything else to say, and that proved she didn't need to say anything any more. It was therefore time to go silent. And in some ways that was a relief. She no longer enjoyed it anyway, and going silent had its own pleasure. If it was a failure, it was a small plop of a stone dropping into the great ocean: a very small sound indeed. Perhaps thousands of years from now, some unhappy child of the future would pick up a copy of *Balthazar's Nighttime* in a cobwebbed digital library and rescue her from her oblivion. But then again, what a stupid, surreal idea that was. No one would be reading in fifty years' time, let alone a thousand. Everyone knew that. The children of the future would be empty-headed clowns. No one in the future would need her, any more than anyone in the present did. But not to be needed was as pleasurable as being needed.

Career? That was a strong word. She looked down at her blancmange breasts, quivering under their film of water and to what end? It would be better if someone were observing her right now, not letting them go to waste. But there it was. One ages out of view, in an enforced privacy. Guiltily, she thought about David then, but she couldn't keep it up. He still hadn't answered five calls on his mobile. Instead her mind drifted back to the party, to the beautiful girls. Was she really less beautiful than they, less unhinged by the present moment?

I can't be the librarian every single second, she thought archly. Not every single second of every hour.

She got out of the pool and sat drying next to the Martini glass while Dally's pet doves made their noises in the trees. She began to enjoy her new solitude. At length, she redressed and walked back towards the main house. A pinwheel firework turned on one of the lawns that the staff had to water night and day, spluttering with green sparks. She went to one of the open bars and asked for a Cuba Libre. The music had started up again and the guests were drifting towards the dining room, where the candelabra had been lit, the dark-green candles clustered together in waxy sheaves. It was a very late dinner, but no one seemed to mind. Boys in pirate dress wandered about asking people if they would like to join the table and ushering them in if they said yes.

It was here she met Day again. He had a head covered with bay leaves and little yellow flowers, and she thought he looked like a Greek celebrant, which was obviously the idea. They smiled and she thought: He's a little less attractive than the last time.

'You don't look like a pirate,' she said at once.

'Pirates never do,' he said. 'I'm going into dinner as Dionysius. None of these illiterates even knows who I am.'

'I am not an illiterate.'

'Then I have an audience of one. The pirate costume looked bad on me anyway. I looked like Johnny Depp.'

'I would think that'd be better than Dionysus.'

'I look weird in an eye patch. Sort of twitchy.'

She let him charm her.

'You aren't the god of wine. You're someone from a toga party.'

'We're at a toga party, aren't we?'

They stood by the French windows leading into the dining room, and the creamy light of the dining room fell onto their cheeks. Her hair was still wet and she felt like a child about to go into a cupcake party. Day was wearing a long *djellaba* with elaborate brocade and his face was open wide, very pink, as if the blood inside it were circulating at twice the normal speed. His eyes opened wide as well, with their mineral green quality, and they laughed as loudly as his mouth, just as his mouth laughed as silently as his eyes. A trick of some kind. She wondered how old he was. About the same as David, or a little younger, critically so, even? The difference that five years make in your forties.

'I'm starving,' he said. 'After you. I've been dancing with some goats. At least I think they were goats. Perhaps they weren't goats. But I think they had four legs.'

They went into the sweet air of the dining room, where the sugar ship now held a mound of almonds. Richard rose and tapped a wine glass.

'Ladies and gentlemen,' he said. 'I have never seen such a crowd of piratical ruffians. Grab your sabres. Our chef, Monsieur Ben, has created a new pastry stuffed with sardines. It's sensational. Afterwards you can loot as much as you want. In fact, I encourage you. *Vous êtes ici pour looter.* Just don't steal my oil paintings. If you please, darlings, not those. Just take a cigar. They're free.'

Issomour

___

Issomour

Thirteen

AS THE TOYOTA ROLLED DOWN THE HILL towards the road, the tall Kebbash who had opened the door for him leaned forward and asked David in perfect French, almost unaccented, and with a distinct politeness, if he would like a cigarette for the road. The old man, he said gaily, always insisted on driving and, by God, he could not be dissuaded from this sad duty, though it was unendurable for all concerned. David reluctantly accepted the cigarette, though he disapproved of the habit, naturally. But now, he reasoned, it would help him get through the hours. He therefore took the crumpled Gitane without a word and let the man, Anouar, light it for him. Their eyes met and they did not duel. Anouar seemed quite courteous and intelligent. There was something boyish and calm in his manner and voice, a lilt and a skip and a small murderous humour. He talked with his head on his side, like a large inquisitive parrot. 'Your wife,' he said sincerely, 'is very pretty. I will one day have a *gazelle* like that, God willing.' But would He be willing?

All six men were smoking by the time the car bumped its way onto the road, which was plunged in porous darkness and empty of traffic. They tore along it at a clip nearing eighty miles an hour, the wheels whining loudly, the windows vibrating as the nuts and screws shook. The engine shuddered. To David, the road suddenly looked like something intimately known. The white box-shaped guardhouses standing next to ditches and the straggling thorn trees were burned into his recent memory. Only the slopes of loose rocks looked higher than they had, less regular, and between them the groovelike ravines where the darkness seemed to collect like a fluid. It was now heavy in some way, this landscape, ominously saturated with its own inner gravity. Bones, marrow, but no skin, no external sheen.

Abdellah drove with his foot rammed into the accelerator and nothing else. He looked at the road and never at David. The men said nothing except when the cigarettes were lit. Only Anouar leaned forward to say a few things close to David's ear.

'We are driving straight through. We will stop in Erfoud to see some people and have a drink. And a nap.'

Before long they passed into the outskirts of Errachidia. The city was rectilinear, with wide avenues thronged with thousands of male students, and a soft light covering it, turning everything a dark gold. They shot over a bridge spanning a surprising river, the waters lit up by rows of lamps, and then rumbled along the flat, hard boulevards of what had once been a French military town. The buildings were uniformly white and so were the robes and hats of the innumerable students. There was still something of the desert barracks about the place, the departed Foreign Legion, and in the great spaces between the apartment blocks one could see – or sense – the flat line of the desert that was close enough to smell. There was no rubbish, and no animals – perhaps the seasonal heat had burned them away – and the young men thronged there in small clusters seemed scrubbed and neat, without animality themselves. It was an optical illusion. The outside never knows anything.

They stopped at a street corner to buy Cokes and sandwiches. David got out to stretch his legs. The air was so hot that his face winced despite his own determination not to betray any discomfort in front of his 'captors'. It was a struggle. Sand bit into his nostrils. Anouar asked him if he wanted to pee and he shook his head. It was impossible to tell what time it was, and through some vague superstition he didn't want to glance at his watch. Instead he watched Abdellah kneel by the wheels of the Toyota and inspect the tyres. Under the orange lamps, he looked more youthful, more lithely menacing. He clucked and said nothing to anyone, and his filthy shoes, David noted, had small cheap gold chains on them. The other men, moreover, seemed awkward around Abdellah, as if the embarrassment caused by his bereavement could not be lightened by the usual bonhomie. They did what he asked, and they did it quickly.

* * *

On the far side of Errachidia the road narrowed and sand drifted across it; low mud walls sometimes hemmed it in, and behind the walls rose the dark cool of palmeries tossing in the wind. Men with agonised blank faces trudged by the roadside with gaggles of goats, and their eyes flashed like cats' as they looked up into the headlights and didn't blink.

David watched the faces of the Kebbash in the rearview mirror. They were chewing dates now, passing around a piece of sticky paper, though not to him.

Perhaps they assumed that it would be offensive to his tastes. The pace slowed as the road became smaller and more cracked, and the father at some point reached down and switched on the car radio. The men sighed, affected by a burst of religious music. David struggled to keep awake, exhausted emotionally by the evening's events, and his hand gripped the shattered metal window handle. He reflected that none of the other men had been introduced to him, or their names divulged. It suggested that now names didn't matter much, because he was not an ordinary guest. Crammed together uncomfortably, they stoically endured the ride until one of them leaned down and picked up something heavy and metallic, and from the corner of his eye he sensed the presence of an old rifle. But it was not directed towards him. It was raised against the outside environment, which seemed to make them anxious as the palm groves thickened and the desert plains made themselves felt on either side of a road that relentlessly narrowed and became more suffocating. They were, he said, nearing Erfoud, inside the Tafilalet, the largest oasis in North Africa. From here came the royal family of Morocco.

David finally did glance at his watch. It was almost midnight. His mind was shrieking silently, and his sweaty hand let go of the handle. Abdellah huffed.

'He says we'll go to the hotel,' Anouar translated from the back seat. 'No one can drive across to Alnif in the dark.'

What he added in French was '*On regrette*'. But what did they regret?

'What hotel are we going to?' David asked pitifully.

'It's the hotel where the fossil dealers go. The Hotel Tafilalet.'

They passed along streets of rose-brown houses with

yellow and turquoise shutters, blue grilles and white crenellations along the roofs. Erfoud sat in its winds and dust, obstinate and sunken, and it was not even yet the sleeping hours. In the hot season, night was precious, a time in which to be alive and do one's business. Horse-drawn carts clattered around them piled with alfalfa and mint, lightbulbs exploded into life out of the dark, out of the arcades of a market where the flies had died down. The pavements were long piles of rubble behind which people sat on mats, staring at the traffic like people who are expecting a downfall of volcanic ash that will bury them for centuries. There were the same fossil shops he had seen in Midelt. The same gaunt men with trays of shark teeth and lumps of crinoids, the same boys running alongside the cars shouting *'Dents de baleines!'*

The Hotel Tafilalet stood on one of Erfoud's main streets, of which there were two. It was done in the *Arabian Nights* style, green and blue, with kitschy *mihrabs*, columns and alcoves that made its lobby seem denser and more majestic than it actually was. It looked like a smoker's den in a private club, with water pipes set up next to the tables and forms cradled inside cushioned benches.

Around the pool a few outdoor tables were set with sheltered candles, and here knots of men sat with their beers and smokes trying to find some relief from the scorching winds that rippled the water. The Kebbash parked the Toyota in the hotel lot and left two of the men to guard it; Abdellah strode through the lobby as if it were his living room, as if his physical shabbiness didn't matter there, and David came behind him, egged on by Anouar. They passed a bar next to the pool, its stone surface encrusted with ammonites. A few aghast-looking Europeans sat there, not knowing what to do, since it was too hot even to go in the pool, and their blue eyes watched the group shuffle into the garden and settle at a table where they ordered cold sodas for themselves, then in a comical pantomime settled David at a table all by himself.

'They will bring you a cold soda,' Anouar explained. 'There is a room upstairs where you can sleep. We get up again at five. I will come for you.'

'But why am I by myself?'

'It is more fitting, that's all. Surely you understand?'

He did understand; in fact, he preferred it. His exhaustion overcame him and he slumped onto the table, his eyes ready to close. He gulped down the 7-Up in its glass of crushed ice, then tried to steady his nerves. The pool was surrounded by tall palms planted on the far side of the walls, and their bushy heads tossed in the gusts. The light was brown with flying sand, like the inside of an old fish tank. The grit didn't seem to bother the locals, who obviously came here to network and trade. Mostly fossil dealers, he imagined, they floated about from table to table with elaborate gestures of friendship and small trays of polished ammonites. Did they, too, believe that these creatures were small demons who had fallen from the skies long ago? As they bowed at each table, they touched their chests with one hand and adopted a pleading tone. To David, they were especially pleading.

'*Monsieur, Monsieur, des très beaux ammonites de Hmor Lagdad! Des purs, des rares! Regardez, et pour vous, Monsieur, un prix étonnant, ridicule!*'

As they pressed desperately upon him, the Kebbash looked over with great amusement. The manager of the hotel had come out to greet them quickly, and the Erfoud dealers also passed by to shake their hands. The men from Tafal'aalt were key suppliers.

David shooed the sellers away irritably. He called Jo on his mobile but there was no signal. He cursed under his breath and considered asking the manager if there was email at the hotel. But when the manager came over, David had nothing to say. Suave and multilingual in the Moroccan way, the manager pre-empted him in impeccable, singsong English.

'Do not believe those sellers,' he laughed, gesturing towards virtually everyone there. 'They are all liars. But if you would like to support their families, it is a good thing to do. One fossil feeds a child for a month.'

'I wouldn't know what to buy,' David said bluntly.

'I would recommend a trilobite called a Spiny Phacops. All the tourists seem to love them. Especially the Belgians. However, I see that you are not Belgian. Nevertheless . . .'

David shook his head mournfully.

'A Spiny Phacops never disappoints,' the manager went on like a busy toy train. 'Bill Gates loves them. Your wife will love them. I love them. Perhaps you will love them, too.'

'I'm not really in the mood.'

'*Awili achnou hadchi.* What the hell. As you wish. I am sending over something to eat, at the request of your hosts. A *tagine,* which is a special dish of the Tafilalet. Your room is ready when you want to sleep.'

He ate determinedly. An elderly Frenchwoman entered the pool, oblivious to the scornful men observing her, and swam mechanically up and down in a pair of goggles.

It was amazing that people came here and stayed in the new five-star resorts lining the roads out of town. The desert was popular with package tours, but mostly they stayed safely near Erfoud. Who was this stubborn old bird doing her laps past midnight? It was probably too hot to sleep in the rooms. He tried to keep up an appearance of stoic English fortitude in front of the table of his captors – as he thought of them. He set his jaw and stared into space, even though his innards were dragging him down and he longed to be alone in that room upstairs. You can't show fear or even discomfort in front of these people. You have to show indifference to both. You have to show disdain. Yet in the end, the most disconcerting thing was that the Kebbash didn't even look at him at all. They ignored him completely. The old French lady shot him a quizzical, mystified look from the pool and he wondered if he should ask her for help. It would be a comical scene.

Eventually Anouar sauntered over and asked him if he'd like to go up and sleep. They took a narrow, dingy staircase to the second floor, and a room with a small balcony overlooking the pool. To David's surprise, the air-conditioning had already been turned on and the room was half cool – as cool as it would ever get, anyway. Anouar was quite friendly.

'Sleep,' the latter said, 'and I'll wake you at five.'

David fell onto the bed and lay there on his side with his eyes open, watching the corrugated white surface of the wall opposite. Then he rolled over slowly and turned on the ancient TV set. An image sprang to life of a moose struggling across a marsh littered with broken trees. 'Climate change,' a distant voice could be heard saying in English, 'in Siberia.' He opened his mobile phone and tried Jo again, but the signal was dead. The moose came to a standstill and stood there bewildered, paralysed apparently by climate change. David closed his eyes. He was going to have equally paralysing dreams. He was going to dream that he was in a hotel room in Erfoud, in which sand poured through the broken windows, suffocating him as he lay innocently in bed, watching a moose.

At five to five, Anouar knocked softly on the door. David was still on his side and the TV was still on. Waking in a snap, he said, 'I'll be there', and got up like an automaton. He went into the plastic-looking bathroom to splash a little tepid water on his face.

In the fluorescent mirror light his grey face appeared. The eyes were brighter and more urgent than the skin, more wounded. Sometimes it's a great disadvantage to have to see oneself in a mirror. It would be better to keep one's pride intact. He fed on the small bottle of Evian supplied by the hotel, then stepped for a moment onto the balcony. The temperature had lowered by about ten degrees so that the air was just about breathable. It was almost light and the wind was still. A maid silently swept the patio around the pool, upon which a detached palm frond floated. On one of the poolside tables sat a single coffee cup, obviously intended for him.

Anouar wished him good morning and escorted him down. David reasoned that he was about thirty-five, moderate in mindset, with a smidgen of education. But where had he got that education?

'Ten minutes for coffee, Monsieur David. Then we leave. Is your stomach all right?'

'Fine.'

David sat stunned with his coffee while birds chattered loudly in the trees. He had never felt so alone, so cut off; the others crowded into the lobby and drank swift pots of mint tea in the gloom where a single oil lamp burned. It took some time for his mind to revive and to resume control of his surroundings. He wondered if he had really slept at all. It wasn't certain. He drank sip by sip and told himself that all he had to do was see this through – sail through it like a stretch of choppy water. All he had to do was appease the furiously cold, implacable father. Above the pool, a clear sky had emerged with the first colour of dawn. Hundreds of doves in cotes nearby that one couldn't see burbled together as if roused. He went outside into the street for a breath of air. Black-clad women padded silently between the turquoise shutters, and out of the semi-darkness a huge radio antenna began to materialise on the top of a hill. From close by there came the sound of hundreds of small mallets and hammers chipping away somewhere, in some open-air workshop near the Oued Ziz. The fossil shop across the street already stirred.

By the town's only intersection, where the post office stood, a cop in white gloves loitered as if waiting for a small crime that might well not happen, and all along avenue Moulay Ismail men and boys slept on dozens of mats laid out under the closed doors. David stood waiting for the Kebbash by the Ziz petrol station, impatient to get going, impatient for first light, and when his co-travellers appeared he was irritated with them for being so dilatory. Abdellah strode out into the road holding a half-peeled orange and stood for a few moments inspecting the arid, washed-blue sky, across which flocks of sparrows were crossing with a jubilant din. His grief was still impressed upon the surface of his face. He held himself stiffly, as if a tremendous energy inside him could not yet be released. He sank his teeth into the orange and spat out the pips, tore the fruit apart and attacked it a second time. It was his breakfast.

They drove through the intersection close to where a huge fossil store called Usine Marmar stood. As they passed the cop, Abdellah rolled down his window and stuck out his hand to graze the white glove of the policeman, though as far as David could see, nothing passed between them.

On the road to Merzouga they passed lines of Berbers on rickety bikes loaded with tool kits. They were Aït Atta, Anouar explained, riding off into the desert to prospect for aquifers and crinoids. They, the men of Tafal'aalt, did not prospect for such things, which were the preserve of the detested Atta. The men of Tafal'aalt dealt only in trilobites, and in trilobites alone. Issomour was the richest source of trilobites in all of Africa, Anouar continued in a lazy, half-serious voice. Why would they need to trifle with fossilised marine plants? They willingly left such baubles to the Atta, while traders from Germany, France and the United States paid handsome sums for the beautifully preserved Comura Tridents that they dug from the faces of their holy mountain. Some specimens sold for hundreds of euros.

Before the sun rose they were at Hmor Lagdad. There was a quarry called Mirzan set among great trenches of scarred red rock. They stopped by a cluster of wretched huts where a group of ragged little girls stood in the dawn with chisels and hammers in their hands. Their father ran the quarry. A forty-year-old compressor stood nearby, inside a deep trench whose walls were inscribed with the delicate forms of prehistoric placoderm fish and floating aquatic plants. Here the father appeared, scampering up towards them with another small girl. She was wild-looking, with matted hair, and she homed in on the white foreigner with something in her hand. She danced around David crying '*Orthocerus!*' The men said nothing, hunkering down instead to a pot of tea. David examined the stone in the girl's hand, which looked like a polished razor shell, and bought it from her on a whim for a few *dirhams*. She pointed at her own chest and said, '*Tuda!*' Anouar pulled him gently away from the group around the tea, however. Abdellah, it appeared, forbade David from coming anywhere near him.

'He says you cannot drink from the same cup, not eat from the same plate. He says your shadows must not cross.'

Anouar said this quietly, out of hearing of the others.

'He says you cannot touch what he has touched, and he cannot touch what you have touched.'

He's mad, David thought methodically. Or it's the grief.

'Is that a custom?' he asked Anouar.

'It's not. It is just his way right now. It will pass.'

'I find it very strange.'

Anouar said nothing. They watched the men haggle over some crudely prepped *Orthocerus* wrapped in newspapers and some fragmented trilobites. While they did so, the girls stood in the rising wind with a baby wrapped in wool, the stonecutters' children, born to hack at fossils all their lives. Goats stood around them, cocking their heads and bleating, but no women. David put on his sunglasses to protect his eyes and rummaged through filthy boxes of assorted spinosaur teeth and ringed crinoid stems. He was beginning to feel their sinister quality, their evolutionary remoteness and otherworldly allure. Anouar came with him, as if he needed to be entertained, or at least orientated. David wondered if Anouar felt sorry for him. It wasn't impossible. They passed some strange 'sand roses' from a place called Kem Kem, then some fossilised turtles embedded in a massive slab of rock that was being raised by hand on a single car jack. It was being sent all the way to Norway as a coffee table. It had the feel of a materialised dream, a nightmare that had gone subtly wrong.

Anouar yawned and kept his eye on the others. The foreman was called Amar Taglaoui, Anouar said with a hint of resentment. He was an *ouvrier* and a poor bastard, but you had to watch him. David shook his head. Around his feet he noticed hundreds of snail-like forms embedded into the small rocks, the sediments of millions of years from when the Sahara was an ocean, and it seemed like a landscape of madness equivalent to what he imagined was going on inside Abdellah's head. Full of life, but dead; rich in forms, but monotonous. He felt sourly depressed. Grief was just a giant confusion in which millions of bits from a life lay about like ruined fragments, and nothing could make them cohere again. Seeing this terrible mood appear in David, Anouar tried to cheer him up, and he threw up his hands as if performing a conjuring trick.

'They pour Coke on these gypsum formations to make them look old. Crooks, David, operators!'

He nudged him to make him laugh. Crooked Arabs, what a thought!

The men rose from the teapot. They came crunching over the shards of agatised algae and the snail-like creatures, their *chechs* flapping because the wind had risen and was getting stronger with every minute, and suddenly the sun shot a low ray across the orange sandstone. They made for the car, and David followed eagerly, noticing that one of the men had an armful of fossil rocks. The little girls waved with ammonites in their hands.

'Where are we going?' David blurted out to Anouar. He knew that none of the others would answer him.

Anouar put his hand on his shoulder. 'Relax, David. We're going to Alnif.'

For a moment, Abdellah paused before turning on the engine. His eye scanned the empty road along which the crinoid dealers would pass back that night on their return to Erfoud. He seemed not to be thinking at all about his son or about David. He had paused en route to buy a few specimens from the stonecutters; he had allowed his mind to wander, apparently, and to entertain frivolous calculations – though in the context of a pitiless struggle for survival, such calculations were not so frivolous, perhaps. Abdellah paused, and his psychic attention seemed to turn to David. He caressed his teeth with his tongue and raised the knuckles of his right hand to his mouth for a second. He quivered. When he spoke, it was to Anouar, who sat in the back seat and would translate for him.

'A wretched place,' was all he said, grinning suddenly but still not looking David in the eye. 'It is dying, as you can plainly see. The desert is what we fish, and the fossils are our fish. Dead fish! It is a joke. God has played a joke on us. Does it make you laugh?'

'Not at all,' David said grimly.

'It makes you laugh,' the old man insisted. 'It makes me laugh.'

'No,' David repeated.

'Soon, there'll be nothing here. No people, no trees. We're the last ones.'

The other men sighed. *Bismellah.*

'I am telling you, we are the last ones,' Abdellah repeated, rapping the steering wheel with his nails. 'We have fossils and our children. And nothing else.'

David hung his head, and the engine roared to life.

'You will see,' the father said softly, as if David really would see when they arrived at their destination, which was Tafal'aalt.

An hour later they were at the ruined ornamental gate of Alnif, where birds nested among the colourless weeds. Across a sloped square behind this *bab*, the villagers and fossil dealers stood about in the first shock of sunlight, unsurprised to see the Aït Kebbash appear among them yet again. The Kebbash went for a coffee at the café, and David leaned against the car trying his mobile phone yet again. Nothing. Dicky had lied spectacularly to him about that. Ruefully, he walked back to the *bab* and peered out at the vast horizontal lines of the desert. Here were the ergs, the open wildernesses. Tufts of pale drinn grass lined the road with a hopeless greenery, and here and there a thorn tree rose into the immense morning light, glistening with a mysterious dew. So this was it, he reflected with all the resilience he could muster in a tight corner. He was trapped in the most definite way. Why had he not simply refused to go? It had been a curious moment of weakness, which was to say of guilt. As he looked back on it, it was incomprehensible. But everything must happen for a reason.

He thought of his wife asleep in her bed in Azna. She wouldn't be up yet. She would be in her deepest dreams, tossing and turning. He thought of her skin that had a smell of library dust in the morning; her musty, haylike hair falling over the pillow, where he liked to kiss it. He would not describe this journey to her later, he decided. In fact he had already made a resolution to himself that whatever happened in Tafal'aalt would remain with him to the grave, even if it was sadder than anything he could imagine now.

Fourteen

THE ROAD GREW LESS DISTINCT AND MORE like a track scratched into the surface of the desert by a cosmic stick, and around it, receding infinitely, the acacias multiplied. Their daggerlike thorns lay all around on the ground. In the far distance they saw the mountain called Atchana, 'the thirsty one' in Arabic. It formed one corner of the vast rectangular plateau of Jbel Issomour close to the Algerian border, which now began to rise to their left, a low shadow on the horizon.

As they neared it, the land grew almost black, its surface cracked and pitted. It was hard, jagged rock, not the sand he had expected, and before long they were rolling across open country, unbound by the puny formality of a road. The car pitched violently, and the Kebbash gritted their teeth. To the left, man-made ditches began to appear, fossil trenches. In the hot season, the workers fled to the Atlas to make a gentler living and they left their tool kits and camping gear by the side of the trenches, where they would remain undisturbed until winter. When the temperatures came down, they would return to find their belongings exactly as they had left them. It was like the equipment of a Roman army that had disappeared two thousand years ago, like the camps you could still see surrounding Masada in Israel. The burned plain to the right had a colour of roasted peaches and custard, and across it a single figure made its way in the full anonymity of a morning sun. The car stopped for a moment and the men jumped out and waved. It was a boy of about fourteen wrapped from head to foot in indigo cloth, following a flock of camels that were far out of sight below the horizon. Anouar helped David out of the car and they soaked up the sun for a few minutes while two of the party ran off to peer inside the fossil trenches. The shepherd threw them a few friendly words.

They have a completely different idea of space, David thought mutely as he watched the kid walk off with his stick. On the far western horizon, nothing could be seen but shimmering thorn trees. They're not even on the same planet. Their planet bore only an extraordinarily slight resemblance to his.

Anouar offered him some water and they drank apart from the rest of the group, urinating by themselves. They walked up to the trench, and Anouar wound his *chech* more tightly around his face. Through the soles of his shoes, David could feel the heat of the ground.

'We'll drive around the Jbel,' Anouar said, 'and arrive through Boudib to Tafal'aalt. It's the back way.'

'Why the back way?'

The Moroccan shrugged. It was too complicated to explain.

'It's the father's choice.'

David felt a surge of pent-up exasperation.

'So it'll add hours to the trip?'

'I wouldn't say so long. We'll be there soon enough.'

Standing by the car, Abdellah watched them with a hawkish, cold suspicion. He had opened the back of the jeep for a while to see that the body was all right, and his concentration lingered there. When he had closed the back of the jeep again, he stood very erect in the snarling gusts and drew his *chech* up under his eyes. Something in his look made Anouar shift uncomfortably and draw apart from David. The two men were forced to look at each other sheepishly, and neither could quite decipher the rage in Abdellah's expression, because it was not entirely the rage that a son's death would cause. It was directed at nameless things, at things that lay behind persons. David watched the old man turn slowly and kick a rock under the jeep. He walked off by himself and brooded, his head bowed onto his chest, where his long, hairy arms were folded.

Now Anouar said, 'It was his only son. It was his only child.'

David felt his heart going dim and tinny, like something spinning on a piece of empty ground. He said, 'I see', and his fear assumed a more definite form. The suggestion of revenge began to emerge from the back of his consciousness, where it had been hiding itself. So it was possible. All his old prejudices recrystallised, and he gripped his useless mobile phone. Oh, he knew what these tribals got up to when everyone's back was turned. He was prepared for some cat-and-mouse.

They even said that al-Qaeda squads roamed this part of the desert. He was sure that that blackmailing subject would come up at some point, and only the week before he and Jo had read in the *Telegraph* about the western oil workers whose bodies were found near the oil installations in Mauretania. They passed across the Algerian border all the time. Dicky had admitted it, and it was incredible to think that they had all *known* this before so blithely sending him off to the badlands. They thought it was a high old joke. His heart was audible to himself in the silence, which was made total by the wind's roar. He thought of his own father for a second, punting on the River Ouse in a straw hat. 'Never trust an American or a Nigerian, Davie boy. Slippery tongues.' He looked at his watch, as if it might tell him something provocative, and still he heard Daddy's plummy, ingeniously innocent voice describing places he had seen in Ecuador when he toured there as a mining engineer in the Forties. The world was a dreadful place, Daddy said, by and large, and the best thing you could do was make fun of it. At least that was an authentically English response.

As he looked up from his watch, Anouar shaded his eyes and went to sit in the car. From the pool of shadow that suggested the form of Abdellah came a sound like the gnashing of teeth. For even if the old man had been crying, he would have kept it down deep and inaudible inside his lungs.

The Toyota hauled itself dramatically up long, serpentine gullies. It groaned like a beast of burden and sometimes stopped, exhausted, while the gears were changed and the brake was slammed, then released. The old man cursed it and talked to it. His teeth were still grinding. The rancid water in the bottles was now as hot as bath-water. But still they rose, inching towards the shrill blueness that hovered above them and which seemed potentially touchable.

The roof of Issomour was so high that, looking back, they could see expanses of desert that shone salt-white, pale yellow and rose. It was windier and hotter, but even here, in the most terrible place of the ergs, there were long, skilfully cut trenches and workers' tool bags lying in the sun, as if the cutters sometimes took picnics between their sessions. Now, Abdellah didn't stop. They raced across this new wasteland with a surprising alacrity, as if chasing animals or avoiding men.

There was a wild intensity in the old man's driving as he savagely changed gears and drove his beast on and on. By noon they were gently descending again, towards the north face of the mountain, underneath which five villages lay: Boudib, Ambon, La'gaaft, Tabrikt and Tafal'aalt. La'gaaft was where the despised *haratin* lived.

In the back seat, the men slept. Their rifle pressed inadvertently against David's own seat. The heat poured down through the jeep's roof, stunning the senses, and the chugging AC produced almost no result. David's head began to slump against the seat belt, and he felt as if one of his eyes was coming loose like an ageing lightbulb. As for Abdellah, he knew that Anouar, his translator, was asleep, so he said a few things to the pimply fool next to him in Tamazight — because even if this David understood a few words of Arabic, he surely understood not one of Tamazight. Roughly translated, Abdellah's remarks were:

'In La'gaaft live the blacks. If they ask you in Tafal'aalt if you have been in the village of the blacks, admit it, but do not say that you have drunk their water. Say nothing — it's better that way.'

And he laughed mercilessly, as David nodded in confusion and said yes.

At the bottom of the long descent lay Boudib. Its houses were shaped like domes, and on its metal doors were painted the forms of yellow trilobites. Its back gardens were fringed with spindly, dying trees, and a prickling dust bowled along its rubble lanes.

At midday, the heat had driven all its inhabitants indoors; even the dogs cowered behind whatever cover they could find. Huge white stones like dinosaur eggs lay piled along the dried *oueds* where the infected trees gasped out their last. The men in the car were still asleep as they accelerated through Boudib towards Ambon, and even in Ambon they still slept. They had seen Ambon a thousand times, and there was nothing to see but the well.

Beyond it, outside La'gaaft, the father stopped for a moment to inspect the tyres, and David took in the sheer mauve face of the north side of Issomour towering above the villages like a static tidal wave. Its surface was pocked with man-made caves from which ropes and ladders hung. The shadow from this monumental cliff was so long that it engulfed the whole settlement. There was the well, around which two figures stood, their faces visible through bundles of rags. The men in the car awoke. As they tumbled through La'gaaft, they were silent, clutching their old rifle, but far up the face of Issomour, David saw a boy sitting on the ledge of a cave, waving with a white cloth as if surrendering, and the top of the precipice above him had a raw colour like blood-oranges.

In each village all the way to Tafal'aalt the houses were the same cement domes with the same trilobites painted on their metal doors. People came out to shout and greet them. A man with a basket on his head, coiled with ropes, stood by the entrance of Tabrikt with a hand raised, and he called Abdellah by name, as well as one of the other men in the car, whose name was Moulay.

David felt all his revulsion revive as they came to the

edge of Tafal'aalt itself, the last village before the open desert. So this was Driss's home. It consisted of two dozen of the domed hovels looking like eggs sunk into sand, behind which he could see vegetable plots guarded by low stone walls and clusters of date palms. The paths between them were white like beaten chalk. As with the other villages, the shadow of Issomour reached right up to the gardens and would soon engulf them.

Abdellah parked his car and strode up to one of the metal doors covered with blue trilobites. He hammered it with his fists and yelled as David was hustled out of the car with his comically neat travelling bags that Jo had packed so fastidiously. The sun shone at its apex, and the blood-orange tinge of the cliffs above them reminded the Englishman a second time of a tsunami frozen in time that might yet be released and come crashing down upon them. He peered up at the stone wall and noted the same ladders and cave openings. What could one think about it? One thought nothing, he realised. It was a zone of barbarism, of prehistory. It was a desolate comedy with child labour. One had to stop thinking, to just endure it. One had to *lie down*.

The metal doors swung open, and inside, sheltered from the sun's glare, three women peered out. Their faces and hands were tattooed with delicate lines of spots. They burst out of the house in their black robes, slipping past the men and running towards the car. The sound of lamentation. The men had been dreading it all along. They set their jaws and looked down, almost in irritation, and David looked up at the sun separated by an expanse of blue sky from the edge of the mawlike cliff. What time was it?

Abdellah waved an ironic hand at him.

'Come in,' he said in Arabic, as if this was the alien lingua franca between them. 'Welcome to my beloved hovel. Please, mind your step.'

It was the house Driss had grown up in, and it carried the energy of his spirit in some way. Even in Paris, as he told Ismael, he had always kept the memory of it close to his heart.

Fifteen

AFTER ROGER HAD LEFT, DRISS SAID TO Ismael that day, he and Angela dug a new bed of sunflowers. Her brisk and yet tender manner with him seemed a little freer than it usually was, as if her husband's presence always constrained it, and after their work in the garden, they went to the house and she made him pots of Earl Grey tea and scones with raisins – by God, he said to Ismael, a stranger food there was never seen upon the earth.

They talked more intimately then, and Angela told him that their business was not working as well as they had hoped and that Roger, in fact, had gone home to England to raise more money from his family. Times were difficult, and fewer tourists were coming to the marina at Sotogrande.

'So,' he asked, 'is Roger coming back with a lot of money?'

'It doesn't work quite like that. It takes a few months for the money to arrive.'

'I see.' Driss nodded. Then it is now, he thought, or never. And it cannot be never.

He said to Angela, 'I have been wondering about that safe and how you open it. It seems like a very clever thing.'

'The safe?'

'Yes, I have been watching Roger do it and I cannot figure it out.'

'Why do you need to figure it out?'

She stood up and he suddenly noticed that hours had gone by somehow and that it was already the end of the afternoon and the olive trees were growing grey outside the windows as they stood under the rain.

'Because,' he said quietly, 'I need the money in it.'

Slowly, they evolved into the same scene they had enacted at the petrol station, except that now they were months along the same lines of thought and everything had changed in Driss's favour. He saw, superimposed upon the face of the woman he had grown fond of, the face of the ancient unbeliever who would never give him what he wanted.

'Driss, don't be silly,' was all she said. 'There's only two thousand euros in there. Is that worth it?'

By God, he thought, it is.

He came round the table, and one of his hands reached out like a whiplashing cable that has snapped.

'No, you can't,' she said softly, and wriggled out of his grip, though he reasserted it. They began to dance.

He dragged her silently towards the safe, which stood inside a large kitchen cabinet where cookbooks and pots of dried herbs also stood. His free hand searched for a weapon with which to intimidate her into some kind of informative submission. A drawer was opened, and inside were the household knives. 'I was not thinking of such a thing,' he said to Ismael, who had gone quiet, 'but how else was I to cut through this troublesome knot?' He found a serrated bread knife and raised it against the side of her neck as she sank down towards the floor and tried to twist away. There was something immensely gratifying about this pose of purely subconscious supplication and the way those hippie sandals slipped off and lay in the middle of the kitchen floor. Finally, he felt, the positions of power were as they should be, and if that involved a humiliation for this weak old lady, it was distasteful but not unnatural. It was the reverse that was unnatural. 'Let me go,' she was crying, but why should she not cry such things and why should he let her go? When the tip of the bread knife bit into her neck, she revealed the numbers of the combination and he memorised them.

When he had taken the money, however, he was not sure what to do with the enormous situation that had suddenly opened before him. He had no real plan, he realized. Night had fallen and he could not very well just walk out of the house without a thought, leaving behind him an angry unbeliever who would now call the police at once. What would he be then? Hunted through the fields by infidels with rage in their gut. It was foolish to think he would get away with it. He needed a little time to get to the road and hitch a ride.

He thought all this as the knife still lay against her neck. One exertion, he thought, and all your problems are solved. Ignore the look of disbelief in her eyes. She is old anyway. Her time has come.

'You cannot do that,' she said to him inside his head.

'Oh, yes, I can,' he replied calmly.

So much blood for so little a reason. He let go when it was done, and he felt a cool, surprising elation as he cleaned the blade in the sink and put it back in the drawer. The house was suddenly as quiet as a house can be, with only the sound of birds calling through the olive grove behind it. There was just him and his lungs and his beating heart.

Sixteen

HE WENT DOWN WITH A BAG FILLED
WITH cash and clothes to the road that ran past San
Martín and soon found his way back to the petrol station
where he had started. A few lorries idled there and some
beat-up cars of immigrants that had obviously just
disembarked from the ferry. The Moroccan families sat
about on the shoulder of the road eating oranges and
pastries, and among them he could move with his prop-
osition without difficulty. All of them, without exception,
were going to Paris and, in that regard, his ambition to
get there himself was sensible. He talked to them quietly
and persuasively, asking them who they were and from
where they had come and where they were going, and
when he offered to pay all their petrol to the French
capital, several relented and offered space in their cars.
He went with a young family who owned a grocery
shop in a place called Marx Dormoy. He asked them if
this place was in Paris and they said, 'Assuredly, it is.'
Very well then, he thought. It had not been as difficult
as he had anticipated, not by a long shot.

At this point in his narrative Driss got up and went
down to the trench to relieve himself. He was well satisfied

by the effect his tale had had on the impressionable Ismael and he was sure, in fact, that the kid believed every word of it. He chuckled to himself. The fossils all round them gave him the goosebumps, because he knew they were evil, that they were not of this world. But now he was entertained enough to forget the damned things. He loved telling stories.

'You were cold as ice, brother,' the kid said as he came back and sat down again by the fire they had assembled on the bare rock. He had a waxed paper bag of figs from the market in Erfoud, and they cut them open with the penknife. Driss nodded.

'Necessity, brother.'

'The world is cruel. My father keeps saying so.'

'He is right. *Cruel* is the word.'

Driss could sense that Ismael suddenly admired him more than he had ten minutes earlier, and this had been his intention. The boy looked at him with wide-open eyes in which the newly minted wonder was mixed with a little fear. It was perfect. The balance between them had shifted in his favour, and he felt more assured as he stirred the fire with a stick and ate into the figs. More than assured, he felt mightily pleased with himself. For the job he had in mind, he needed Ismael wrapped round his little finger, and there he was, like human thread. He would, from now on, be a more willing partner in whatever Driss had in mind; he would look up to the older boy and do what he was told. Driss cut up a fig for him and offered half, and all the while he talked, because Ismael wanted to know about Paris. Paris was where they all wanted to go. Paris, where the girls are true sluts.

'So,' he said to Driss, 'you went to Paris after all?'

'Of course I did. Didn't I say so?'

The family from Essaouira drove him all the way there through the night. They stopped at motorway filling stations in the dark and during the following day, and he and the father took turns driving the car. The father was a fat brute from the coast; he had made a living making chessboards for tourists in the *souk* of Essaouira. Sly and rolling and over-curious. He explained to Driss the arcane ways of the French, which were different from the more familiar ways of the Spaniards. Driss listened without retaining a single word. He remembered a place near Perpignan in the early morning with cattle standing submerged in mist, and he thought: It was not so hard after all. The Nazarenes are not as clever as we make them out to be. He wandered with the family into a food court in some motorway services, where the unbelievers ate in open-plan cafeterias awash with alcohol. The French girls were in cutaway jean shorts and tiny T-shirts, and they looked over at him with a short, momentary disdain. The bread was stale. In the shops there were hams wrapped in silver foil and model fire engines, and there were chairs where the lorry drivers were massaged electronically. Everyone stood around automated coffee machines and said nothing. Strange, the ways of the unenlightened.

But then he decided not to tell Ismael too much about Paris. It was better left as a mystery. The weeks on the rue du Faubourg-Saint-Denis behind the Gare du Nord, in the Indian neighbourhood of tandoori houses and sari shops filled with gold jewellery (he thought with a smile of the glass busts of women in the windows with vulgar necklaces draped around them); the *hammam* on the rue d'Aboukir; and the long nights alone in the Brady cinema on Sébastopol watching soft-porn movies. What was the good of describing it? His fruitless search for a job in the newspapers, the useless economies, the endless boredom and loneliness. Nothing had happened there but failure anyway. He had not found a job even as a janitor, nor even as a supermarket stocker, which everyone had said was a sure-fire thing. And the two thousand euros? Ismael asked.

'Even when you buy a sandwich,' Driss replied sternly, 'it costs the same as a week of *tagines* here. The infidels steal every *centime* you have. It flows through your fingers like sand.'

'Ah, I thought so.'

Every night Driss had been forced to walk the streets around Château d'Eau, following clusters of middle-aged Chinese whores who dressed in black like female undertakers and who migrated to the bus stop there when the Métro was winding down. Nocturnal solitudes on the well-named Passage du Désir and the African cafés all along the rue du Château d'Eau, which was the only place he could afford to pretend to have a nightlife. Paris.

'The City of Light,' Ismael said hopefully.

A bitch of a den of infidelity, Driss said, a sewer. Though one night, having decided to relinquish his sixty euros and seeing as he was already lost amid Unbelief, he followed a sad Chinese girl back to the *chambre de bonne* on the very same street where he lived, into a courtyard filled with sacks of cement exactly like his own, and up a winding staircase to a room exactly like his own, six feet by six, with a cat that smelled of carpet cleaner. And this girl, who spoke no French, took off her clothes and stuffed her sixty euros into a box under the bed and asked him, he imagined, if he wanted *la pipe*.

Well, of course he wanted *la pipe*, he said. Would he go to a streetwalker and not get *la pipe*? He would not spend

sixty euros and not get it. They laughed and Ismael said,
'By God.'

'And these Chinese girls walk the streets at night?'

'They are the only girls left on the street apart from
the Albanians, who are all thieves and cut-throats. So
that is how we do it there.'

'And they are all dressed in black?'

'Like the undertakers of the unbelievers. They are
dressed in black, and I must say they are fearsome to
look upon.'

'But nevertheless you had *la pipe*?'

'I had to see what it was like. So I did.'

'It was well done. How was it?'

'Less than magnificent.'

They laughed again, but more uneasily.

Driss said that he used to walk over the bridge that
crossed the railway lines behind the Gare du Nord and
pass from the neighbourhood of the Hindus to that of
the North Africans – the lines divided them – and, once
on the far side, he walked all down the boulevard de la
Chapelle under the Métro, where the boozers lay in their
calms and the blacks sold their drugs; past the Lariboisière
Hospital to Barbès and the Tati store, where he bought
his cheap shirts; and from there into the rue de la Goutte-
d'Or, which made him think comfortingly of a Moroccan
town, and the rue de la Charbonnière, where the restaurants with *grillades* and the halal places were. Here
gathered the Muslims with their food and their gossip.

It was like a dream, he said to the impressionable Ismael,
but not necessarily a very nice one. He walked and walked,
he admitted, and the more he walked down the rue Myrha
and the rue de Sofia and the boulevard Barbès and even
the small and orderly rue Cail that was round the corner

from where he lived – with its line of garish Indian restaurants and the blossoming trees at the far end – the more he realised that life was elsewhere and not in Paris, and that he was not the one to live in this place and make it his. So, in a sense, he said to Ismael, he had wasted his time and everyone else's, and soon, though it was against his will, his thoughts were turning back to the desert and especially when he was alone in the Brady or wandering down the rue de l'Aqueduc towards nowhere, adrift among the migrants from countries he had never heard of, among the skins darker than his own, eating a peach or a bag of nuts and feeling that he was slipping down a long slope towards a pit, for that was how walking down the rue de l'Aqueduc always felt to him.

'How so?' the younger boy asked.

'I cannot really explain it. A great anxiety and unhappiness. That is what the world of the unbelievers does to you.'

The boy nodded.

'I see, yes.'

'But I mean it truly. There is no happiness there.'

'The Koran has said so.'

'The Book is entirely correct. There is no mistake.'

Driss rolled another joint, and for some time they listened appreciatively to the clean, murderous sound of the wind sweeping across the plain, across the fossil trenches of the quarry, and across Hmor Lagdad as it had done for millions of years, even perhaps when it had been a sea. Something lay behind it, an indistinct white noise of some kind, and they could hear it with ears that knew every texture of that wind because they had been listening to it all their lives. Soft wind and hard wind, slow wind and quick, benevolent and malign. The compressor glowed with a metallic light all its own, reflecting some radiance so far-off that they could not otherwise detect it. The moon, behind storms of sand high up in the atmosphere? Then how could they see the stars?

'All the same,' Driss went on, as the fire began to die. 'I have been thinking how we can make some money for ourselves and then leave for the city. It's what you want, isn't it?'

'Assuredly.'

'I knew it was. You are the ambitious sort, like me.'

They agreed on this fact tacitly, and Driss lit the joint. Neither of them was sure how stoned they were now. All that could be said was that things had become indistinct around them. Ismael asked him what he had in mind, and Driss smiled cryptically and said, 'Something that needs some pluck, my dear Ismael, something that requires you to lose all your sentimentalism.'

'I am not sentimental.'

'Up to now you've been. You'll have to be a warrior from now on, and not think too much. Can you do that?'

Ismael said that he could, though he couldn't know, and there was annoyance in his voice. Driss soothed him.

'Very well. I'll explain it to you after we've finished our smoke.'

'I hope you will,' the other muttered, and lay down on his side with his hand beneath his head so that he could see the road as well. And yet there was nothing on it and would not be. All he could see were the white posts along its edge.

'Perhaps we should sleep first,' Driss said. 'You're tired and so am I.'

It was not a bad idea, Ismael thought. He closed his

eyes, and they said nothing until sleep did come to them, if lightly and without depth. Driss lay flat on his back and savoured the taste of the *kif* in the back of his mouth mingled with the sugary mint tea he had drunk earlier. The *kif* was good and strong, from the high mountains, from fragrant leaves, and it made him dream fluidly: that he was walking down through a fir forest in the height of summer, with the bees droning in the glades, with a sound of water from somewhere. Allah, he thought, knows where I am, even if I do not.

He came down the slope thick with pine cones, and at its bottom, barely revealed between the trees, he saw a woman standing by what looked like a well. She was white, like Angela, but young, and her hair reached down to her arms. She was turned away from him, peering into the well, and around her bare feet flies played silently as if attracted to something about her that he could not see. In the heat he could not think, and he came down slowly with an axe cradled in his hands, the woman's head turned away from him. One's foot breaks a twig and the *gazelle* turns her hoof, her gaze. She turned slowly and he came out into the sunlight in the clearing, and he thought, Am I evil? Am I who I am? It was high noon, and from the depths of those woods came the sound of cuckoos and the drone of heavy flies.

Seventeen

TWO HOURS BEFORE DAVID ENTERED Abdellah's house, the same sun that struck him carved out the shadows of Azna against the gentle slopes of rocks, and the early-shift cooks peeling potatoes on the back steps of the kitchen looked up, blinking, and noticed prickly pears shining with yellow blooms. They stopped for a moment and shaded their eyes. The light, moving from behind the house's towers, struck the open ground where their peelings lay and lit the metal buckets filled with slop. From the dining room they could hear a strange music played on fiddles, a distinctly European racket. It wasn't music. It made them wince inside themselves, mostly in embarrassment for those who claimed to enjoy it or who were damned to pretend to do so. Nawfal, the second cook, had seen four Chinese men dressed in white suits playing those screeching fiddles. The infidels apparently considered it soothing and entertaining, and they listened to it intently as they devoured their halved grapefruits and bowls of crunchy rabbit food that belonged to yet another darker sphere of incomprehensibility. The boys from the villages on the valley floor stared at the sun and secretly wished that a cloud would come and blot it out, and Nawfal, meanwhile, returned from the dining room with a basket of half-eaten croissants and encountered the mournfully ubiquitous Hamid at the threshold of the boiling kitchen.

'They tell me they took the infidel to the Tafilalet,' Nawfal sneered, slamming down the basket and going to the back door to light a cigarette against Monsieur Richard's explicit orders. 'Is it true?'

The boys listened avidly. 'It is,' Hamid sighed.

'They'll cut off his fingers one by one,' one of them said, and they laughed. Hamid, too.

'They'll cut off his feet, boil them and eat them with their goats.'

'Perhaps,' Hamid agreed.

'They'll cut out his tongue at the very least,' Nawfal opined, sucking on his cigarette and blowing out a ring.

'God willing,' some of them sighed, and Hamid's glance of disapproval had no effect. They smiled among themselves and began peeling again. Hamid regaled them with an inevitable proverb. 'The tongue has no bones, but it crushes all the same.'

Personally, he wished no harm to the wretched David. And yet justice was not always kind; it had to be faced. He walked to the fridges and opened the tall aluminium doors. He reached in and picked out a box of eggs and a plastic box of butter. One could feel dismay, but it made no difference. David had earned his bout of bad cosmic luck. It was the mutinous mood among the staff that was worrying him more. He felt that if something unpleasant befell David, they would calm down. They would feel justice had been served.

He went outside by himself and stuffed a croissant quickly into his mouth. Sometimes one wished for rain, for clouds. That damned sun, making everything sick. He had just been upstairs to the masters' bedroom and glimpsed them asleep in each other's arms, protected by the heavy velvet curtains they had imported from Paris. It made him a little sick, but he never let it show to them. There were certain divides that could not be reached across. There were moments in which amorality was a wise course.

* * *

At the same moment that the sun was striking the prickly pears of the kitchen yard, it had sliced through the shutters of Jo's bedroom and turned the four-poster bed into a small lake of gold. She was awake, eating breakfast in bed and reading a two-day-old *Herald Tribune* as the rays enveloped her naked toes and warmed them. Her eyes were gold and blue also as she looked up and thought to herself that it was the first time she had woken up alone in eleven years, alone and calm and undisturbed and not at all lonely. She had gone to bed drunk and there was a cocktail glass standing on the night table that she didn't remember. Her sluggishness made her read lazily, half wondering instead what David was doing at that very moment (eating a baby goat with his fingers? taking a piss in a tin shack?) until a knock on the door shook her out of her daydream and she called out, 'Who is it?'

The door opened. The *haratin* boy pushed his head through the crack.

'Madame,' he said gravely, 'Monsieur Day has sent you a card.'

'Monsieur Day?'

'Yes, Madame. Here it is.'

A card was mounted on his tray, which he held as if it carried a bevy of drinks. It made her smile.

'You can put it down on the chair,' she said mildly.

The boy hesitated.

'What is it?' she smiled.

'Monsieur Day says I must wait for a reply.'

'Are you serious?'

'Yes, Madame.'

'You can wait outside.'

She threw on her kimono and read the card.

Dear Jo,

*Do you have a terrible hangover like me? I recommend
a raw egg and Worcestershire sauce, never fails. It was
fun dancing with you playing Mary Poppins. I'm sorry
I broke your plate. Come over and have coffee and croissants. The raw egg is all prepared and waiting for you.*

Pirate Tom

She frowned and examined the loose, carefree hand-
writing. Had he really been Pirate Tom and had they
actually danced? She didn't remember anything. The tone
was odd, but at the same time he seemed to feel confident
about using it. She tried to remember the previous night's
party. A lot of people, a lot of noise. A lot of drinking
and the pink sugar ship. There had been more Gnawa
and, of course, the fire-eaters of Taza, who had been
ridiculous. Day had been there, too. He had been watching
her – she remembered that. And she did dance with him,
now that she thought about it. Pseudo-waltzing to Gary
Glitter. They had walked to the gate and back. She had
called him Tom. She was sure she had called him Tom.

She told the boy she would take a shower and think
about it.

'I will wait,' he said solemnly.

Under the jets of tepid water her head gradually cleared without rendering better memories of the night. She didn't recall coming back into the cottage at all, nor collapsing into her creaky bed. She laughed quietly. She was such a crappy lush; drinking like a fourteen-year-old, staggering about. And she probably had talked in a loud voice and acted like a middle-aged slut. But there was nothing wrong with middle-aged sluts. They were the best kinds of sluts. Day was a sort of middle-aged slut, too. And she was a little aghast at herself, but not as much as she would have expected. Day was shameless. But shamelessness was the single thing she needed most now. It would purge her of fourteen years. It brought out something precious and necessary in her. It reminded her that death was still a long way off.

She relished the feel of her hips as she turned herself inside the rotary action of the huge white towel and breathed in the smell of expensive cotton and the Crabtree & Evelyn musks. Her face was bright and sun-kissed in the mirror, with a slightly peeling nose. The important thing is always *now*, isn't it? The spinning brilliance of the now.

* * *

She came out onto the porch, and the boy stood up quickly, as if he knew he shouldn't have been sitting. Was that the way they trained them?

'I'll come with you,' she said with great certainty.

'To Monsieur's Day cottage?'

'Where else? That's what he wanted, isn't it?'

But then she remembered that of course he wouldn't know that, unless he had read the card on the sly.

'Yes, Madame.'

'Lead on, then. Is it far?'

He laughed. 'Of course not, Madame.'

Of course he read it, she thought gleefully as they stepped into the sun and the hot laterite paths that stung the feet through one's sandals. And then she added to him, 'You can call me Mademoiselle, if you like.'

'Whatever you like, Madame.'

They walked side by side through the labyrinth of tiny houses, turning down a short alley bordered with tamarisk trees. The boy left her at Day's chalet, where the porch was already set up with breakfast and where the American lay in his pyjamas reading the same two-day-old *Herald Tribune* which she had already devoured.

'Look,' he said, picking up a fruit from the table. 'The lads have found us papayas and sent them down for breakfast. How do they do it?'

'Connections in high places,' she said, sitting in one of the wrought-iron chairs. Unsurprisingly, the cottage was exactly like theirs. The same design, the same frills. The same flounced curtains. She looked with curiosity at the slice of papaya.

'There's a picnic today,' Day went on. 'I should – we should – go. There's a waterfall somewhere.'

'I don't really feel like a picnic.'

'Sure you do. You can't mope about worrying about your husband all day. You weren't moping last night.'

He shot her a mischievous look, and it forced her to do the same.

'I was being a bitch last night. I'm feeling very guilty today.'

'Have some papaya. It's guilt-free.'

'Waterfall,' she murmured distractedly. 'Is that for swimming?'

'I would imagine. The voyeurs among us want to see you in a swimsuit.'

'You're not very subtle, are you, Mr Day?'

'I come from a city where subtlety is fined.'

'I can't fine you. I can just put you down as you deserve.'

She drank some of his strong coffee spiced with cardamom. Day was very neat: his clothes were folded, his books were stacked. She struggled to recall what he did. A financial analyst? She had little idea what financial analysts did, if they did anything. His eyes were grey, though before they had been green. So his eyes changed colour.

It was turning out to be a strange weekend. Her calls to David were still going unanswered. Where was he?

'All right,' she said, more alertly. 'I'll come to the waterfall. I can't really believe there's a waterfall in a place like this. Are you sure Dally and Richard didn't create it themselves?'

'I am not sure of anything. Men who can summon papaya and velvet curtains can create anything. Do we care?'

She shook her head.

'Long as it's cool.'

'Water is water.'

'Yes,' she said, 'that's the thing about water.'

He seemed to be holding her in his hand in some way, just holding her and watching her. He was one of those men whose grooming almost puts you off. He stretched out his long legs and stared at her mockingly. Those pyjamas – he must have brought them from New York. She wondered if he wore them every night in his sixty-million-dollar bed in SoHo as he tangled with his whorish dolls. She peered through the half-opened door into the room where everything was frighteningly ordered. Curiously, a baseball lay on the floor, as if he had been practising and had dropped it there. It lay there like a weapon, mute and shining, and when she looked up, the grey eyes suddenly caught her as if she, too, were a ball spinning in mid-air and she had to be *stopped*. She came, therefore, to a mental standstill. The papaya was deliciously cool on her parched tongue. The trees nearby rustled like paper kites. She wiped her mouth and swigged from the potent coffee. Suddenly there was nothing more to say and the man sitting across from her entered her invisibly, without lifting a finger, with the deftness of a thief who knows his way in the dark, though who knew how.

* * *

By late morning Dally had organised four jeeps by the front gate, and while he waited for the picnickers, he posed in a *djellaba* for a photographer from *The Times* Style section. 'International revellers,' the caption would later read, 'are entertained by Mr Dally Rogers Margolis and his friend Richard Galloway in the remote *ksour* of Azna. Pictured below, Sofia Prinzapolka drinks tea from a sixteenth-century Berber cup while bathing at the *Source des Poissons*. Guests say it's the best party east of Marrakech. Hash brownies are served for breakfast with imported bananas. Right, some bemused villagers look on as the annual picnic drives down to the Hadda water-fall.' Dally arched his neck. The girl asked him to stand by the wall and look out at the desert.

'Way cool,' she kept saying.

'I'm used to it,' he said without affectation, simply because it was true.

'Move a little to your right.'

Dally was proud of his picnics. He worked at them and they usually came out right, though he lost sleep over them sometimes. Would strawberries be too predictable if they arrived in the frosted cups with the grape designs, or would they fall flat if they were served with crème fraîche as soon as everyone poured from the cars at the other end? Would the parasols be silly carried by the boys in white gloves? Would dust get into the crème fraîche and the perforated shortbread? No one knew, and Dally didn't know either. Richard was more concerned with the larger operations and wasn't much help. But then again, photographers much preferred to snap Dally in a big straw hat sitting on his walls or striking a pose by the waterfalls at the Sunday lunchtime event he had now organised four years in a row. He was more photogenic than Richard, less stern.

The guests began to arrive at the gate in their swim-suits and sun hats and clogs. They looked like a bunch of refugees from a Club Med. Dally yelled at Hamid, whom he spotted at once: 'Hamid, get them in the cars smoothly, will you? It's just awfully hot.'

Richard was there, in his Sunday best. He was so formidably handsome when he dressed up, Dally thought. He was wearing a pair of Loake suede boots in the heat and cufflinks. It was that indifference to discomfort that stirred one to admiration.

'Dicky,' he called out. 'Have we got enough cars?'

Richard came up with a whiff of Annick Goutal.

'We're fine, I think. Where is Jo, the Henniger girl?'

'I didn't see her. Why?'

'Dally, we have to keep her as far away as possible from the snooping scribblers and the photographers. We don't want her face in any bloody picture. If any of them asks who she is, lie, or say you don't know. Steer them away from her.'

'I knew that, laddy. I'm not that naïve.'

'I know, sweet. But Hamid and the boys are gormless. Make it clear, will you? Keep your eyes peeled during the picnic. I think that girl from *The Times* is sniffing about. Everyone knows about David. They're gossiping like a bunch of schoolkids.'

'It's probably the most exciting thing that's happened to them all year.'

'We don't want anything exciting to happen to them. We want hush-hush and make them think about something else.'

'Well, the strawberries for one thing. I've had them iced. I know it's weird, but they look like internal organs. Totally freaky. We've put them on beds of watercress.'

Richard scanned the mob of faces for Jo. He was determined to ride down to the waterfalls with her.

The staff held a flock of rose-tinted parasols above the heads of the complaining guests, who were coughing in the dry dust of noon. The seating arrangements inside the jeeps were organised, with male-female and same-sex flirtations discreetly accommodated. The ice chests and silver plates and champagne glasses all came in a separate vehicle, tended by a tense and authoritarian Hamid, who always felt that his reputation was on the line when operations of this kind were in full swing. A crate of iced prawns jostled in the back next to the oblong dishes of frozen strawberries.

'Drive slowly!' he barked at the driver.

Richard finally saw Jo and Day sauntering into the sun's glare.

'Over here,' he cried, waving a little too determinedly and catching her eye at once, but she seemed suspicious, or so he thought, and he was usually right.

The convoy turned off down a precipitous track above Tafnet. It was shaded by thin, pale-green trees and high walls of sandstone that the local youth had scored with amorous, but discreet, graffiti. Sitting awkwardly between Richard and Day with the windows rolled down, she felt the humidity of the river flowing in its deep groove and the faintly acid scent of the okra gardens irrigated by its waters. It was a new way of feeling the intimacy that this landscape offered; its close-knit architecture of water and shadow and rock. You felt that it had been created by real needs over considerable time, rather than by a desire to impress or to be grand. She liked the smell of birds that were sheltered by it, and the sudden glitter of a small canal as it swirled around a water wheel. She liked the dewy sweat on the air that smelled of dung. Someone had told her at the party the night before that the Berber names for the months were still a corrupted form of Latin. She didn't know if it was true, but it was a seductive thought that the world of Apuleius was still alive in an underground way, that the women crouching on their heels in the palm shadows were still partly pagan and that they made her pagan, too.

The road was steep. It passed under ponderous, fractured cliffs, winding past plots of fig trees and then slopes of iron-red dirt, dark as fresh liver, where tiny black goats stood stock-still with quivering ears. Richard told her all the place names as they went, because he and Dally walked down here almost every day by themselves with their swimming trunks, reading poetry if the fancy took them.

'Every time we make this walk, I remember why I am not in London. I sing a ballad to Pan, and a few other gods, too.'

'Not Mammon?' Day asked innocently. 'He was a god.'

'The Phoenicians didn't quite make it this far west, Tom. Here we are a pleasure-loving band of complete hypocrites. I am going to look for a house for you.' He turned to Jo with beady eyes. 'I've de-Americanised one and I'm going to do *him* next.'

'You haven't de-Americanised anyone.' Day laughed. 'Dally?'

'He's a work in progress.'

They heard the waterfall crashing into its pool, echoing high up into the rocks that formed a small amphitheatre around it. A fresh, joyous sound, like that of children playing, and wholly unexpected. The cars stopped by the edge of the wide pool where the river widened. The waterfall was half in sun, its bottom half dark. The water foamed and rippled away from it.

Hamid organised the setting up of the picnics, the rolling out of carpets, the placing of ice chests and hampers. The party spread out, and a few guests slipped off their outer clothes and plunged into the cooling waters.

Jo sat with Day and kicked off her shoes. She was in a strange mood, not wanting to be there, yet wanting to be there. Looking across the water, she noticed at once that there was a series of interlocking pools reaching back into the edge of the oasis. Day said nothing, sipping a glass of cold Prosecco and warily watching the young girls splashing under the torrent. Something about them irritated him. Their loudness, their weak sense of self. It was only Jo who interested him now. Her deep cold-ness attracted him because, being the exact opposite in temperament, he could only interpret it as woundedness. Yet he was predatory and she could never be. Personally, he doubted that a womaniser could ever be entirely cold, as portrayed in popular morality. It was the wounded who were cold. *They* were incorrigible.

Day, mildly uneducated, didn't know what she was talking about half the time – the references she dropped all around her were like heavy stones – but he was skilful enough with people to know how to roll with this small problem. One nodded and said 'yeah', and he didn't mind. It was a sign of her naïveté, her lack of worldliness.

'Olive?'

She looked disgusted as he thrust one up to her mouth. 'Don't feed me,' she said.

It was only belatedly that they saw the Moroccan musicians whom Richard had brought down with them, and who now set to playing.

'In the water,' Dally suddenly shouted.

And the small herd stirred obediently, like ruminants motivated by thirst. Two dozen heads dispersed over the pool's surface, fanning out around the roaring falls, where a stunted rainbow had formed. The Berbers looked on glassily, on the brink of bemusement. Day took her hand without warning.

'Oh!' she stuttered, and then realised that she was being whisked off into the water.

'You are a great protester,' he muttered.

'It's going to be really cold, I know it.'

She quailed, then like an elastic band felt the tension inside her reverse and spring forward. She sailed past him into the green water. The shock made her laugh aloud. A few people turned to see who could scream so winningly. Day was delighted. All he had been waiting for was this sign of impulsiveness, since impulsiveness is the womaniser's best ally.

But I am not being a womaniser, he thought then, crossing the thought out in his mind as soon as it occurred.

'It's like a fjord in Norway,' she gasped.

Separated from the party, they found themselves climbing into the next pool down, a long oval body of water surrounded by low-hanging shaggy palms, and the unripe green dates were so close to the pool that their reflections were stable in the water, across which water-boatmen skimmed in quick bursts of energy. She didn't know why she was going there with this odd man who did not arouse all her sympathy, or why she was so light-hearted about floating on her back and looking up at the clusters of dates. She let herself melt into this clear, devastating water that seeped away from them into irrigation channels, and slowly, mediated by this same water, the idea of sex was developing between them, as it had been for the previous twenty-four hours. The drums and pipes from the neighbouring *wadi* made them both giggly and childishly uninhibited. Day went underwater and came up with a dead palm frond to prick her with.

Only a matter of time, she was thinking already. And it was curious how it was always like that: a desire that was inevitable, preordained. She remembered that feeling from adolescence. It was akin to ball bearings rolling down an incline.

His hand was upon her shoulder and she didn't make a fuss. His unshaven cheek brushed hers. Men were such opportunists, but if they weren't scavengers, nothing would happen. The sexual planet would not turn. She certainly gave in.

'I shouldn't,' she murmured predictably.

He laughed, in the cruelest way, and it was nearly a mistake.

'But obviously you want to,' that laugh implied.

'Maybe,' she wanted to say to him. 'But I want to pretend that I don't want to. Do you understand that?'

They found dry land again. They walked through the dry, bristling palms in the paradoxical humidity. They heard the water wheels and the doves, the voices of women walking through the lines of dates with long sticks. The latter greeted them with cries of '*La bess!*' The decayed fronds underfoot skewered her soles, and she couldn't pull herself away from the grip of his cold, wet hand. It wasn't coercion, or even overbearingness. It was just the accurate reading of her own coming-and-going that crushed her a little.

'Do you think they hate us?' He nodded at the furtive women in the depth of the grove.

'Not at all. Not the *women,* anyway.'

They saw the party frolicking under the waterfall, as if it were a silent film. It looked absurd.

'I'm not so sure,' he said, pulling her towards him and without further ado kissing her on the mouth.

It went on and on. The girls splashed in the echoing *wadi*, and she was sure the Berber women went silent. 'It's where they come to get fertile,' she pondered, deep in a red and bloody mood.

When she broke free, she found herself gasping. She turned away, and his hands around her went limp.

'I'm swimming back, not walking,' he drawled. 'The spines are getting in my feet.'

'Mine, too.'

'Well, wade back.' He laughed.

She looked at his naked back moving off towards the pale-green water.

'Do they have crocs here?' he wondered aloud. 'I thought I saw a hippopotamus back there. Must have been a guest.'

Her heart was beating too strongly and she breathed slowly to make it stop. The drummers on the other side desisted and she heard Dally's hysterical voice making some sort of irrelevant announcement.

Day turned and shot her a little wink. Oh, come off it, she thought. She decided to walk, letting the dead fronds underfoot tear into her skin. It was now one o'clock, and so hot that her head would not clear. The frozen strawberries were laid out in the shade with an array of small silver spoons and cups of vanilla ice cream that had already melted. The scene was somehow dismal. Hamid frowned, crowed a little and threw up his hands in exasperation.

Eighteen

AT ONE FIFTEEN, DAZED BY THE SUN, DAVID stooped as he stepped down into the house's interior and took off his sunglasses. The sweat poured between his eyes and down the bridge of his nose, which was struck at once by a burned scent of cloves and human salinity. It was the smell of animals living communally, in a kind of ceaseless fear of the future, and when the metal doors were slammed shut behind him, he found himself with Abdellah, Anouar and one other man in near-complete darkness as they fumbled their way along a bare cement corridor haphazardly overlaid with cheap, filthy carpets. The whole structure was made of this same cement, which had probably been hastily poured and shaped. There were several rooms on either side of the corridor, all with the same patchwork of coarse carpets. In each one there was a crude square window whose wire and glass were insulated with newspaper.

They walked into a large bare chamber with a gas stove and a metal kettle bubbling on top of it. Here were glass cups and a tin plate with a pile of fresh mint and next to it a large block of sugar. The lamentations around the car seemed to grow more vocal, expressed by more voices, but above and around it the wind moaned and soughed and sometimes drowned it out. The window crackled as it was hit by flying sand, which sounded like rain. Abdellah lit an oil lamp.

They sat in a sprawling sort of way while tea was made. Anouar said gently to him, 'You cannot drink now. I'll bring you some in a minute.'

The old man planted himself on a square of cardboard, his throne, and picked up a small chisel with which to hack at the block of brown-tinged sugar. He worked at gouging out some rough lumps and dropped them into the kettle where the mint was brewing. Then he crossed his legs and leaned back against the wall. Anouar cut the stalks of mint and crammed them into the kettle as well while the two men murmured to each other. The father unwound his *chech* as if it pained him, slowly unravelling it to its full length and laying it down next to him. His cropped white hair glistened slightly as he looked down at his own fingers and then spread them for a moment over his face.

David could hear the body of Driss being removed from the jeep and being carried into the house through a different door. The lamentation thus reappeared in the corridor outside the room, loud and reverberating; it unnerved him, and he waited to see what effect it would have on Abdellah. But the old man said nothing. When the tea was ready, he crouched with Anouar and sipped it from his tiny glass cup with loud slurps. They went through four or five cups in this way while the wails from the corridor worsened. It was this that made Anouar uncomfortable, and which made him shift awkwardly from one foot to the other. He asked the old man what he should do with the foreigner.

217

'Take him to Driss's room,' Abdellah said a little absently.

Anouar rose, but the father then signified that he wanted him to do something else in addition.

'That friend of Driss's. Is it Ismael? Where is he?'

'He is in Tabrikt hiding with his father.'

'What is he afraid of? The police won't come here. Go to Tabrikt and tell him that I would like to speak with him this afternoon, if possible. Tell him Driss's father wishes it, and he should respect me. I know he won't come to the burial.'

'He is afraid.'

'Tell him it is understood that he has his reasons for not coming. But nevertheless I want to speak with him anyway. I want to know what he has to say for himself.'

'Very well.'

'Tell him to come quietly, when no one is looking, when the burial is over and done with.'

Anouar motioned for David to rise, and they ventured back out into the corridor with his travelling bags, where the women stared at them thunderstruck. Anouar pushed David quickly down the corridor towards another room at its far end. David went uncomplainingly, grateful to be hustled away from the Furies. They darted into another stifling cement room with a newspapered window, and Anouar slammed the door shut behind them. The floor here was covered with newspapers as well, and a single rug. Around the bottom of the walls, dozens of trilobites were stacked, each specimen numbered and named in roman letters as if in expectation of a Western buyer. A mattress lay in one corner, with plastic bottles of water and a small transistor radio.

David understood at once that they must be Driss's

things. It couldn't be an accident that they were making him sleep in Driss's bed next to Driss's transistor radio. His stomach turned and he was tempted to say something harsh, but Anouar pre-empted him.

'It's the room of Driss, as you have guessed. There is no other room for you to sleep in. The father wanted you to feel his spirit here, too. He thinks it is fitting.'

'Fitting?'

David trembled visibly, and his eyes seemed to Anouar to lose their formidable colour. Moreover, his knees were weakening, Anouar could see.

'Lie down, David. You must be tired.'

'I didn't have to come here, you know. It was my choice.'

'Lie down. It's the only bed we have for you.'

David felt himself spiralling downwards, helplessly propelled towards this sordid mattress where the boy had slept, maybe for years, since childhood.

'I can't lie down yet.'

He went to the window and looked out. It was like peering through the periscope of a submarine, because it was at ground level. The whole house was more or less subterranean. The boy's personal effects had probably been cleared away, but there was still a pile of magazines and a razor standing in a plastic cup. He stared at them in horror. And there was the amiable, slightly blundering Anouar with his huge ochre-coloured palms spread out like an old painting of Jesus making his gesture of compassion. Except that Anouar's gesture was not quite compassion. It was a sort of insistence. He told David that he was going to the burial now, and while he was away, David should keep the door bolted.

'It's for your own safety,' he said.

'My own safety?'

'The women are hysterical with grief.'

'What happens now?' David wanted to scream.

'Well,' Anouar concluded, lowering his hands finally and giving the sinking Englishman as warm a smile as he could afford in the circumstances, 'I will come for you at dusk. Get some sleep.'

He swept out as if in embarrassment, and David bolted the door behind him, as he had been ordered, and he did it quietly, without a fuss. Perhaps it was better after all. Soon silence overwhelmed him. He went to the window and watched the acacia thorns rolling along in the wind. The shadow of the giant cliff was advancing towards the house and would soon engulf it as promised, but when? He bit his lip and counted to a hundred. The mobile phone still offered no signal. He collapsed on the mattress, and exhaustion suddenly gripped him. 'It's an outrage,' he said aloud, but of course there was no outrage that he could actually define, so gradually he calmed down, because after all he had no choice. He swallowed a multi-vitamin pill from his bag and lay quite still, controlling his fidgety hands, for soon they were going to bury Driss in the tumbledown cemetery behind the houses, where a few white stones marked the largely forgotten ancestors.

The trilobites stood there in a light that slowly mutated and declined. The labels fluttered in the hot breezes passing through the glassless window, and the Greek and Latin words scrawled on them could as well have been mellifluous spells. Psychopyge, Asaphus, Dicranurus. The latter was a spiderlike form with splayed legs and two coiled ram's horns, and came from the Devonian period. To pass the time, he opened some of the news-paper packages and looked at the spined, armoured,

crablike beasts that had been hacked out of the face of
Issomour by Driss. They were as hideous as anything
from his own nightmares – as fierce, negative and
chilling. So the distant past had been a nightmare, too,
and the Sahara had once been a vast nightmare ocean
filled with teeming life that had been as ugly as anything
the earth had seen before or since. Demons indeed. That
superstition now seemed less improbable. He picked up
an exquisite tiny specimen called a Comura, with a
single row of perfectly articulated spines, across which
he ran a finger. It was marked 'Buyer, USA'. The wide,
smoothly armoured head of another animal was just as
primitive, like the disturbingly simple design of a horse-
shoe crab. It was incredible that wealthy men collected
such things, bought them indeed at exorbitant prices at
the Butterfields auction in San Francisco and then used
them to decorate their bathrooms in Palo Alto and
Manhattan and Venice Beach. A single bathroom renovation of a Silicon Valley executive probably kept a
Saharan village like Tafal'aalt alive for a year. And these
specimens had been painstakingly prepped until their
surfaces had a polished sheen to them. They looked like
beautiful Neolithic tools, elegant in their fashion, and
Anouar had told him that the more detailed their corrugated eyes were, the more valuable they were, the more
dealers were prepared to pay for them. And so too with
the extravagant, sometimes curly spines. So this was
what Driss had spent his time doing, and these were
what had filled his waking mind for twenty-odd years.
Comuras and Psychopyges.

He lay down again and forced back the tears ready to
erupt down his cheeks. How could one spend a whole life
digging, trading, preparing these nightmare life-forms

from another geological era? It must be enough to drive people mad. It *had* driven them mad.

London was distant now. He thought of the agonising lawsuit that he had lost. The old woman in Chiswick Park misdiagnosed through one of those forensic fuck-ups that strike as rarely as lightning, but with roughly equal force. He hadn't spotted the tumour for what it was; he had not concentrated, perhaps, or his antennae had not been as sensitive as they usually were. Some part of his unconscious might well have led him astray, deluding him for a fatal few moments. There was no accounting for what had happened. It had been human error – his error – and all the fury of the gypped medical consumer had fallen upon his lone head. Too late to catch her tumour in time. The woman was dying, and making a considerable amount of noise while doing it. She was decaying because of his error, and it was just enough that he would have to pay for it. And now this – it could hardly be coincidental, could it? It must be the unconscious at work again. The unconscious working as a noose.

For some time he had had that feeling of oncoming doom. He wondered if Jo, too, had noticed it. They were so rarely intimate any more, she probably never got close enough to notice. All she could sense was his never-ending irritability, his morose closure. Another thing for which he would eventually have to be forgiven. And yet in the end, he had not done anything wicked. It had just been an accumulation of accidents. One accident after another. Or do we produce our own accidents? Are they the sum total of our little neglects?

He slept. The usual nightmares arrived, then departed.

He woke to the colour of the cliff burning in the first moments of a Sahara dusk, the ropes and little caves exposed to a light that seemed oxidised. For a while he didn't move. He wanted to just absorb the dread pouring out of that wall of bitter, luminous redness. He was sure the burial was already over.

In fact, it had passed quickly. The wind was high and the plot of gravestones carved into the desert was unendurable even as the sun went down. Driss's mother had died years before; it was the aunts and cousins who wept and cursed. The men had already absorbed their grief into themselves and stood silent and unmoving as the wind hurled debris around them and made them feel their desolation.

They were lost in their own thoughts as the bandaged body was lowered into its slot and the prayers were said. Abdellah thought of his son's young face as a ten-year-old when he had taken him prospecting across the mountain by himself. A face like an apple, with the burnished freckles of young boys. He remembered it as if it were yesterday, and the Dicranurus they had picked up by the trenches. Driss still had it in his room. Abdellah bit his lip. His tears were all expended and nothing more would come out of his eyes, nothing, in fact, but vision itself.

As night was falling and the mass of Issomour was losing its sparkling definition against an indigo sky, he went to the edge of the village where the dried *oued* was full of majestic boulders and waited for Anouar to arrive back on foot from Tabrikt. Almost as soon as the sun disappeared, the air cooled considerably and he drew his *chech* round his head. His mind was empty, numbed with horror, and no violent words passed through it, not even as his anger rose and fell and rose again, because, after all, life was not words and neither was reality and they changed nothing. Many times during the journey from Azna he had considered what he should do to the Englishman, but in reality he didn't know; his mind was as yet unresolved. There was only one thing that mattered to him and that was whether, when confronted with the most painful necessity of telling the truth, David would do so. To tell him the truth about how Driss died: it was the only thing that now obsessed him. Upon the question of that truthfulness, everything would be decided from now on. If David lied, it was one thing; if he had the courage to tell Abdellah truthfully what had happened that night, the ending would be of a different nature. There it was. There was nothing more that a father could ask of a man who had killed his son. The question of vengeance in itself was merely vulgar and had no force. He was therefore waiting before he made any decision. He had had to wait until Driss had been buried and until he had talked to Ismael. But a lie from David could not be forgiven, that much was clear. The lie would be far worse than the original accident. Far worse, he decided. For whereas an accident is no one's fault, a lie is an individual man's specific fault because it is deliberate. It's a real act, something willed, and it is more difficult to forgive than anything.

After thirty minutes Anouar came out of the dark, picking his way along the *oued*, and behind him came the boy, swaddled in black rags to conceal his identity. Abdellah stirred himself; he beckoned the boy forward impatiently, and Anouar threw off his *chech* for a moment and got his breath back. The boy was tall, thin, very like Driss. He had been in the house on countless occasions, since he and Driss had been apparently inseparable at times. They walked along the *oued*, finding a place where the wind was tamer. Ismael was extremely nervous, and his shoulders rolled as if their owner wished them to disappear, and his eyes had that wild, vacillating look that you see in the faces of minor criminals as they are being led away by the police.

'Calm down,' Abdellah said sternly. 'It's not you who has done anything wrong.' And his voice made itself respected, so that Ismael crouched down, as if this would make it more inaudible in the grand scheme of things, and his face was long and birdlike, his eyelashes like a girl's.

'Tell him,' Anouar said in a friendly way. 'He wants to know what happened, that's all.'

'It's a terrible thing to ask you, Ismael. But I have to know everything.'

Anouar sat down, and for a while they all waited for the moon to appear over the edge of the Issomour cliffs. Anouar passed out cigarettes and lit them one by one, so that gradually the mood became more serene, more affable and more conducive to talk. Ismael sighed theatrically and asked how the funeral had gone. He was greatly sorry he hadn't been able to attend. He apologised. Then he said:

'I was with Driss all the way. We left here together with the Psychopyge specimens wrapped in paper. You remember?'

'I do. Where were you headed?'

'To Midelt. We thought we'd sell them there. There's a German dealer there, you know. He would buy them.'

'Ah, Meissner,' Abdellah nodded. 'He is a crook.'

'But you were alone on the road together, so late?' Anouar asked.

The boy shifted, and his face became a little petulant.

'We were hitching rides. And sometimes we could sell from the road. We heard there was going to be a big party up at the faggots' house. Lots of rich foreigners driving by. It was common sense.'

'So you were waiting for cars?'

The boy said nothing, staring down at his own ankles. Abdellah lit the oil lamp he had brought with him and made a merciless study of Ismael's shifty, twitchingly evasive face. The boy was a notorious liar, and he had many times suspected him of being a minor thief as well. One of those who roamed the trenches at night looking for places he could dig himself. One couldn't trust him. He wasn't afraid enough to tell the truth now, but Abdellah would hear him out, because there was no one else. No one else had been there but David.

'The foreigners drove up in their car,' he said to Ismael. 'And then?'

'We ran towards them. They slowed down.'

'It's not possible,' Anouar said.

'They slowed down *a little*. There was a European man driving. He clearly saw us and that we were holding up boxes of fossils for sale. When we saw him slowing, we thought they were interested. We sprang forward with joy. They pay anything when they are in a car.'

'It's true.' Abdellah nodded again. 'They're very stupid when they're behind a wheel.'

'That's what we thought. We thought, aha, he is going to roll down his window and pay us ten times what he should.'

'You held up the Psychopyges?'

'We did. But we made a mistake. The man didn't stop.'

'They knew it was a demon.'

226

'Whatever they knew, they didn't stop.'

'That much we know,' Anouar interjected.

'But he saw you both?' Abdellah insisted.

'By God, he did.'

'What happened then?'

The boy had tears in his eyes.

'I admit it. I ran away. I was too scared.'

'Where did you run to?'

'I ran into the hills. Up and up until I couldn't run any more.'

'You little shit. You pathetic fool.'

There was nothing to say; the boy hung his head.

'You ran while Driss was lying there?'

Ismael stammered. 'He was already dead. I watched the man turn him over.'

'What did the European do?'

'He — he — went through his pockets and took out the ID.'

Of course, Abdellah thought. It was so obvious. Men always act in this way. They think God is blind. As if they won't be found out.

'When you ran, did you turn back to watch?'

'I saw them arguing, the man and the woman. The woman was screaming at the man. The man wanted to find me.'

Anouar and Abdellah laughed, though it was not really laughter — it was a pained sneer. They thought of David running after Ismael and it simply made them laugh. It was comical enough.

'Well, well.'

Abdellah got up and strolled in a circle around the crouching boy. He wanted to kill him, and yet Ismael had only acted out of self-preservation. He was a petty thief, and he acted accordingly. For all he knew, Driss had been a petty thief, too, and he was not quite convinced that they had been standing by the road just to sell fossils. Ismael was a devious boy. His word was nothing. He would lie at the drop of a hat to exonerate himself.

Suddenly Abdellah rose and lurched towards Ismael, laying about him with his hands, smacking him on the head and then beating him with the flats of his hands until he couldn't thrash any more. But there was something half-hearted about it all, the hands not really connecting, the anger half feigned, so that the boy knew it and didn't react unduly, merely rolling back on his heels and turning his face away.

'You fucking wretch!' the father cried, but again a little forcedly. 'You worthless scum! What will you do for me when I ask you? When the time comes, what will you do?'

'Anything,' the boy cried.

'You're a liar and a thief. I should kill you right now. Anouar, where is my pistol?'

Anouar said nothing while the boy flinched, and Abdellah's arms ran out of energy.

'You say anything, you little shit. Would you do anything I asked you?'

The boy nodded.

'Well, I didn't ask you. But you owe it to me.'

For a long while, none of them spoke. The moon continued its languid rise and the innumerable man-made caves punched into the vertical surface of the mountain became visible. Abdellah sat down again and lost himself in thought. Anouar lit another cigarette. Furtively, Ismael glanced back over his shoulder down the *oued*. Perhaps he could just run back to Tabrikt and have done with it. He was thinking of running away to Casablanca anyway. He and

Driss had spoken of it many times. Anything was better than this shit-hole. He clenched his fists but didn't move. Abdellah stopped watching him after a while and looked up at the ladders suspended across the face of the cliff. He stroked his chin. Really, it was difficult to think. The moon was in the way. It was too bright, too penetrating.

He let the boy cover his face again and felt his anxiety fragmenting, dissipating. Why not let fate take over? It would anyway. Ismael, for his part, thought incessantly of that day at the quarry when Driss had told him all about his past life in Paris.

Finally he dismissed Ismael and strode off back to Tafal'aalt, with Anouar at his heels. He pounded on the metal door. The women had prepared a goat *tagine;* the men who had come with him on the journey to Azna were gathered in the main room, smoking and drinking tea. They looked up as he entered, and there was a storm cloud on his face that made them put down their glasses and wipe their lips. He didn't like this reaction and immediately tried to put them at their ease.

'Relax, my friends. It's a sad day, but there it is.'

Invoking the One True God, He Who Is Merciful at All Times, they murmured into their glasses again and uttered words of comfort to the father. Abdellah sat with Anouar beside him and began drinking with them. The normal jokes and sexual innuendos were left to one side this time, and silence was allowed to pervade the reunion. When the *tagine* was brought in, Anouar leaned over to Abdellah and whispered, 'Shall I bring in the foreigner?' But the old man shook his head.

'Take something to him instead. I am too tired to think about him now. And eating with us is out of the question.'

'Very well.'

Abdellah stretched out his creaking, aching body on the oil-stained carpet and tore into the communal bread. And to think that the wind was already scouring Driss's grave not a hundred metres from here. He dipped the bread into his mint tea and found that his hand shook so obviously that everyone else was aware of it. He could not stop it, and after a while he ceased feeling ashamed of it. He let it shake. Why should it not shake? His whole body and mind shook. When you go mad, he thought to himself, this is what it is like. You begin to shake first. Then all of you shakes. You shake until pieces of you begin to fall off. You become a wolf, a bear. You no longer hear the world. You curl into a ball and Satan begins to talk to you. Your hand goes on shaking and you eat your bread like a fool. You think, I am poor, and nothing else. And then you realise that no one is listening to you or your thoughts. You are alone with facts.

Nineteen

WHEN ANOUAR KNOCKED ON HIS DOOR,
David flicked open the bolt quickly and yanked the heavy
door open. His face was ashen, with big glass eyes like
a doll's – or so Anouar thought. Perhaps he had been
praying to his dreadful, ridiculous God, whom the infidels held in such exaggerated and futile regard. 'It's you,'
the Englishman blurted out, and stepped aside to let
Anouar enter with a large metal dish of goat *tagine*. As
he passed, Anouar caught a whiff of curious aftershave
that smelled like apricot stones, and yet David had not
shaved and indeed he was looking a bit shabby.

'Is everything all right?' he asked David.

'I'm just starving. Where were you?'

Anouar said nothing. The room was in darkness
because David had not been able to figure out the combination of matches and oil lamp. So Anouar did it for
him. He laid the tray in the middle of the floor and
organised the lamp while David sprawled next to the
tray with a lugubrious groan. He seemed to unfurl like
some tired, dented rodent.

Anouar was fascinated by David. By his fastidious
cleanliness, his obvious wealth, his refinement, which

was genuine, not affected, and by his comfortable sense of superiority. The latter quality in particular absorbed him. It was not just a superiority to the men of Tafal'aalt, after all, but – Anouar supposed – to the whole of creation. He was sure that David would even feel superior to the king of Morocco if he were put on the spot. It was a flabbergasting thought, and that in turn made David a flabbergasting man. Anouar could see this whole phenomenon in the way David folded his handkerchiefs and the way he picked up a glass with two fingers, but never three. He was a gentleman. Only a gentleman would use two fingers. Only a gentlemen would feel a passing contempt that he could not disguise, however hard he tried. The gentleman was like an unconscious robot in some ways. Everything he did was automatic, instinctive, blind. He didn't think about making mistakes. Fascinating!

Anouar tried to imagine what world had produced such a man, but it was impossible. England was a place of green lawns and terrific, fat women. They had peaches there and enormous carrots and beaches made of stones – he had seen them on the TV at the Café des Ksours in Rissani. The men there lived in perpetual gloom and unhappiness, no doubt brought upon them by their infidelity to truth and their indelible taste for buggery.

Yet David was a handsome specimen of arrogant pride and exact manners, and Anouar noticed everything about him that was an expression of pride, respectability and exactitude. The marriage ring, for example, carefully adjusted upon the appropriate finger; or the gloss of the shoes that was produced by a dainty vigilance that never let up. He had noticed that David had a special cloth for dusting his shoes that he took with him everywhere he went. When the shoes dimmed a little, he leaned down with this cloth and rectified the situation. He breathed on his watch and cleaned it. He wore cufflinks even here in Tafal'aalt. Never had such a thing been seen there before.

Now David ate with the metal fork Anouar had provided for him, but he used it with noticeable restraint. Anouar sat with him and asked him questions about his homeland, but David did not seem willing to tell him much. He was more concerned about what Abdellah was going to do.

'Nothing,' Anouar reassured him. 'I think he would like to have a conversation with you, that is all.'

'That seems rather improbable. I feel locked up in here.'

Anouar was a little mortified by this comment.

'But you lock yourself in,' he reported. 'It is not the same.'

'You know what I mean,' David insisted.

He ate methodically, keeping an eye on the deltoid-shaped flame of the oil lamp. His own thoughts about his hosts were far less speculatively romantic than Anouar's about him.

'All is confusion,' Anouar said truthfully. 'Would you like some *kif*?'

'You mean marijuana? No thanks. I'm a doctor. I don't believe in marijuana.'

What a fool, Anouar thought, and lit up anyway.

'I wonder if second-hand marijuana smoke makes you stoned?'

But Anouar didn't understand irony.

'Never mind,' David sighed. 'I'm sure it does.'

'It's as you wish, Monsieur David.'

'The *tagine* is pretty good.'

'They killed a goat kid an hour ago.'

'Oh,' David said, and his heart sank. It wasn't like buying a shank at a supermarket, was it? He stopped eating for a moment.

Anouar relaxed with the *kif*. It was strong, fresh shit from the green Atlas foothills, pungent as mint, and it went straight to your head. He could tell that David was curious about it, but that his upbringing made it difficult for him to accept a polite offer of a puff.

'I can hear people walking past the house,' David said.

'It's the diggers coming back from the mountain. They come back at dark, when they can no longer see what they are doing.'

David went to the window. Shadowy forms filed past between the houses, clinking with hammers and stones, and the tangy spiced grease in his mouth trickled back into his throat and he swallowed hard, disgusted and grateful at the same time. So they work from dawn to dusk, he thought.

It was a nice phrase until you thought about what it meant. And it wasn't for anything useful or productive. It was futile, in the end. The diggers were obviously paid nothing, and the middlemen and dealers made the profits. One day a European just like him would stride into this same room, point out a Dicranurus and have it wrapped. The money would keep the family alive for a few weeks. Flour, oil, butter, tea, bread, newspapers, tobacco. But the Dicranurus would then have a glittering career on the far side of the world.

So what, though? It was the same all over the world. One didn't give a second thought to the sweatshop workers in Indonesia who assembled one's hundred-dollar DVD player. It wasn't necessarily an injustice. They were paid what everyone else in Indonesia was paid. They didn't pay Paris rents in Jakarta and they could eat quite well for a dollar a day. Whereas he and Jo spent thousands on food every month and ate quite badly. They weren't any happier because they had a soulless little house in some soulless London street with white doorways. Indonesians didn't envy them. No one envied them. The tone was usually a kind of bemused pity.

A young boy walked by, shouldering a large leather bag. Then the alley fell silent. Anouar announced that he was leaving and that Abdellah would come by shortly to have a talk with him.

'Just you and him. To clear things up.'

'Is he coming with a knife?'

'I don't know,' Anouar said simply. 'One must be prepared for all possibilities. Don't you think, David?'

'I don't have any opinions about that.'

'He's high as a kite,' David thought as the door closed behind Anouar. Perhaps they were all high now. A house full of high Berbers: it was not a particularly comforting thought, but then again, perhaps it *was* a comforting thought, and after a while, as he stood by the window watching the moon, he heard a strange sound from the other side of the house. It was a low communal singing, the voices rising and falling in mournful sequences. The men were singing around the dead goat. As they sang, David thought he heard an *oud* playing behind them. The sound was so sad that he couldn't move from the window until it had stopped. He went to the door and peered into the corridor. A single lightbulb had been left on at the far end, lighting a pile of tools stacked by the end wall. A woman sobbed very quietly in one of the rooms there. He closed the door and held his breath.

A few seconds later, the light went off. The men gathered in the main room seemed to have fallen asleep, and David went back to the window, where he pressed his face against the wire mesh to suck in the cold air. The scent of iron in the air, the heat that moved and crept. He was panicking and his heart rate was picking up its pace, becoming so emphatic that he could feel it with his hand, and a feeling of terror encircled him completely and he gripped the bar of the window as if to stop being swept away. He knew that Abdellah was walking down the corridor towards him. He'd merely waited till his companions were asleep. David thought blindly of the parachutes with swastikas he had made at school and the way he had never been found out for a crime that had caused at least one mother to faint. He laughed. The Issomour cliff was a wall of silver, with the buckets suspended on ropes looking like fairground contraptions of some kind, and across the rubble road that ran through Tafal'aalt scorpions ran in the white light of the moon. He was still not sure if he was sorry. More sorry for what he had done, that is, than he was for himself.

'That kid was going to rob me,' he said under his breath as the door moved and began to open. 'He was going to kill us by the road and take our car. Dammit.'

Abdellah was carrying a candle waxed to a saucer, and he had shaved his head. He spoke perfect French, it turned out.

'This is very difficult for me,' David began.

'Sit,' the father said, and took out two apples and a huge SOG combat knife, which he placed next to him as he sat down.

So David put himself into a cross-legged position and watched with a calm horror as Abdellah picked up one of the apples, leaned the blade of the SOG against it and began to peel.

The old man bent over his task with a remarkable concentration. He removed the peel as a single intact coil and laid it next to him. Then he cut the apple into four pieces and handed one of them to David. A drop of juice hung off the blade as he wiped it against his knee. Between the two men there existed a mental chasm — centuries of antagonism and mutual ignorance. But such a chasm, David considered, would have been relatively easy to span. It wasn't just that. There was a deeper misunderstanding between them, one that went so far back into the mind that its beginning could not be conceptualised. Thousands of years without trees, without lawns, without ease. Just this wind. They had minds perfectly adapted, not to wood, streams and fruit, but to stones, dust and wind. They were moulded by stone. They were formed by elements that other people only tasted impartially, occasionally.

'Is it good?' Abdellah asked.

'The apple? Fine.'

The old man smiled drily.

'It is very regrettable, this whole business,' he went on. And David felt a mild outrage that this wily fox spoke such fluent French and had pretended otherwise. Of course he spoke a European language. Moroccans were brilliant linguists, and Abdellah's clients were all Europeans. The fossils in this room were all priced in euros. It was so obvious now.

'It was an accident,' David said sullenly. 'It was one

of those things that happen in the dark of the night, *dans les ténèbres, vous savez?*'

'I know what an accident is. Life is full of accidents.'

'Then, if you'll forgive me for saying, I am not sure why I am here. I came here as a favour to you, and because my friends thought it would be a good idea. But I am not sure why I accepted.'

'Because you felt responsible.'

'Yes. But I'm not sure for what.'

'You felt responsible for something.'

Abdellah picked up the knife again and proceeded to the second apple, which he peeled in exactly the same way. It was as if he had done this thousands of times blindfolded, as if the apple was sullenly inclined to pop into his free hand superbly naked.

'I will leave that to you to imagine,' he said. 'There was one thing that I wanted to show you. It was the fossil that Driss was carrying when he was struck by your car. It was recovered by the police.'

David blushed suddenly, but the father's voice rolled on unconcernedly as if blushes were only a matter of nature and did not need to be observed with any special care.

'I hadn't heard about that,' David retorted.

'It was returned to me because it was so valuable. It's right behind you. It's called an Elvis.'

Before David could turn, the old man had lithely risen and picked the thing up. He sat down again and tore off the shreds of newspapers from a creature armoured with a row of crazy spines, widely spaced eyes and three distinct humps. It was labelled with the single word *Devonian*. Abdellah admitted that he didn't even know its technical name, but that only three specimens had been found in the Sahara, and dealers had decided to give it the superstar name of Elvis.

He didn't mind telling David that Driss had stolen it from
his own father and gone off to try to sell it somewhere.

'But,' he added mildly, 'this happens all the time. The
young boys are frustrated. They feel they are going
nowhere and have no hopes. They don't want to be diggers
all their lives. It's a miserable life. They want to escape.
They don't want to live like their fathers. So they steal
an Elvis, which they know will sell for ten thousand
dollars in the United States, because even if they sell it
in Midelt for a thousand euros, they can still go to
Casablanca and find a girl. Yes, they can! Casablanca is
full of loose girls, and a thousand euros will get you a
long way with a loose girl. And I do not mind telling you
that I didn't mind when I found out. I understood him,
and in a way I wished him luck. It's only a fossil after
all. It's a lump of rock, literally. If he had sold it to you
for a few hundred, I would have been happy for him.
Really happy.'

Abdellah's eyes filled with tears. How much better it
would have been if David had stopped and bought that
damned Elvis. David would be in Azna drinking cocktails
with his wife, and Driss would be in Casablanca in the
arms of a loose woman. Not bad, compared to what had
actually happened. As it was, it was this Elvis that had
caused Driss to run away and try his luck on the open
road. It was not even greed; it was just bedazzlement.

'But frankly, I have no idea why you people have such
a thirst for these stupid rocks. What do you see in them?
All we know is that you want them and that you are
prepared to pay money for them. That's all we need to
know, too. Perhaps you are completely deranged. Who
knows? Some of us believe that these are the most evil
creatures that have ever existed, that they are the forms

of dead demons. That is what they look like, you must admit. They must have an influence upon our minds, an influence that is evil. And that is precisely what attracts you to them.'

'Really,' David stammered, 'I couldn't tell you.'

'Do you know why we called it an Elvis?'

Abdellah got up again and, without saying another word, began to gyrate his hips. He danced for a while, then sat down again, sighing heavily and shaking his head.

'I see.'

But David didn't see anything at all.

'Well, David, it is all a mystery. He took my Elvis and ran. The next person he met was you, unfortunately.'

He pulled the lamp closer and turned it down. They ate the last segments of the apples, and the wind battered the house, making it sing like a whistle as air flowed through its cracks and glassless windows. The sobbing stopped. David looked down at the Elvis, which seemed to be moving. If it sprang to life, he would have to run. Its eyes glistened. Abdellah took out a long white clay pipe and lit it from the oil lamp.

'Tell me,' he asked, 'what cereal do you eat in the morning? I prefer cornflakes myself. I prefer it to cooked goat kid. It's the one good thing you have given us, apart from ice.'

He chuckled and rolled back on his haunches.

'I'm glad you like ice,' David sneered.

'I like everything that is cool and cold and fresh. You people seem to think we like living in this furnace. You think we like the camels and the sand palm trees and the one hundred and four degrees in the morning? Ah, not at all. I dream of Sweden most of the time. I have seen it in the colour magazines. A fantastic place, by the looks of it. It's the place I would most like to live. How wonderful it would be to go to Sweden and stay there. It must be so deliciously cold there.'

The old man raised one hand and made a strange gesture, as of evoking icicles. Then his face changed.

'Tell me,' he went on. 'Was my son alone that night when you struck him with your car?'

David replied automatically:

'As far as we could see, he was alone.'

'Are you sure?'

'Absolutely.'

'Well, there we are, then.'

Abdellah wiped his hands and scraped together the split pips from the apple and they sat awkwardly listening to the wind picking up, and Abdellah tapped out the contents of his pipe prior to refilling it. He did this as slowly as a man can, indifferent to the infidel's boredom. But then, it had occurred to him, David was not even an infidel in the strict sense of the word, because he was sure David did not even believe in his own God, let alone Abdellah's. It was darkness, pure darkness, and a civilised man couldn't imagine it. And yet he rather liked the guy. He wondered if he should offer him a puff of his pipe instead of cutting his throat, as he had originally intended to do. Come to think of it, he could always do both. There was an idea.

He got up and flung the end of his unravelled *chech* over his shoulder, taking the lamp with him and leaving David sitting on his piece of cardboard.

'Monsieur David,' he said, as he was about to close the door behind himself. 'I would bolt the door when you sleep, if I were you. Anouar will bring you some tea later on. You have been very helpful.'

'You're welcome,' the atheist said, a little idiotically.

'By the way, you are perfectly free to go wherever you like. None of the doors is locked. If you want to go outside, please do so. Just don't walk to La'gaaft. As you know, that is where the blacks live.' His voice became spirited. 'You'll regret it.'

But David didn't bolt the door straight away. He wrapped himself in his sleeping bag and turned off his own lamp. He was aware of the possibility that he had made a mistake, but it was a mistake that revealed itself only in the demeanour and half-conscious body language of Abdellah: he was too friendly. And why the tirade against La'gaaft, which looked identical to Tafal'aalt? And the hatred of the *haratin*, who had been neighbours presumably for centuries? The room gradually became cold, and he began to shiver. He took a banana from his bag and ate it savagely. 'Here I am,' he accused himself, 'eating a fucking banana in a pillbox. Is it me or is it because I'm white?'

A little later he took an Ambien but didn't sleep. He locked the door, then unlocked it. He couldn't decide which was worse, confinement or protection. A woman was walking up and down the corridor, in the dark, talking to herself. He decided to daydream. Where was Jo? Sitting by herself wondering why her phone didn't work? He knew her. She wasn't enough of a party animal to make the time go by swiftly. She would be killing every minute with a hammer, as her mother used to say. She'd be standing on the wall at night with a pair of binoculars. It was terrible for him to take this for granted, but her unhappiness didn't make her faithless. It merely made her repetitive.

But still, it was this same repetitiveness that made him love her more, the more he considered all her qualities rationally – and he was thinking more rationally now than he had in years. Would he love her less, for example, if she was snorting cocaine at that moment? Of course he would. It would mean that she had forgotten him for a while, at a time when forgetting was out of the question. When it was a crime. Her repetitiveness was her fidelity, which was the knot at the heart of her mutinous unhappiness. But neither of them would cut that knot. They had made a profound decision.

Twenty

ON THE LARGE GLASS TABLE THAT
dominated the salon of the second floor the servants had
set down dark chocolate-coloured terracotta plates of figs
and segmented oranges with vases of white orchids between
them. Since the windows had been opened and the curtains
drawn back all the way, the desert air came in and it was
not nearly as hot as it had been the previous night. A change
in the weather, a momentary cooling: it was enough to
loosen her mental hinges, to open the hatches (she thought
of herself as a warren of hatches, like an old cargo ship),
and let her bend down to put her nose to the lines of cocaine
that Richard had carefully cut with a paper knife.

'No, honey, not with your nose. We have *the tube*.'

The tube was like a thin pencil made of engraved Arab
silver with one end shaped like a cat's mouth. He handed
it to her and watched her try to use it, sucking up half a
line with one nostril. Her profile from his angle was beautiful: precise, aquiline, wonderfully edged. She wasn't
smiling like everyone else. Though he had no interest in
women, he could not help trying to admire her hetero-
sexually. Did men fall in love with her, coming to a moment
when they *had* to look past her dowdiness, her scholarly

affect? Because there was no quickness in her, no vividness of reaction. She was always old, in the noblest sense of that word. Even when she snorted a line of coke through a silver tube, her profile never decomposed. It was like someone studying a rare nematode in a lab, every nerve devoted to the task. It must take a very particular kind of man, he thought as he watched her inhale his exactly cut line, and it was not David or Day. It was likely that she had not found him, and never would. There are women like that. One sees them everywhere.

When she had finished, she sat up again and quickly wiped her nostril.

'Believe it or not,' she said, 'I haven't done it in years. Maybe never. I can't remember.'

'Take your time. It's quite a boring drug anyway. I only do it because Dally insists. What about you, Tom?'

Day refused the offer. 'It's a bit Eighties for me. These days, it just makes me fall asleep with aching nostrils. I can do without aching nostrils.'

The French girl was at the table, snorting away feverishly. Her Moroccan lover looked at her aghast but didn't interfere. Her face had gone pink and shiny and her eyes seemed to be bleeding in some way.

'Mohammed, the whole place is full of reptiles. You're a reptile, too. A sweet little reptile.'

'She had a zoo as a kid,' Mohammed explained to the table. 'She had a pet lizard called Mohammed. I think she ought to be decapitated for that.'

Jo held herself still so that this alien force could surge through her at its own speed. She took a small ham sandwich from the table and crammed it into her mouth. Everyone laughed. Day caressed her foot under the low table, where they were all barefoot. And then the cool air struck her face and she was aware of the light film of sweat that clung to it.

'Usually,' Dally chimed, 'they can't eat a thing. Especially not with my A-Force snow from Marseilles.'

Richard purred to Jo directly. 'I'm glad you're feeling a bit better. David'll be back tomorrow. But personally, I'm glad you got to have a day and a night by yourself. I think you needed it.'

She wanted to reply by blurting 'What?' but she knew he was right. A marriage is a stifling affair much of the time.

'It would be great if I wasn't worried,' she said dutifully.

The staff came round with hot napkins as Swann grew belligerent. He was more left-wing than he looked.

'Are you sure they don't hate you, Dicky? I think you're being complacent. They'd never accept you as an infidel. I don't care what you say.'

'Why should they accept him?' the French girl wailed. 'They have every reason to hate Americans.'

'Is that so?' Richard felt a headache coming on with this one. 'I would have thought they had more reason to hate you.'

She looked genuinely astonished.

'But we have excellent relations with the Arabs. We share the Mediterranean with them. But you wouldn't understand.'

'Oh, I understand. You mean you have them in your ghettos, so you feel close to them. Do you feel close to them when they're burning cars in the suburbs and ransacking your synagogues?'

'That's a – how you say – *problème sociale*.'

'No. They dislike you for the same reason they dislike us. We're not Muslims and we lord it over them. It's against what they regard as the natural order of things, which would be them lording it over us. I understand them, though. They are rival imperialists. I don't hold it against them.' By now he did not have the heart to tell her that he was not American, and she probably would not have cared. 'Besides, in America the Muslims are prosperous and peaceful. They don't spend their time rioting in the suburbs and pelting police cars with rubbish bins.' Richard put on a sickly voice. 'Why do they do that in France only? It must be — how you say — *solidarité*.'

'It doesn't matter,' she shouted. 'We're not killing hundreds of thousands in Iraq!'

'No, darling, the local *mujahideen* are. But I am not arguing with you about Iraq. I was a protester against, after all.'

'Then you know how they feel. I can hear them talking in the kitchen. All the Arabs feel that way. You'd have to be stupid not to feel that.'

Richard took out his nutcracker and turned his attention to a large bowl of walnuts.

'You're bitter because of 9/11,' the tiresome one droned on. 'As if you didn't have anything to do with it . . .'

'There were these beautiful statues of the Buddha in Afghanistan,' Richard said, as if to himself, very quietly, 'and one day the rulers of that happy land came to them with a pile of demolition bombs and destroyed them. I suppose, if you were high on coke, that you could argue that poor old Buddha had it coming to him. Perhaps the statues said something offensive or there was something lewd in their complicated hand gestures. I know how it is. One gets so *hotheaded* about Buddha and his ways. It sometimes seems that the only way to respond to it is by . . .'

Jo suddenly found herself laughing out loud.

'It's the coke,' Mohammed drawled, giving her a wink.

'Mohammed,' the French girl protested, 'back me up against these babbling Americans. They're arguing . . .'

'No, we understand that, when in doubt, we Americans must be blamed. I would miss it if you didn't blame us. I'd feel less important somehow. Believe me, we're masochists. We enjoy it, and it makes us feel bigger than we actually are. It makes us insufferably arrogant. I wish I could make the Arabs understand that. I wish I could make *you* understand that. They'd be amazed. Blame us less and we'd be a lot more humble. We wouldn't think we were the centre of the world.'

'Excellent speech,' Day said, slow-clapping. 'Why can't we put you on Al Jazeera?'

'I don't believe you,' the girl snapped. 'You'd think you were the centre of the world anyway.'

Richard gave her a shelled nut. 'It's an understandable delusion. We *were* for a fairly long time. Now I think you should go back to being stoned. You're very cute when you think you're surrounded by reptiles.'

'I *am* surrounded by reptiles.'

'Centre?' an old man whom nobody knew blurted out from the end of the table. 'Of ze world?'

'Is there a dance tonight?' another of the girls asked Dally.

'We're all too fagged, really.'

'Fagged?'

'It's an English expression. Exhausted.'

She shouted across the room. 'He says they're too fagged.'

Richard cut new lines on the glass tabletop and the servants lit the brass oil lamps. Everything turned deep gold. Jo's pupils shuddered with pleasure. A mood of subtle depression soon spread around the crowd.

'We'll be going down to dinner soon,' Richard said, 'and I want you all properly toasted before we do. I'm tired of sober guests. Sober guests are my problem right now. I must seek them out and remedy them. Dally, I believe there are some in the library.'

'What?'

'Sober guests. I will seek them out and remedy them.'

He leaned down with the silver tube. Day looked over and passed his hand over Jo's belly, which also contracted with an unnoticeable pleasure.

The table was laid with the same orchids, which found themselves reflected in the surfaces of the tureens. Their stamens were inflated, elongated, and the flesh of the corollas had reached their maximal plumpness before they would die in a few hours, and certainly by morning, their baby-skin pinkness beginning to deepen and the stamens thickened with golden powder. It seemed to her that this dinner of the third and final night was different from the previous two. The men were all in dinner jackets; the dresses were fancier. There were rollicking multilingual speeches, and the eyes were wild and unstable, as if an atropine dropper had been handed round and they had inhaled an airborne pollen from those orchids coated with an unknown stimulant. The decorum that had held the previous two days together frayed, and something wonderfully ugly emerged. Her blood was up. A sexual note had appeared. It is difficult, she thought coldly, for women to be promiscuous, precisely because it is too easy. When they put themselves out for it, they get used in a nanosecond; then again and again. And meanwhile they begin to think anxiously about the birth canal. But what if the birth canal were no longer much of an issue? Would those small and swift exploitations matter as much as they once had in the days of fertility and youth? Men, too, became sadder and more hopeless as they aged, and there was mutual recognition. One became free.

She looked over the scornful Moroccan boys lining the walls. They were Dally's magazine fantasy. Would she give in to them? Were they beautiful? It didn't really interest her. Beauty didn't really interest her. There'd be no struggle. Her struggle was with Day, whom she would give in to, but not because he was merely available. It was rather because he had bothered with her, when men rarely did. He had taken the time to consider her, to take her into account. To measure her qualities and faults and weigh them like ounces of gold and slag.

When she looked over the Europeans girls next, she saw at once why men were more attracted to them. They were *internally* playful in a way that she could never be. Their faces were full of unmalicious malice. They knew what men wanted. They were bitches in the magnificent sense of the word, and they ruled their domain without forethought.

'And I am not even one per cent bitch.'

The tureens were full of turtle soup. Amphibious claws peeped up around their edges, and the European girls shrieked. Day was sitting next to her, unrelenting in his way, and his breath had turned pepper-hot like a cheap curry. She wanted to spit in his face, but he leaned over. 'You're looking beautiful. It's the coke.'

'Don't look at me. I'm pink!'

'What's wrong with being pink?'

'I look like a cake. I look as if I have icing all over me.'

His eyes shone like photographic paper.

'Icing — would I object?'

They went through the whole dinner chattering and forcing their laughter at other people's jokes, but hour by hour silence was falling around them, as if they were walking together into a sandstorm and letting the peripheral sounds disengage from them and the lights of the world gradually go out. They were listening only to each other. He talked about his house in Bali, rarely visited but frequently embellished. Bali, that place that had been turned into an extension of a folkloric airport. 'What do you like about Bali?' she asked, as the chocolate cake was being carved up and some Arab coins were being excavated from its centre.

'I'm not very romantic about these things. I like hot weather and cheap restaurants. I like affordable spas because I'm old. I thought Mick Jagger lived there, and then it turned out he didn't.'

'No girlfriend? I thought all white guys had a girlfriend in Asia. In fact, I think you have a few sluts on the side, Mr Day.'

'Oh, do I?'

'I'm not judging. I think men need sluts.'

His eyebrows rose.

'Original,' he murmured. 'Personally, I think women need to *be* sluts. They can't manage it except when they're drunk.'

'That's because you don't know how to ask.'

'Me?' He laughed.

'Yes, you. You haven't forgotten about my husband.'

'Well, we oughtn't to forget about him. It's just that, in a way, we have, haven't we?'

She nodded.

'I'm sorry about that.'

He stirred, his face opening wider a little: 'I never thought this would happen at all. I am surprised. I think you have me all wrong, Mrs Henniger. I didn't mean what I said about sluts. I was being facetious and ridiculous.'

'Just banter.'

'Yes. Everyone needs to banter at dinners.'

Seduction, she thought. How she hated seduction.

Then he faltered.

'I feel as if I have been quite phoney with you in some way. Playing a part. It's not me at all. I didn't want to meet a married woman because I thought she would be a quick, cost-free . . .'

'But we have our uses, don't we?'

And she smiled as brilliantly and as unharshly as she could.

'I wouldn't say uses,' he objected, but they burst into laughter, and the damage, so to speak, was done. He laid the edge of his hand against hers as it lay on the dazzling white of the tablecloth, among the silver napkin rings and engraved forks. It was the slight, inconsequential gesture of a man already familiar with her body, already swimming among her waters. It was as light and animal as the motion of the huge moths fluttering against the lozenge-shaped windowpanes just out of hearing of the table.

Soon the French windows were opened and the dinner disassembled into the night. There was no dancing that night, no music, because Richard wanted a more sophisticated finale to his weekend. The gardens were just left to the guests to fill up. An Italian TV personality had materialised out of nowhere, and as she stood on the lawn adjacent to the dining room, two or three photographers bathed her in hysterical flashlight. 'It's Monica

Luciamora,' someone whispered near to them as Day and Jo made off across the same lawn with an armful of biscuits and strawberries and two glasses – the bottle was waiting in his cottage.

As she hurried through that blinding spectacle, with smoke stinging her throat, she refused to think about anything. The dread inside her was pushed down; she was firm. He snatched her hand, and its copious sweat put him off a little. Poor thing, he thought, she's such a freckled English perspirer. She can't take this climate. As they crossed into the *ksour*'s narrow alleys, she actually closed her eyes, letting herself be led, and the man leading her was struck only by how easy it had been.

When she opened those same eyes, she was inside the quietly opulent room with the sashes and Berber knick-knacks and the orderly laundry boxes of the American she didn't know. She saw a pair of leather slippers lying by the writing desk. One of Richard's one hundred cats crouched in a corner lapping from a saucer of condensed milk. Day was peeling the foil from the bottle slanted in its ice bucket, and he was telling her that, technically, the wire cage underneath was called the *muselet*. Here, he was saying, is how you open a bottle of champagne, by holding it firmly by the base and turning the bottle, not the cork. A red wine is held by the neck, a woman by the waist and a bottle of champagne by the *derrière*.

'Mark Twain,' he said quietly as the cork came out without a pop. 'But those priorities can be rearranged later in the evening.'

'Oh, they can, can they?'

He poured, and there was a hiss.

* * *

253

She kicked off her sandals and went straight to the bed. Her body felt as light as tin that has been beaten patiently and incrementally for days and nights. Her spinning top was slowing down and losing its impeccable balance. She flopped melodramatically into the bed, letting her hair splash on the crispy-crunchy laundered pillows and her legs separate wildly to form what she thought was a sexual pattern on top of the tribal coverlet. 'You're stoned,' she said to herself. 'For once it's you, not David!' But Day didn't seem to notice. He unleashed the energies of the champagne and then poured out two glasses like a waiter in a third-rate bistro. He didn't hear her heart beating at all. Was he supposed to hear it? He turned and watched her rolling on the bed.

'It's the same as your bed,' he remarked drily.

All her long-stifled, fermenting hatred of David was turning into champagne bubbles and evaporating into nothing. As it evaporates, even hatred has its sweetness. Day came to the bed with the two unsteady glasses and they sipped in silence, avoiding each other's eyes. Then she took his cufflinks and bit them open. He seemed paralysed by her for a while, looking down at her as if she had ripped into his own skin. His mood did not grow gentle, as she had expected, and in a way it was better. He undid his buttons with one hand while she made unflattering remarks about the hair in his ears. He chuckled. Slowly, she took him in her legs like someone grasping an insect with a pair of pliers. They rolled over, and his dry mouth began to kiss her arm. It took a long time for him to make his insistence final. It was because she could not – even now – make up her mind. At any moment she could withdraw, run out of the room, and keep her system with David intact.

In the wall mirror she kept seeing his naked feet, and they reminded her of pig's trotters; she didn't mind, but it made her think again. As he took off her pants, she struggled a little, and it was because she wanted to struggle. 'All right,' she thought, 'rape me if you can. Let's see.'

But he wasn't raping her. If anything, she was raping him. Yet when she did struggle, his hands held her down and the door on escape was shut finally and for good. He put his whole weight into the denial. Instantly, her mind gave way, shattered into pieces.

And those pieces began to whirl clockwise. She saw the fan turning in the opposite direction, and the result was vertigo. The bed turned as well, so that there seemed to be gears turning within gears. There was a look of triumph on his face, and a wetness around the eyes. His eyebrows had arched up as far as they would go and his pupils were like wet, boggy moss. She hated that look, but it was too late, and without warning he suddenly pushed his arms underneath her and lifted her up an inch. He held her there for a while, then let her down again. The muscles along his sides moved with a long, jittery electrical shock, like a horse when it's pricked. She groaned because she couldn't hold her lungs down.

The curtains had been left open and the moon burst across a scene that looked like petty warfare. A shoe, an orange, a broken glass, a knife laid across a sill and forgotten long ago. There was a smell of dank grapes and orange zest, and the product he splashed expensively under his arms. While he slept, she moved her hands across the sheets and into little pools of drying semen. The sameness of men came as a sudden revelation that served to calm her down. It never occurred to them that they were remarkably similar to one another. All pieces of the same contiguous ectoplasm. She lifted her head a little and caught the moon shining on an unknown piece of pisé wall. There seemed to be a distinct human noise of some kind coming from the open air, like someone breathing. The fan whirred over them. Her broken pieces slowly came together again and she realised that she was not going to fall asleep. She knew that she was being watched, listened to, because nothing was secret in the *ksour*.

It was Hamid, in fact, who stood outside in the shadow of the pisé wall listening intently to the lovemaking inside the cottage, which he had expected, but which nevertheless shocked him profoundly. No one had asked him to come down here and spy, but he had been drawn by an irresistible curiosity. The infidels, he now realised more than ever, were extraordinarily shameless in their copulations and betrayals. And to think that he had felt sorry for the Henniger woman as her husband was hauled off to the desert to answer for a crime that in all probability he had not even committed. Though he never said so to the other members of the staff, he considered David's gesture quite noble; it was surprising and even honourable. No one had forced him to do it. And as soon as he was gone, the wife entered the cottage of another man. So this was their vaunted female freedom. That was their miserable liberation.

He crouched with one ear pushed forward, his incredulity warping his senses so that he heard only the erotic struggle of the unbelievers. Then, when he had heard enough, he leaned against the wall and composed himself. He heard the woman pad her way to the bathroom. Truly, as was said, a woman without discretion was like a gold ring in a pig's snout. The lights came on for a moment and then were turned off again. He moved away at last, disgusted with himself for continuing in the service of Richard and Dally, whose friends were so worthless. He continued because he needed the money and because his father's hospital bills were mounting. He was trapped inside a necessary dishonour.

He made his way back up to the gate, where paper lanterns were hanging on long bamboo sticks. The party that night had acquired a curious atmosphere due in no small part to the vast quantities of cocaine that had been distributed earlier. The drug provoked a mild horror in him because it was unfamiliar, alien and its effects so unlike those of *kif*. It was not clear to him why people took it at all. They seemed to derive no pleasure from it, and it did not, like *kif*, improve their mental functions. On the contrary. It made them supercilious, bellicose and even worse-mannered than they usually were.

As he reached the roadside wall where he traditionally smoked his nocturnal pipe and tried to get a grip on the day's misfortunes, he felt suddenly immensely tired. Tired of the breakfasts with their epic wastages, and of the volumes of toxic alcohol constantly being stashed, prepared, wasted, spilled and vomited up again. Tired of the lost jewellery and the braying men from London and Paris rolling around like toys in their hideous inebriation. Tired, for that matter, of the constant gossiping and superstitious suspicions of the semi-literate, provincial Moroccans with pathetically dated prejudices and childish boasting. To tell the truth, he had liked Jo. And now ...

He looked out over the dark immensity of the plain, with the dense oasis in the foreground. Far off, where the desert met the sky, there was a pale, elongated glimmer of straw-gold light. The wind was cool, indifferent, and he wondered if half the night had really passed so quickly.

He had carried Richard half drunk, half stoned to bed with the help of Nawfal, and that bitter boy had spat into the master's glass of fizzing Alka-Seltzer. Shocking, too, in its way; but not so shocking as the treachery of Madame Henniger. They had laid Richard on his Glaoua bed and then gone looking for Dally, who was unconscious in a flower bed with a French lad whose eyes were wide open. Terrible, terrible. And Hamid lit his long clay pipe with a burst of repressed indignation. The birds were beginning to sing. From the desert came a smell of iron and rot, a distant tang of decomposing salt. Terrible, to think of Richard and Dally entwined on that bed, snoring, dribbling, thrashing about in their perfidious dreams. His mind raced ahead, then, to his future life, which he was convinced would be far more glorious. A job at the Intercontinental Hotel in Casa, and then, who knew, perhaps a post in the Seychelles or Dubai running an executive floor among decent, respectable people. Such, anyway, are one's dreams. He shrugged and sat on the wall, smoking with great seriousness as the night ended. So it was already Monday morning, and within a few hours the guests would begin to leave. By God, it was not a moment too soon.

Twenty-one

DAVID WOKE AT ABOUT THE SAME TIME. The walls were faintly visible because the lamp still burned, and it was a surprise that they were not white, but a pale red with scratched words and numerals cut into them. Everything in the room was coated with dust, including his fingernails. Next to the mattress he now noticed a glass jar with a biro standing inside it and a small toy, a Dalek from the *Doctor Who* television series. There was a pile of underclothes roughly folded and a notebook. Driss's things; the few things a teenage boy needed in his room. He was sure they were rubbing his nose in this, making him feel the presence of the dead boy. It was their idea of torture. Because they were sure that he believed in ghosts.

He sat up and his mouth craved not water, but a stiff Scotch. He was astonished that he had come so far without a drink, not a single drop in so many hours. It was still dark, but he realised that he must have slept, because he felt refreshed as he opened the bolt of the door and slipped out silently into the corridor, making his way to the back door next to the kitchen, where a muzzled and suffering dog lay asleep. His muscles had recovered their snap.

The animal opened its eyes but did nothing as he stepped over it and into the cool moonlight that breathed life into a small vegetable garden. Since the wind had died down, its various leaves stood upright with a kind of tender defiance and the half-dead palms shifted uneasily as if being disturbed by gravity. He felt like a schoolboy on a lark, stepping round the gardens and into the wide-open stony space in front of the houses. The moon was low now, and its radiance so weak that the outline of the cliff was indistinct, the numerous cave openings and ladders merged together in a great scar. The horror of that vertical surface where the children slaved was dimmed also. One forgot that only the children were small enough to wriggle into the caves with their hammers. Yet he was still appalled at the thought, because Driss had been one of those children and his labours had ended up in a grave behind the gardens.

He fumbled his way to the edge of the *oued* and then picked his way along it as far as the place where it converged with a larger dried river bed. It was a great confusion of piled-up white stones, and beyond it the open desert began abruptly. The flat earth shone with a dull silver dust. Carpets of blistered stones stretched away from him, a petrified sea. Long sulphur-yellow ridges with black crests would be visible by dawn.

I could run was his first thought. I could run all the way to the nearest road. Then I could walk until I ran into a car. I could beg a ride.

He looked desperately across the half-visible plain and there was a part of him that was prepared to jump, to make a dash for it. Run, a voice inside him urged. But that was always his instinct, to run, and famously one tires of running. Just then, he saw something flicker against the scabby wall of the cliff. It was a campfire. Next to it sat a man he didn't recognise, a middle-aged digger in a dark-brown *burnouse* who was sharpening some of his tools with a whetstone. The *chip-chip* sound of this operation produced a tiny metallic echo that came across the open space with a comforting human regularity. David walked over to him.

'*Salaam aleikum*,' he tried, raising his hand.

The man didn't bother looking up.

'It's no use running,' he said in Tamazight.

David didn't understand and therefore didn't reply.

'I saw you looking,' the man went on. 'You looked like a thirsty man gazing at water.'

David shook his head: 'Sorry, can't understand.'

'Are you awake now? You know very well I am here to stop you wandering off. No idea what I am talking about? Very well, it doesn't matter.' And he added an Arab insult: '*wlad lekhab.*'

The man stopped sharpening the axe he was working on and put it down. David shook his head and began to retreat. The man laughed.

'Come, I will show you something weird. Did you know there is a lake just over there? A lake with flamingos.'

He got up and beckoned David to follow. The wind suddenly rose and wailed around them as they struggled across the *oueds* and plunged into the darkness. David turned longingly to reassure himself that the fire was still there, and then followed the willowy digger as he trudged across a sheet of flat blue-tinted stones. After a few hundred yards, the man knelt down and pointed to a sloping shelf of rock that was inclined at a gentle angle within pockets of hardened sand. They would not have seen it if the first light had not suddenly broadened behind the edge of Issomour. The surface of the slab was covered with writhing forms as subtle as stencils, and among them was a huge fish with a beaked mouth and fins that could have been claws. An ichthyosaur, a Devonian mermaid. The man smoothed his hands over it and gave David a slick grin, switching to French.

'We call them the flamingos. I can hack it out for you.'

'I don't want you to hack it out.'

The man's stick traced the outline of the fish. We're at the bottom of a sea, David thought, reaching up to his own throat with his right hand and caressing it.

The man's voice rasped. 'Where are you from? London?'

'I can't buy a fish,' David said in his tumbledown French.

'We can make it into a kitchen table. Think how pleased your wife will be!'

Already, the waltz between them was becoming threatening, but also liturgical. The man circled him tutting, while his stick tapped scales and tailbones of the monster fossil that could never make a kitchen countertop and his eyes sought out the truth behind the unbeliever's facade. David, for his part, felt his resistance weakening, his knees giving out, and eventually he willingly crouched and let the man stomp around him crying, 'It's a steal, a robbery, and you can't even see it!' and as he did so, he covered his eyes with his hands, then reached out and ran his hand along the spine as if appreciating what was magnificent about it, which was its completeness, its manifest evidence that life had existed long before them.

Abdellah's jeep, meanwhile, moved at the edge of the *oued* for a few moments before its headlights came on. The sound of the engine suddenly pierced the silence and echoed along the bottom of the cliff. Looking up then, David saw a small child's form swinging up one of the knotted ropes.

'Ah, they're looking for you!' the man crowed.

He stood up and waved.

As the jeep roared up to the slabs of fossilised sea creatures, David made out the enraged face of Abdellah behind the windscreen and the softer countenance of Anouar. The father descended, slammed his door shut and strode over to the two men who had been nailed by the headlights. The digger was deferential, and they exchanged four or five curt phrases, but Abdellah was concentrating on David.

'So I see you have come for a walk. Of course, you saw that there is nowhere to run, nowhere to hide.'

'I wasn't trying to hide,' David replied coldly.

With a quick, silent dart, the digger vanished.

'It doesn't matter,' the other said. His voice was terse, impatient, and his body seemed to be on the verge of uncontrollable violence.

'You said I could walk about,' David protested.

He realised that he sounded as if he was pleading for his life.

'I did,' the older man admitted. Then he grinned nastily. 'Were you trying to beat the dawn?'

Abdellah barked at Anouar to turn off the headlights. Darkness returned and suddenly they were alone together in the wind, straining to hold themselves upright as grit blew into their faces and the straw-gold break in the night sky had widened to become a gash of dirty sunlight.

Abdellah reached into his long, straggling overcoat and took out the SOG knife that he had used to peel the apples the previous evening. Its fearsome blade thus came between them, and it shone more than their skin, so that all David knew for certain was where the knife was. He took a step, and from the corner of his eyes he took note of the undulations of the earth around him and the vastness into which he could escape. Abdellah did not advance accordingly, however; he stood where he was. He was himself undecided as to what to do and his consciousness was not lit up by any dominating idea except that of pain. He lurched forward for a moment, then stopped again, gripping the knife so hard that it began to shake. Then, letting himself retreat mentally from a terrible idea, he raised the blade so that it pointed towards the distant town of Alnif.

'Anouar is going to take you back now. Your bags are loaded in the jeep.'

It was Anouar walking forward, his face open with fear and loathing and some incoherent compassion that could not break into the open as it wished.

'David,' he called, 'don't be afraid. You can get in the car now.'

'You had better,' Abdellah thought, and lowered the blade to his side. He, too, stepped back a little, and some force inside him passed from his body and seeped into the open, where it was bound to disappear. So it was, for him.

He turned and walked back to the jeep, without climbing into it. He walked on towards the *oued*, with the sky breaking into gold and grey above his head. A dog from the village ran out to greet him, and soon there came the sound of chipping hammers from high up on the cliffs, a gibberish sound like that of thousands of birds converging upon a corpse. A cock crowed from Tafal'aalt. The old man walked on without slipping off the hood of his *burnouse*. His eyes were held down to control the emotion welling up in his mind, and he was — in some secret place of himself — glad of his ability to control what was darkest in his personality.

He went back to the house and prepared a pipe and a pot of tea for himself. From the cliff face came the tinkling sounds of the children tapping away at the stone, and it could only remind him of the little Driss of fifteen years ago, strapped to a long rope and dangling from a ledge so high up that they felt a small fear for his safety. He smoked quietly and let those memories spin through him, the fragments of remembrance of his only son, to which he must now cling with a dogged single-mindedness.

After his pipe and a boiled egg, he went into the boy's room and lingered among its effects, sure that there remained there a subtle, far-off smell of the living being who had once inhabited it. He remembered Driss locking himself in here with his immoral secrets when he had returned from France, never telling his family where he had been or what he had done in Paris. He had lain there smoking his *kif*, going out only at night. He had gone back to Hmor to look for a job at the quarries, to recuperate his old job in effect, but who knew if he had been successful? He had come back much changed, much — he said it to the women — worsened. A bite in his voice, a new arrogance and intransigence. He had always been difficult, but now he had been aloof as well, keeping his meagre earnings to himself, refusing to answer their questions about what he might have earned in Europe. He had gone with such braggadocio and false *élan*. I will come back, he had seemed to say, better than any of you. Richer, more knowing, more resourceful. So Abdellah had let him go without a word and the boy had come back a word miser. It had been strange and unwelcome, because no son of his should ever have been a bitter recluse.

Finally he closed the door behind him and walked slowly back to the main room, where he lay down for some time listening to the wind. Driss. He was right there in the dying cemetery and his soul was somewhere nearby with all its memories. Driss with the long hands and the small scar on the left one, Driss of the wandering eyes and the unscrupulous habit of slipping banknotes into his socks. When he was a boy, there was something green in his eyes that gradually disappeared. Who had ever known him? He used to listen to that music called *raï*, hours alone in his room with the plugs in his ears, and when he was away in Erfoud or Rissani, they would hear of the dishonour he had brought upon them. He sold drugs and illegal trilobites, apparently, but then it was no more or less than what the other boys sold; he was no worse than the others, he was just more indiscreet. He just couldn't hold his tongue.

During the following night, Abdellah regretted that he had not killed David. It was not that he was convinced of David's guilt. It was that whatever the unbeliever had done or not done, he could not forgive him for the death of Driss. He regretted he had been weak in that moment at first light when he had held the knife and the unbeliever had seen it. All power was in my hands, he thought, and I did not use it. So Driss, his life and his death, had gone entirely to waste because no punishment had been exacted. He went to the grave after midnight and sat there thinking about his weakness, which previously had seemed to him like a strength. But what he had wanted to avenge truly was the fact that he simply had never known his son at all. The unknowability of Driss had therefore been made eternal by a mistake on the road, a miscalculated angle or distance. *Bismellah.* Deep in his grave, his son remembered his past, but no one else was admitted to it, and the riddles from now on would recede and grow more complicated, since life is but a sport and a pastime, as the Koran carefully reminds us, and because it is a game and nothing more, one forgets that the point of life is death.

The Forgiven

The Forgiven

Twenty-two

WHEN JO WOKE IN DAY'S ARMS, SHE FELT
A moment's suffocation and then caught her breath,
bringing her panic under control. Where was she? The
windows were open and the AC was silent, and so the room
was as hot as an oven, her skin prickly and wet. A sensation of drowning just before her eyes opened, then the
awareness of night as it slid into day. She unpicked herself
from the alien male arms and went to the bathroom to
wash her face. The mirror was covered with fingerprints.

She had never been unfaithful to David in all those
years and, for that matter, the thought had never even
crossed her mind. Even when they had slept apart for the
last two years, it had not occurred to her to venture out
into the sea of other men, for what would she do there
but wave and drown? Look at yourself in the mirror:
haggard, exhausted, sweating. Can one ever recover
instantly from such a mistake? It was the potency of the
secret one would from now on have to carry round with
one that hurt the future and made it less liveable. Even
if she couldn't remember the lovemaking with Day (what
an inappropriate phrase!), it would still exist inside her
as a weight she would have to carry round, a semi-memory

but still a form of knowledge. Had she enjoyed it? She didn't know.

The sound of the taps didn't wake him. She crept back to the bed and gazed down at him with a dry amazement. Had she really made love with this snoring animal of pretty dimensions? What had made her do it? A string of moments of madness, a bottle of fermented grape juice, a clever man and a subtle, aggravating rage against the husband who was not there, and who in many ways was never there. It was hardly a real argument for betrayal, but she hadn't needed to be persuaded anyway.

Her first thought was escape. The door was wide open, and there were pieces of clothing everywhere, including her sandals and her hair clips, and from the soft open night came the enticing sounds of parties gone haywire and people walking about on tiptoe. These were all things she had wanted to drown herself in when they'd set out sulkily from London two days earlier, in those days of innocence: an all-night party with elegant touches, and nights filled with mysterious humanities. She went out and took a big gulp of that soupy air, then steadied herself against the door jamb. The dawn was not even faintly there yet, and it was strange, because she was sure she had glimpsed it before falling asleep.

Between the sexually fetid darkness of the room and the open night, what a difference. The latter fresh, innocent and plump like a girl who has just washed her hair, the former already stale and suffocating. Cicadas in the earth walls, water flowing down the runnels that fed into the pools. A promise of something. Whereas in the room there was just the remains of something already completed and for ever done and the man asleep in his cups. She stepped out and left it behind.

As she went down the path of embedded shells — they made little pictures she hadn't noticed before, images of fish and tomatoes and gibbous moons — she found alien words flowing back into her mind, to the effect that even the most frozen, deadened heart has two or three drops of love at its bottom, enough to feed the birds. It was an American who had said it long ago, but she couldn't remember who. She walked swiftly away from the room where Day slept and soon she was drifting back among the guests, and it was still surprising how few of them she knew or had met. Had a new crop arrived earlier that evening? They were even younger, louder, and they ignored her as she slipped between them with her middle-aged ease. On one of the wide artificial lawns some kind of *raï*-inspired hip-hop was playing, MC Rai, though she would not have known it, and the kids were rocking to it with pinwheel fireworks turning on three sides, smoothly replaced and relit by the staff when they burned out, the bars sprinkled around under the trees lit from underneath so that the immense glass pitchers looked brilliant, packed with floating ice cubes and pieces of fruit. There were bowls of sugared yogurt that were kept chilled and silver racks of hard-boiled eggs, and the staff held long spoons with which to mix drinks in the tall glasses and scissors to cut up the bunches of fresh mint. A brisk trade in mojitos, in caipirinhas and gin and tonics and 'moroccojitos'. The boys dancing in borrowed slippers, high on *majoun*, and wet from head to foot.

She went past the spinning fireworks, which made the staff laugh and elbow one another, and into the stone courts that surrounded the main pool, around which the braziers were going strong in gusts of sparks that blew across the flagstones and died out. She felt them breeze past her, then sting her arms momentarily. Fifty people at least stood and swam in the pool, their arms raised above their heads. On the court's far side, the long tent with its cushions and pipes was crowded with people lying on their side, indifferent to the time of night, or early morning, as it now was. She wondered what to do, locked inside that deafening music. Unthinking, she dropped fully clothed into the pool and sank under the surface, letting her hair drift upwards and stretching out her arms as wide as she could.

As she floated there suspended among the forest of dark limbs, her hair static and fanned out in the water, she suddenly felt like a child again. She let out a big fat bubble and began to choke with an enormous happiness. She saw herself running along the bank of the River Ouse near Piddinghoe with her father, catching moths with a net, with a suet pudding in a cheesecloth that her mother had given her. Moths, or mussels – she couldn't remember. Her dead father was now alive, turning back to catch her eye. They recognised each other and he said, 'You have a little stream inside you, always alive, always running, my wee Muff.' The dead are always inside us, she thought. They are what make us alive, though one only sees them underwater.

Then she resurfaced, slightly dissolved and cleaned, and found herself among bobbing heads moving to the beat of 'Raivolution'. She hauled herself out and went to lie in the tent. A boy came to offer her some ice cream from a tray, and then a joint. She didn't hesitate. She accepted. Above the walls, meanwhile, the first glimmer of dawn had appeared, a blush against the jagged outline of the mountain. She smoked thoughtfully and waited for something to happen, and when it didn't, she felt herself fragment again and she wondered if she was going mad or if that same mountain really was higher and sharper than it had been. The serrations rose into thin spire-lights like those of a cathedral. She thought back to their first hours in the country on Friday, and it seemed incredible that she could look back on that former self as naïve and inexperienced. In forty-eight hours she had been completely destroyed from top to bottom, but at the same time liberated and rebuilt. If David had remained at her side, nothing would have happened at all; if they had not killed that boy, nothing would have happened either. Nothing would have happened and she would have remained the same, lumbering forward in time towards her predestined discontents. It was, she thought, Driss who had liberated her finally. It wasn't even ironic or paradoxical or anything like that. It was too tremendous for such concepts. Were it not for Driss, she thought bitterly, she would not have slept with Day. There was a grim logic to it, and she had gone along with it. Driss, Day, David, her Three Ds.

It was Richard who, picking his way through his own party and spotting her from afar, came to rejoin her to his grand weekend. He was looking relaxed and intensely appealing, as gay men sometimes do when they allow their considerable flair to engage the female eye without hesitation, and he knew how to put her at ease and cajole her into satisfying his curiosity, which in any case was never overbearing.

'Here you are at last,' he said, sitting himself down next to her and then adding, 'It'll be dawn in an hour and you're going to enjoy it. It's going to be one of those days.'

She doesn't look depressed, he thought.

'I can't wait,' she said.

'Nor can I. And our David will be back before lunch.'

'I wasn't afraid he wouldn't be.'

'I suppose,' he said, lowering his eyes, 'you are probably sorry you ever came here. Maybe you'll consider coming back at a later time, when all this has blown over.'

'I would consider. David. I don't know.'

'You could come alone.'

She nodded. 'Yes.'

From now on, in fact, alone might be better. Aloneness had suddenly appeared as a wide-open possibility for the future.

'It might be better like that,' he went on. 'If I may say — I know it's impertinent — you didn't seem very happy. I mean, in general. You didn't seem like you.'

'It's been rather a difficult time all round. Part of it is me. I haven't been working. Things haven't been going well at home — I can't concentrate; I can't get it rolling. You know how that is sometimes?'

He took her hand and said, 'Oh, Jo, what cases we are!'

'You have those periods, too, then?'

He said it was sometimes better just to stay depressed the whole time. Dally had told him about a recent study of shrimps exposed to Prozac. The beasts, it was found, swam in more brightly lit waters than normal shrimps and there they were easy prey for larger fish.

'Am I one of those shrimps?' she laughed.

'We all are.'

'I feel like one now, I must admit.'

'But you disappeared — what happened to you?'

'I got waylaid by a pirate.'

'I see.'

His look was knowing, but non-committal.

'Such things have been known to happen.'

'Not to me.'

She had blurted it out, and regretted it. Too late. He gave her a small chocolate from the tripod table in front of them and watched her dutifully peel away the foil.

'It can happen to anyone. Circumstances conspired.'

'They certainly did, Dicky.'

'I am kind of glad in a way. I don't mean about the boy. I mean about you. It knocked David off his perch. That was a good thing, wasn't it?'

She sank her teeth into the truffle and felt it melt over her tongue. Sometimes a humble champagne truffle can open all the bolted doors inside you and you can lick it off your fingers gratefully.

'In the grand scheme of things,' she said, 'it doesn't matter if he was one way or another. I wasn't thinking about him. For once I was thinking about myself. I dare say I won't be the same again – in a hundred tiny, vicious ways. That's fate if ever I saw it. But just now I jumped in the pool, and I have to say, Dicky, I never felt more alive than when I was under that water. I don't even know why. I felt I had walked through the Looking Glass.'

'Then maybe you did.'

'Yes, in a funny way, I think I did.'

'What's on the other side?'

Nightmares, she thought.

'I don't know yet,' she murmured. 'All kinds of odd things. A different future anyway.'

'You didn't know what the previous future was.'

That was both true and untrue.

'I could guess,' she ventured. 'I just didn't like it much. I was glad it evaporated, anyway.'

'There you are, then.'

He had a brilliant smile for her, and his hand pressed upon her with a slow, deep sympathy and an assurance that he would never judge her. It made her eyes fill with tears that they nevertheless contained. The anguish brimmed up but stayed within her eyes, held in suspension by her iron will. No time for crying, this. She had lost nothing but her own self-deceit.

'The only future worth entertaining,' Richard said, emphasising that odd last word, 'is the one we can't imagine at all. The one we'll never have except partially.'

'I would be grateful for anything that wasn't like the past. I'd get on a plane anywhere. I would.'

'Are you going to divorce him?'

'I can't do it quite yet. But I have to, don't I?'

'That I can't say, sweet. Divorces aren't my area of expertise. It's usually best to wait a while.'

'Yes, but I found out this weekend that I could and I must.'

'I see.'

'You see, the bottom fell out somewhere along the line these last two days. I can't remember the exact moment, but it fell out and I saw it fall out. And I thought, okay, now I know it for a solid fact.'

'Was it David's breakdown?'

'He didn't have a breakdown. It was his true self that was allowed to come out. I thought he was actually relieved to be his true self for a change. He had an excuse to be his true self and he seized it. He was secretly thrilled.'

'So it's even worse.'

'Yes, it's even worse. The man I loved revealed as a cheap stranger.'

'Well,' Richard tried, thinking that he might as well represent David honourably for a change, 'put yourself in his shoes. It cannot have been easy.'

'It's not his fault,' she snapped. 'Like I said, I'm talking about me. I'm the one who's had the breakdown.'

It's been years coming, he thought.

'You need to calm down, I think. It sounds like you've been up all night and are tired out. Maybe you should sleep now, before David gets back.'

'It's the last thing I want to do. I can't sleep now. I've never felt more awake. I'm so awake I'm dangerous.'

'All right. Let's dance, then.'

'Wait a moment. Before I do anything — I know it sounds silly — I need you to take my pulse.'

'What?'

'Please, just take it. I was sure it was irregular a little while back. I want you to just take it right now and tell me.'

He protested at how ridiculous this was, but he did it anyway, and strangely enough it was indeed a little erratic. He said it was perfectly normal.

'We're both drinkers,' she said morosely. 'That's the problem. Of course, I wouldn't dare put myself on the same level of boozerdom as David, but we're both in it together. It was the drink that made him drive so badly, and I'm only telling you because I know you'd never tell the police, and you'd say — and you will say — that it makes no difference now, and I agree, it doesn't. But I'm telling you anyway. I have to get that off my chest. It was one hundred per cent our fault. The kid did nothing wrong except step in the road and try to make us slow down, and David — David is so terrified of them — and he was so boozed up . . .'

'As you say, it no longer matters much. I knew all that anyway. It was quite obvious.'

'We're rather an obvious couple, aren't we?'

'Aren't all couples obvious in the end? Look at me and Dally. No one would ever accuse us of not being obvious.

279

In a way, I think one should strive to be obvious. It's the sign that you've finally made it as a couple.'

'I don't agree. But I see what you mean.'

She looked crestfallen for a moment.

'All I ever wanted,' she resumed, 'was for us to be unobvious even to ourselves. What an insane ambition!'

'It's everyone's ambition.'

'And then we grow old and wear our trousers rolled?'

'Yes, more or less.' He chuckled. 'Who cares about ambitions anyway? What do they ever come to? At fifty, I've noticed, everyone is in about the same state of protracted despair.'

It's not despair, she wanted to say angrily.

'The funny thing about tonight,' she went on, 'is that for the first time in years, I felt young again. I don't know what it is. I committed adultery with a ridiculous man, as women always do. I woke up feeling like a god. I went for a swim and underwater I had a revelation. Well, revelation is a strong word. I had a *flash*.'

'How do you mean, young?'

She shrugged, because she felt that it didn't really need to be explained. The word itself was so potent, so tyrannical, that it never needed to be explained or emphasised.

'I felt I was alive again,' she said bluntly. 'Like coming out of the Ice Age. I felt the past coming back and giving me life.'

So there's no going back, he wanted to say then, but if he did say it, he was afraid the thought would be so conscious in her mind that she would impulsively act on it.

'In that case, run with it,' he said kindly. 'It won't last for ever. If you have that feeling for one night, then live that night to the full and hope for the best.'

'Yes. I just don't feel guilty any more. I don't need to be forgiven by anyone.'

'I've been saying that all along, haven't I?'

'You have, but it's such a huge thing to believe, isn't it? That one doesn't need to be forgiven by anyone.'

He was not sure what she meant, so he let it go. But soon their minds had wandered in different directions anyway, and she took his hand as a final gesture of solidarity and kissed it. There, there, he thought. He wondered what the rest of her tortured day was going to be like, the husband returned from his farce in the desert, the departure on the same road that had brought them such misfortune. It was not going to be a day she would relish. And yet it was beginning magically, with desert birds and the cruel line of the mountains as fresh as something being torn in front of their eyes and the stars fading out unnoticed. Things might yet resolve in ways unexpected.

'I'm going to dance for a bit,' she said. 'While it's still dark. I don't want it to be dawn yet.'

'I'll come with you.'

'Can't we clear our heads with something? Some lemonade?'

'Nothing simpler. I'll see to it.'

They walked slowly up to the walls for some fresh air, and Hamid brought up the lemonade, the glasses, the ice. She drank it all voraciously and the two men watched her, bemused. On the slopes below them, small goats stood in the dark, their ears pricked, and the egrets stirred. The anticipation of first light and the endurance necessary for it. She sucked on the ice cubes and wet her hands with them and ran one through her hair, letting the ends drip. The nerves all along her limbs vibrated quietly, set into life by the cooler air blowing up from the plain, and the cold water slid between her breasts. She wondered if there was a condemnation in Hamid's eye, but none seemed to be there. She thanked him for the lemonade and avoided that same eye, climbing back down with Richard and leaving the haughty servant watching them from above. They went to the dance floor in the main courtyard, and she fell into his arms and they danced for a while until she became too hot, and then she took off her shirt and went topless like the others until the moon went down into the side of the mountain and the sky began to lighten. She didn't care whether it did or not. She was no longer waiting for David to return, and by the same token she was no longer not waiting. She lost herself in her own movement, and it was a long time before the music was cut and breakfast was served under starched cotton shades, with no sense that anything had ended.

Twenty-three

'BETWEEN YOU AND ME,' ANOUAR SAID TO David on their way to Alnif, 'I am emigrating to France next year. I have a cousin who owns a restaurant in Rennes. It will be hard, but at least it is not Tafal'aalt. I have talked it over with my father and he cannot prevent me. It's life or death. Well, almost.'

There was a long pause, and the shadow of Issomour crossed their path with its deep-blue menace.

'I am sorry about Abdellah,' David said at length, but dourly, as if he had saved up these words for hours and only now could utter them. He tried to mean them as earnestly as he could, and to not let his obvious relief taint them. Anouar nodded hastily.

'We could tell that you were sorry. It is why he let you go.'

'Oh?'

'He judged you to be sincere.'

David shuddered and said nothing until they were back at the lopsided square of Alnif, with the birds nesting in the old *bab* and a bitter wind scouring the dirt streets. They drank a *café noir* at the hotel. Anouar leaned close to him for a moment.

'Abdellah instructed me to drive you straight back to

Azna, no stops. And I will do it. If you wanted to stop to buy some fossils, however, we could spend an hour in Rissani. I know a good man . . .'

David shook his head wearily. 'No, thanks. Just get me back to my wife.'

A moment later, he added: 'Do you think Abdellah found it in him to forgive me?'

'I am sure of it. He *must* have forgiven you. Otherwise you and I would not be drinking a *café noir* in Alnif!'

There was a grim certitude in his voice.

'I see,' David murmured.

'He is not a vindictive man,' Anouar went on in a slightly injured tone. 'He has been thrown into a great crisis. Driss was his livelihood, his principal digger. What is he going to do now?'

'I cannot say,' David admitted. In truth, this dimension of Abdellah's misfortune had not occurred to him.

David thought about the great lump of cash he had stuffed into his travelling bags, now unused, unwanted, irrelevant. It was shameful now, in fact. And yet everyone knew he had brought it with him.

They drove past Rissani. Wild camels nibbled the drinn by the road, the shoots of grass flattened by wind against the black gravel. In hovels clustered against the road fossil preppers came out waving fake Psychopyges and Comuras embellished with car-repair resin. 'Fraudsters!' Anouar laughed, turning his hand in the air like a screw. 'The shame of the nation!'

He pressed down on the accelerator and the battered Toyota jeep sang like an old harp. They drove through Erfoud without even stopping for a glass of water, and on the outskirts of Errachidia the mobile phone finally picked up a signal. He talked breathlessly.

'It's me, David. You must still be asleep. Everything's fine. I am being driven back by one of the men from Tafal'aalt and we're just outside Errachidia. I have no idea what time it is. We'll be there in a few hours, I suppose. Just in time for brunch. God, what an ordeal. I hope you weren't too worried. Anyway, it's over. I'm getting chauffeur service all the way home. I'll have a word with Richard about this when I get there. He knew all along, and I must say I'll have a hard time to forgive him.'

He was not sure if this was true, however. He would forgive anyone and anything in exchange for a hot bath and a gin and tonic. Moreover, he also felt that he had now earned these little fussy pleasures, and his forgiving Richard his deft deception was a small matter when compared to the forgiveness he himself had earned in the house of Abdellah. Such things did not come easily. He was even sure that his ordeal had made him stronger in ways that the others would not readily understand. It had made him even coarser as well, but he didn't mind. At the same time, the bitterness of the thoughts that whirled through him surprised even him; they were like crumbs scattered from a meal that has gone bad, but at least he had eaten them and got sick and pulled through, which was more than could be said for those idiots dancing the night away in Richard's *ksour*. What did he have in common with those pot-smoking retards anyway? At least, through his accident, which had not been his fault at all (was it wrong to protect one's wife from roadside depravities?), he had seen the Berbers as they really were, which was more than any of them had seen. He had, in a sense, switched allegiances. For all his brutishness, Abdellah had impressed him. To live in a place like that and survive was magnificent in its way, and the greed David had feared from them had not in the end materialised. They were not, he decided, driven by money in the same way that materialistic Westerners liked to think. And then, yet again, he thought about the bag of money. It would be unacceptable to return with it, because Richard in particular, and Jo, too, would spitefully assume that he had stubbornly refused to hand it over on principle. They would get it wrong, but how would he defend himself from the charge?

He began to think that he would give it to Anouar. He knew very little about the man, but if he was thinking of emigrating to France because he had no other way to make a decent living, he could surely use two thousand euros. Two thousand was a huge sum for a man from the desert. It would take him all the way to Paris and maybe even enable him to live there for a few weeks. It would not be an insignificant gift. For once, a gesture of his would mean something. It would change someone's life.

They rolled into a dusty, run-down *bled* straddling the road, and Anouar went into a small shop to fill the water container. A few palms waved in the wind over a rectangle of houses. David got out as well and walked along the edge of a straggling garden where a few children sat with mud pies and frazzled toys. They did not look up. He had taken the bag with him, and he must have cut a slightly ridiculous, and even suspicious, figure. Nevertheless, they ignored him as he passed, lost in their own thoughts. Above them the sun had risen rapidly and bore down brutally on the plots of partially whitewashed date trees and rickety fences, forcing him to raise a hand to keep his vision intact. He came to the edge of the gardens and a line of walnut trees, and as he stood there slightly stunned by the morning brightness, Anouar came up behind him with a miraculous thing, a heated croissant.

'Where did you get that?' David laughed, and as he took it from Anouar's hand, he swung the bag in his direction and added, 'Here, this is for you.'

'For me?'

'Yes, absolutely for you.'

Anouar took the bag with genuine surprise.

'What's in it?'

Does he really not know? David thought.

'Never mind. I'm going to ask you something. Don't look inside it until you are back in this same village on your way home. Can you promise that?'

'By God, I can.'

'Very well, then. We'll leave it at that, shall we?'

Anouar nodded awkwardly, looked down at the bag and scowled. It felt, to him, like something of an impo-sition.

'It is my pleasure,' David said, 'to give that bag to you. It's a very nice bag I bought at Timberland in London. Very strong.'

'Ah, then thank you.'

'You're most welcome. You're a decent man, Anouar.'

'Decent?'

'Yes, decent. It's the least I can say.'

'And you, Monsieur David, are very tolerant.'

Twenty-four

AT THE BEND IN THE ROAD, JO WAITED IN
a belted pink dress and a large straw sun hat that Richard
had given her, the brim so wide that it kept her entire
face in shade and its ribbons reaching down to the middle
of her back. There were mustard flowers inserted into
the band. 'A bit too Renoir,' he had said, plopping it onto
her head, 'but no one here knows who Renoir was or is,
so you're safe.' It was his hat and she liked wearing it
for that reason. Richard knew what was best for her.

She sat on the wall listening to the waterwheels in the
forgetful sunshine, baking and content. To make the little
lizards scatter she kicked her sandals against the pale-
green cushionlike prickly pears. It was perfectly silent.
The air smelled of cedars. The mountains shone, paradoxically, like ice, a brown, sullied ice that shines all the
same. When the wind picked up the tassels of her dress
and the hat's ribbon, she felt herself fluttering all in one
piece, with the oils of lemons brushing her tongue and
a whiff of thyme. She hadn't called David back until
midday, and they had had a breathless conversation in
order to get all the prosaic questions out of the way first.

'I went to bed early,' she said, 'and read some of Dicky's

old copies of *Punch*. It made me sad reading them. Made me think of Granddad.'

'Never mind,' he had said banally. 'At least you weren't awake.'

'No,' she said.

David's voice was strained, as if it was coming through glass, and it struck her as slightly unearthly, the voice of a man who has been fasting all night, or else drinking. It was no longer quite David's chirpily angry, wounding voice, and its normally deep reserves of spite had dried up. It was a wounded voice, deliciously rehumanised. She was astonished.

She heard the car from a great distance. But instead of standing in the road expectantly, she sat as she was. She had a tray that Hamid had brought down for her with an ice bucket and a half bottle of white wine with two glasses. She thought it would make a healing gesture. He wouldn't expect it and that would be to the good.

The car neared her, and suddenly, out of the blue, she grew nervous. Had he given all that money to the family? But worse than that, it was also possible that they had done something to him that he had been unwilling to divulge on the phone. She stood up and strained to catch sight of the jeep. Its sound had become subdued, and soon she realised that it had stopped by the track, its engine idling. Standing on the wall, she could see it.

David was talking to a man next to it. They were talking quietly, in a civilised manner, as if they had things to impart to each other before they parted. A second later the car was veering round the bend. It stopped by her and Anouar rolled down the window, and he thought that she ought to recognise him, which she did not.

'Taxi?' he joked.

'Going up the hill?'

He gave her an affirmative thumb.

David got out painfully and was in her arms as Anouar waited patiently, eyeing with apprehension the tray with the ice bucket and bottle. 'You didn't!' David whooped, looking over at the ice bucket as well, but forcing himself, she thought, into an exaggerated enthusiasm.

'Let's have a drink before we go into that infernal place.'

'You're a sweetheart,' he sighed. 'I'm parched, too. We've been driving since dawn.'

They kissed again in the bright sun. Her face crushed into his dirty shirt and it smelled of goat-kid grease and mint. Anouar watched them with a dumbfounded smile. He quietly asked David if he would like to be driven up to the gates.

'No, it's okay, Anouar. We're going to walk up there ourselves. We need to talk.'

'Very well. Then I should be going.'

Anouar got out for a moment and they shook hands heartily. They had grown to like each other, but in the distant, impermanent way that an unusual circumstance necessarily imposes. They wished each other luck; Anouar thanked him for the Timberland bag, but not in front of Jo. A few words, a few confusions, then he drove off. The dust from the car hung above the road a few moments, then dissolved. Jo and David drank the wine, enjoying the fussing wasps around them, then left the glasses on the wall and walked slowly up to the house in the fragrant heat.

* * *

'What did they want with you, then?'

'The father wanted to talk with me, that was all. I didn't understand anything. But I understand that.'

'Did they ask you for money?'

'Not a penny.'

'Then where are the two thousand euros?'

'I gave it to them anyway.'

'You did?'

'I did. Do you find that hard to believe?'

'I don't know. Yes, I guess I'm a little surprised.'

'Well, I gave it to them. Not because I was forced to.'

She lowered her head. She didn't know what to say. Did her skin smell of Day? She looked at him piercingly. It was not something they could ever talk about again, but the implication in her tone was clear. She had understood everything he had done. He, too, sensed that while he had been away she had not been on his planet, as it were. And while it could not be mentioned again, it could not be forgotten either. It had altered for ever the relation between them, and they both knew it. 'It's all right, Stumblebum,' she whispered into his chest. 'We can go home now. It's all over.'

'Home,' he echoed.

The early-afternoon sun struck their faces, and their words dried up. The staff ventured out from the welcoming shade of the gate with cold wet towels, and soon the festive atmosphere of Azna was upon them again. It enveloped them with music and agitation and yapping Western voices and the bustle of cars and jeeps being loaded for guests who were about to depart for the airport. The ends of weekends are often a relief.

* * *

Richard was horse riding with Lord Swann near Tafnet as the Hennigers reunited. He had not experienced much anxiety as a result of David's foray, because he knew that the impoverished diggers of the ergs were sufficiently afraid of the Moroccan police not to pull any xenophobic stunts. Besides, the weather had turned milder for some reason, and all his old love of riding had suddenly resurfaced. His nag was called Britney, and he liked murmuring her name into her ear as he patted the long, silky neck coloured like young chestnuts and reminding her that she was named after a mad, declining pop star. Between sunshine and horse smells and the baffling Lord Swann, his anxieties and concerns evaporated nicely and his meticulous mind returned to its usual preoccupation with improvements to the house and the upgrading of its electrical systems. His carefully planned weekend, moreover, having partially unravelled, was now winding down entirely and he was frankly looking forward to getting rid of this uncontrollable mass of guests who were continually plying him with unanswerable questions. He was disgusted with them. They brought all their *idées fixes* with them, dragging them around on leads like the corpses of so many dead poodles. Why did so few people have the gift of travel, of subtle displacement and simple curiosity? Which was, in the end, merely a question of imagination. Try imagining where you are, and not lumbering around with your festering discomforts and dissatisfactions. And yet almost nobody did. Take Lord Swann. He was a perfect parasite, but amusing enough in his way, and he had been round the block. Investments in Hong Kong, and all that. But he never asked anything about the Berbers, who seemed to him to be elements of an immoveable decor and nothing else. A form of statuary. Of course, he affected to be concerned about them, because that is what everyone nowadays was taught to do. But he really detested wasting any breath on them. They were a source of terrorism, of course; that made them interesting during heated debates.

As they plodded through a meadow of garish, parched wild flowers with silver-coated leaves and a colour of wet mustard, Swann was saying, 'I knew Henniger a while back from the club. He used to treat my aunt's carbuncles. I am sure he has since moved on from carbuncles. Never liked him much, though. Shifty.'

'How do you mean?'

'Not really one of us. He played cards with Darcy and always won. I hate a man who always wins.'

'I went to school with him, you know.'

'Really? How traumatic for you. Did he lurk about?'

'He used to put out a little school paper called *England without Darkies*. It was sort of a spoof to make us feel ashamed of our racism.'

'Was he a lefty then?'

'I can't remember. I always thought he was a bit of an idiot myself. I still think he is an idiot. Come to think of it, he *is* an idiot.'

'Many people say that about me, Dicky, and I have always admitted that they are, by and large, correct.'

'There was just something *off* about him,' Richard said, daydreaming. 'I always thought that his father beat him or something. There was that look in his eye, the beaten-dog look.'

'A beaten dog always looks for revenge. Perhaps that's why he always had to win at cards.'

'Perhaps.'

'I was surprised to see him here with that stick-insect wife of his.'

'She's hardly a stick-insect, old man.'

'She's pretty enough, but not my type. No curve on her.'

And Swann implied that Richard was in no position to judge these things. They laughed. Now they were at the top of the little hill where the shepherds passed in summer. They looked down at Azna, suddenly revealed in its entirety as in a military map. The restoration was so lavish that it now appeared, Richard thought proudly, as it might have a century ago in its heyday. It was a personal triumph, a vindication, and it seemed to him that he had never seen anything as beautiful. Since he would never have children, it was the next best thing. It was a genuinely personal creation.

Then, in a darker mood, he thought of his emotions when Abdellah had appeared outside his gates on Saturday morning. Out of nowhere, the desert had asserted itself. It was as if these men could call on you at any moment, knock on your door when they felt like it. They could extort you, terrify you, and at a moment entirely of their choosing. And now, because of David's unforgivable blunder, they knew where he lived.

'Are you off now?' he said carelessly to Swann as they trotted back.

'I'm taking the girl to Tinerhir to the Hôtel du Sud, or whatever it's called. She wants to get a bit of desert. Myself, I'd like to go to Málaga and play the tables.'

'One is always so exhausted after these weekends.'

Swann nodded ruefully. He would never give them himself, unless orgies could be organised. Alas, the age of orgies appeared to have ended.

'Did they bury the Arab boy all right?' he asked Richard brightly as they swung onto the path above the gates, where the palms were not yet diseased.

'I assume so. That's the way they do things here. They brush them under the carpet. No one wants any trouble in the end. I expect our unfortunate Englishman bribed them up to the hilt.'

Swann sneered. 'Quite right, too. Silly bugger. Cars do have brake pedals, you know.'

'That's been my attitude all along.'

'I wonder how much he paid?'

'That's one of those things a gentleman doesn't ask.'

David and Jo lay by the pool all afternoon. Cicadas purred in the walls and David slept, though his nightmares were mild. He imagined he was inside a giant Boeing turbine armed with a toothbrush with which he was cleaning the blades. Sometimes these sorts of nightmares made him laugh in his sleep, and he did this now. 'Shredded,' he said aloud, as the turbines began to turn and the dwarves inside them were mashed up. Jo smiled. In the main courtyard of the *ksour* the expensive cars assembled and departed, the Mercedes convertibles and the Land Rovers with three extra tyres, the Peugeot 605s rented from the Casablanca airport and the Alfa Spiders with Spanish plates.

The staff milled around hauling luggage and complimentary picnic hampers for the road while people snapped their last pictures of the weekend, exchanged email addresses and numbers, and then screamed their excessive goodbyes. It seemed to have nothing to do with them, Jo thought. And, indeed, no one came to the pool to take their leave. The Hennigers were apparently pariahs, though no one among the guests had actually thought about it consciously. No one even thought about them at all. The bad taste left by the accident had to be expunged as soon as possible, and people were now in a hurry to leave, to get back to the European Union.

'We'll see you at Azrou for dinner. The Hotel Panorama?'

'No, the Hotel Amros. We'll order trout.'

Rendezvouses along the roads back to Casa were arranged in this way, and as each car revved its engine by the gate, Richard and Dally stood in the shade passing out small garlands of flowers, sometimes dropping them into the passenger seats of the convertibles with a blown kiss. Come back next year!

To Jo, they were nothing. She lay very quietly, waiting for hummingbirds that never came. Her eyes were fixed on the distant mountains that grew paler as the day wore on. A quiet, hysterical panic simmered inside her. She had not seen Day since the early morning. He had vanished into the crowd, knowing that David was returning. She supposed that he'd wanted to spare her an embarrassing moment. It was considerate of him, but it left all the threads of the previous night hanging loose. His presence was still inside her, like warm and quick stickiness; she realised that she had to be patient. She would have to let it subside away from her with time. But it was not easy. She was grateful that that night they would be driving, not sharing a bed in a hotel. For the rest of her life she would not have the excuse of being coked up to explain her night of aberration. But then, doesn't everyone have a night of aberration somewhere along the line? It was a spurious rationalisation, but it would do. She got up and went for a swim.

After three, the house seemed silent. Most of the weekend's partygoers had now left, anxious not to drive at night. Whereas she and David were anxious to drive at night, and they didn't know why. To leave unnoticed, she supposed, as undetected as thieves.

She breaststroked her away across the dark-blue pool. When she rested, she heard dogs barking in the valley, their echoes reaching far and wide. There was the retort of a hunter's shotgun and one of the cooks calling across the field behind the south wall. A little later, as she dried off, she leaned over David's sleeping face. It was colourless and mask-like, and the chin twitched with the probably insalubrious dreams that so often disturbed him and which she was never curious about. In this sun-drenched corner of paradise, with the heliconia and honeysuckle bursting around them, it was like a window into a subterranean world that she could never enter and which she knew was always starved of beauty. A sleeping face can be as terrifying as a flight of steps leading down from a trapdoor and disappearing like a rope cast into a well. She wondered if years from now during a bitter argument she might ever tell David to his face what had happened. But he had made her lie, and in a way they were quits. She passed her hand over his eyes as if he were dead, closing lids that were already closed.

The desert night swept in, with its taste of distant salt. She sat up on her elbows and her heart was wild with hatred and foreboding. Where now? She saw nothing ahead but confusion, dire liberation. If only she could stop now, in this moment, for a dozen years. She listened to the birds settling into the grassy eaves of the house, a flock of cold mouths gathering in the twilight — dinosaurs with red eyes.

* * *

'I find it odd that you won't stay the night,' Richard said over their early supper on the terrace as they lay on silk cushions and agitated starlings flapped about in the sultry dusk air. Hamid served them a salted lemon *tagine* with cinnamon-sweetened *couscous* dotted with steamed prunes and lines of sugar that melted as they watched. 'It would make far more sense to start out early and get to Azrou by early afternoon and then chill out there. I would have thought, after your experience with driving here at night . . .'

'I see what you're saying' – David interrupted him brusquely – 'but we've thought it through and we are anxious to get back as soon as we can. I'm sure you can appreciate that.'

'Naturally I can. After what you've been through. I just don't want you to get into another accident!'

'Oh, lightning doesn't strike twice,' Jo said nervously, unsure if this was true.

'It's your choice. I am more than happy for you to stay on an extra night and set off in the normal way.'

'I had a sleep all afternoon by the pool,' David countered. 'I feel fit as a fiddle. I think we'll drive through the night and just get back to Tangier in a single leap.'

'That's one way of doing it. We'll give you a better map. Why don't you stay a night or two in Tangier and recover a bit? There are some boutique hotels there now. You don't have to stay at the Angleterre.'

David shook his head. He had refused to say anything about Tafal'aalt and nobody had asked; and now he had no intention of playing it 'normal' and pretending he'd do this and do that just because Richard wanted him to. He wanted to get back to England, that was all. He'd relax when he was in that plane in Málaga airport.

'The whole country feels jinxed now,' he said.

'It's certainly *not* jinxed,' Dally retorted, giving him a cool stare.

'Not for you, maybe. But for me. For Jo and me. Nothing like this has ever happened to us.' His hand was shaking.

'Yes, I see,' Richard muttered. 'I can see why you'd want to get out of here as soon as possible. In any case, your car has already been loaded. There's a picnic hamper in the back seat. The bottle is non-alcoholic cider.'

It was a cruel jab, and Richard almost regretted it as soon as he had uttered it. But, in another sense, he was speaking his mind honestly. Morocco wasn't jinxed; David was just an incorrigible boozer.

'Anyway,' Jo said in conciliatory spirit, 'it has all ended peacefully at least. Not for that boy, I know. But for everyone else. It could have been a lot worse.'

Very much so, Richard thought tersely.

'Did they have interesting carpets out there?' Dally suddenly asked, changing the subject. 'I've never seen anything from that far out.'

'I didn't really notice.'

What a couple of snobbish queens, David thought savagely. How the fuck do I know what the carpets were like?

'I don't feel there's a jinx,' Jo said quietly. 'It's just a mistake. Traffic accidents happen all the time.'

'It's undeniable.'

Richard looked at her thoughtfully, and caught the subtle tobacco tints in her sad eyes. If only she hadn't married David. If only. The man carried around a cosmic gloom with him.

'By the way . . .' She looked up quickly. 'Did you see Day before he left?'

Richard and Dally looked at each other as if this possibility had only just occurred to them.

'Why, no,' Dally whistled. 'He got off without us seeing him. How did he do that, Dick?'

'He's a slippery guy. I dunno. I see him once a year and I never know who he is, really.'

'Who is Day?' David asked irritably.

'An American who comes to our parties.'

Richard and Dally smiled for and at each other, and in the moment of their complicity, Jo's intention to ask another question faded away. She let it go. There were other things to deal with now. David's feral alertness was on the prowl again; he had recovered the dangerous spring in his step and it was an open question what he would do with it. He felt humiliated and he wanted revenge, but there was none to be had. He glanced venomously at Hamid, who stood by the railing with the sky forming a darkening backdrop behind him. That inscrutable individual was aloof as always, but Jo imagined that she caught his eye once or twice and that a flash of sympathy greeted her. Yes, everyone was sympathetic to her, but no one could do anything for her. Hamid saw that, and she knew that he saw it. And he saw, too, David's trembling hand, which betrayed that characteristic addiction of the infidel. They were miserable wretches and he understood it. All they had over him was money. She looked away from him. A slight wind kicked up and his *djellaba* flapped. He stepped forward a pace.

'Tea before you leave, Monsieur and Madame?'

She shuddered and gave no reply. David shook his head, and their ambivalent hosts wished them gone.

As the staff and the two elegant hosts escorted them to the car, the first stars came out, fierce and steady, and the hillsides emerged from their dusky indecision as crisp black silhouettes. The air was fresh. Hamid opened the gates and stood at the far side with his metal lantern.

'Do send me a line when you get back,' Richard said, leaning for a moment on the driver's-side window. 'We always worry until we know people are safe back home. Otherwise we feel oddly responsible for them.'

They kissed, shook hands, said what people say when they are reluctant to concede that they might not be seeing an acquaintance ever again. It was over in a minute. Hamid wished them luck in Arabic and waved them down the road. The car roared off, a little angrily, Richard thought. Typical David. He was furious for having been bested in some way.

The gate slammed shut and Dally poured Richard an aged Lagavulin in the library. They made a fire, ate some mince pies and drank quietly as the wind moaned around the delicately painted casements.

'What a ghastly weekend,' Dally eventually said, sighing and putting up his feet on a leather pouf. 'We're lucky to be still alive. Did you talk to that French girl? Amazing that people like that actually exist.'

'I told Hamid to lock the outer doors,' Richard said, and his tone was strangely vacant, but domineering. Dally was startled. But Richard tipped his glass and sucked in the saline nectar with its odour of smoked peat and settled in to listen to a bit of wind. It was quite entertaining after three days of non-stop futility.

He went over the puzzles that had been thrown his way during that time, the conflicting personalities that could not be resolved, but over and again he returned to the piercing and unrelenting eyes of Abdellah. There was something not quite right with them. When you looked into them, they did not return the favour. They were alive, proud, vivacious even, but they did not see you.

David tore down the Tafnet road a little recklessly, until Jo held his arm for a moment and more or less ordered him to slow down.

'We won't get there any quicker.'

'The quicker, the better . . .'

She sobbed. He had nothing to say. There was just the bitter impulse to move on, to whirl about and forget. They reached the main road, and David turned north with a stabbing turn of the wheel. He flicked on the full beam and searched for the controls of the CD player.

'Open the map,' he ordered impatiently. 'I think this time we'll get there very quickly. We won't be lost.'

She obeyed, flattening it on her knees and turning on the glove-compartment light. She memorised the route, then turned the light off. In the full beam, the same whitewashed posts and abandoned buildings from Friday night appeared again. They were speeding up a long, tiresome hill. At the top of it lay the place where they had hit Driss.

'I think we should stop,' she said quietly.

'What?'

'I think we should stop and pay our respects.'

Three days earlier he would have said, 'Are you nuts?' But now he was inclined to agree. They *should* stop and pay their respects. He therefore took his foot gently off the accelerator and allowed the car to slow a little.

She felt a deep relief that he did this. So perhaps he had changed after all, and in a permanent sense. They neared the place where a police ribbon still stood tied between two plastic posts. There was a stony hill rising from the right side of the road, which they had not noticed before. It was dotted with cactus, and down it came running a male human form, its head wrapped in a red-and-white *chech*. This manic and unexpected figure timed his descent so perfectly that before they had reached the crest of the hill where the road began to descend again, he was standing in the road directly in front of them, where he raised one hand in which they saw a palm-sized trilobite, a Psychopyge. He shouted, '*Arrêtez!*' and David slammed on the brakes.

Desert grass quivered ominously along the disintegrating edges of the road. Ismael had in fact been sitting alone on this stony hill for the better part of the day. He sat under a coat held up on three sticks, brooding and scanning the surrounding landscape for signs of approaching cars. During the afternoon many of the guests from Azna passed in their stupendous vehicles, and he had had to skip down the hillside each time to see if it was the two infidels he sought. It was repetitive and exhausting. The night fell and it became easier. There was hardly any traffic on the road now. He sat and shivered and prepared the old heavy pistol that Abdellah had given him with a gruesome solemnity. He went over in his mind the events of Friday night, which he had kept resolutely to himself.

He and Driss had waited in the same spot. They had hitched a lift from Erfoud with the Elvis and a few other specimens and had got off at the bottom of the hill, where the cement truck left them. The desert is a grapevine and everyone knew about the party of the faggots of Azna. Driss was in a dark mood that evening because of the quarrel with his father.

'We'll stop the first car,' he said to Ismael as they hid on the hill. 'They'll be loaded with cash. They'll be soft – they won't resist.'

'What if they resist?' Ismael remembered asking.

Driss waved his hand. 'What a stupid question. Are you a girl? They're unbelievers. What the fuck do you care?'

'They always stop,' Driss remarked later, as they were eating a tin of sardines with their hands. 'They're stupid. But when they stop, Ismael, don't be a coward. Act.'

'I promised you I would,' Ismael shot back. 'You think I'm afraid?'

'You're always afraid.'

'No, I am not. It's not fear. It's excitement.'

'Excitement?'

Driss laughed scornfully.

'We'll be wanted by the police afterwards. Did you think about that?'

'What do I care?'

They sat by the road and waited. A wind whipped up the dark sand and grit, and Driss wrapped his head.

'Of course I thought about it,' Ismael muttered. 'We'll be in the city by tomorrow morning.'

He remembered now the look on Driss's face. To think it was only Friday night that this magnificent warrior was still alive.

'I'll leave it to you to shoot, then,' Driss said. 'It'll be your initiation.'

'You'll see.'

He strode confidently towards the Hennigers' car now without a thought in the world, his left hand gripping a small Psychopyge and his right hand gripping the revolver, which was loaded with six shells. He saw the woman wind down her window with a searching, sympathetic expression; the man relaxed his hands on the wheel and turned off the engine. This proved that Driss had pursued the wrong strategy. People are by and large trusting, especially infidels. He simply walked up to them and said, '*Salaam aleikum.*' They had an astonished look on their faces, as if they wanted to ask him his pardon now that they suddenly recognised him. But what they didn't understand was that grace was not his to give.

Ah, he thought sadly, if only you knew. The woman

half leaned out of her window, angling for a view as he crossed the beam of the headlights and into the darkness next to her. He dropped the fossil and raised the revolver without any effort. There was no sound from either of them as he slipped quickly round the back of the car and caught the man opening his door. David's eyes were not at all frightened. They were merely filled with lame curiosity and wonder. Ismael smiled at him with a cruelty that came straight from the bottom of his heart, because he remembered the Englishman digging a little hole in which to bury the ID of Driss and he knew it was the kind of thing a *gaouri* would do. And David, for his part, suddenly understood and was not surprised either. It seemed to him then that there was nothing he could have done either way, and that the idea of freedom of choice was completely absurd. It never occurred to him why he had not been forgiven, because he had forgiven himself. So he looked up with tired, resentful eyes and felt everything go into a slow motion that made it bearable. He held up one hand and tried to utter a single word, but it was too late. His tongue never formed itself around the word, and he had to say it straight to Ismael with his eyes, telepathically, as it were. He was sorry in that split second of repentance. Because when you thought about it, there was not much to say and he had, when all was said and done, failed to say it. He closed his eyes and let the turbine shred him.

Acknowledgements

I would like to express my immense gratitude to Caroline Dawnay for her intelligent and soulful help in editing and sustaining this book, and to Emma Parry for setting it in motion.

Lawrence Osborne is the author of one previous novel and seven books of non-fiction. His short story 'Volcano' was selected for *Best American Short Stories 2012*, and he has written for the *New York Times Magazine*, *Condé Nast Traveller*, the *New Yorker*, *Forbes*, *Harper's* and other publications. Born in England, he lives in Bangkok.

www.lawrenceosborne.net

Read On For

An Essay from Lawrence Osborne:
Off the Grid: Morocco Beyond Marrakech

A Conversation with Lawrence Osborne

Recommended Reading:
Some of My Favorite Writing on the Region

An Essay from Lawrence Osborne
Off the Grid: Morocco Beyond Marrakech

Although well travelled by tourists, Morocco remains a country where secret places abound. The desert is vast, as are the Atlas and Anti-Atlas Mountains, and here, far from the cities and cultural centres, one can find places removed from the camera-wielding crowds. Admittedly, many Berber desert towns are popular with tourists; they're reached via the modern-day equivalent to the camel: the air-conditioned bus. But travellers equipped with their own four-wheel drive can move beyond the more traversed watering holes. The deep desert beckons.

The road that leads to the desert town of Erfoud passes through the Rif Mountains before descending towards Er-Rachidia, a former Foreign Legion outpost that sits on the edge of the desert plain. It passes through the gritty fossil-selling town of Midelt and then on to the remarkable Gorges du Ziz, the road spiralling down among abandoned *ksours* (fortified Berber villages).

Erfoud has become something of a destination in recent years due to its proximity to the magnificent sand dunes of Merzouga. But it still feels like a frontier town, its economy based on fossilized trilobites and aquifers. From here, you can drive across the open desert to Rissani, a former slave market and now center of the huge oasis around it: the Tafilalet.

Rissani has a tumbledown market and scores of shops selling

fossils and gems. Traders from the deep desert show up here, bringing pieces of meteors for sale. It's an interesting stop for a night, but beyond it the roads peter out and a four wheel drive is necessary to reach the places that are even more remote.

There are two enigmatic mountains that reward the adventurous. One is Hmor Lgdad, 'the red-cheeked one' in Arabic, and Jbel Issomour, a place famous for its prized trilobites, which are sold all over the world.

Insider tip: it is very highly recommended that you only make the trip to Jbel Issomour with a guide. The easiest way to do this is to stop in Rissani and find a fossil seller or guide to take you to the various fossil villages around the mountain.

Issomour makes the most rewarding detour, though the journey from Erfoud is arduous and requires an expert guide. It's a plateau mountain that rises from the desert like something not entirely natural. Enhancing the supernatural feel are the miles of fossil trenches around it. Hundreds of people labour in cooler months here, but in summer they depart for the Rif and leave their tools by the sides of the trenches for months at a time, undisturbed by even the wind. The effect is eerie. Circumnavigating the mountain by Jeep provides access to a ramp-like track that leads up to the top – a rough *wadi* that requires strong tyres.

The drive across this plateau is remarkable, since it is roadless, off-the-grid, and bare. On the far side, another *wadi* leads down to a series of oases that are dying from the gradual encroachment of Bayoud's Disease, which afflicts palm trees. At their edge lie tiny hamlets devoted to fossil mining.

Their houses are often shaped like eggs, with metal doors brightly painted with images of trilobites. Visible above, on the looming, almost menacing cliff faces, are the caves where locals hack away for the precious fossils, each one trailing ropes. With a bit of courtesy, it's possible to spend the night with a local and watch the diggers set off at dawn. But by ten, in summer, the heat is unbearable and those not working in the caves will stay indoors.

The drive to and from Issomour is as remarkable as the mountain itself. Along the roads are fossil prepping shops and quarries; the pretty village of Alnif boasts a beautiful *bab* (gateway). Closer to Erfoud, you will even find unexpected lakes with flamingos. This is the eternal desert, untouched by the mega-resorts now springing up everywhere around Saharan towns.

A Conversation with
Lawrence Osborne

Q. Is *The Forgiven* based on a true story?

A. Yes, though I reworked it to fit my own idea of a story. The characters are mine, and I was very familiar with the landscape in which the story occurs long before I heard the tale that I eventually used. In fact, the original story immediately reminded me of a place where I had spent a lot of time years before. And it seemed probable. It resonated with what I remembered of my own sometimes difficult relations when staying in the Sahara – that feeling of not knowing where you are, or not knowing if the surface and depth of other people are aligned or whether they exist in the same context as you do. The Westerner there is always alone and slightly bewildered.

Q. You've been all over the world as a travel writer. Why did you choose Morocco as the setting for your novel?

A. I had lived there for a while, and I also made a trip into the desert near Erfoud and Rissani to explore fossils. The mountain of Azemmour had been so impressive to me – I could not stop thinking about it for years. There was a kind of dread about it that was difficult to express. And the villages around it, which I have described (though the names are altered slightly), were always incredibly ominous and strange to me. Even the shapes of the houses, like eggs buried in sand, and the enormous cliff face filled with fossil caves: it seemed like the improbable corner of what we call the world economy. Child labour hacking out trilobites for European millionaires. Of course, I wanted to write about our updated version of the colonial relation, though the word *colonial* is simplistic. I wanted that as a backdrop to my morality fable. One of my heroes is the French filmmaker Clouzot, and *The Wages of Fear* was very much an inspiration for me in writing this book. You might remember that that film was set in a place very like Erfoud, though of course in Latin America.

Q. *The Forgiven* features an incredible cast of characters – different ages, nationalities, social classes. Are any of the characters based on real people you've met during your travels?

A. Most if not all are based directly on people I have known. That doesn't mean I met them in Morocco! Though some of them I did. I met quite a few fossil dealers in Erfoud and in the Tafilalet region, and also quite a few foreign desperadoes of various kinds. Some of the other characters are very familiar to me from my English and French upbringing, and indeed from my own family – so they are types I know very well from childhood. I didn't have to invent them very much – their way of speaking and thinking are very clear to me and so, too, is their psychology, which is nevertheless quite complex and too easy to caricature. They all found their way into the characters of *The Forgiven*. To me, place creates character, not the other way around. So the setting – the place – twists and reshapes the characters into a certain form . . . that I suppose is the whole point of the story. In the Sahara, you are not the person you were in South Kensington.

Q. What's next for you?

A. I am working now on a collection of short stories set in far-flung places where I have lived and travelled, exploring themes that are quite similar to those in *The Forgiven*. I am fascinated, I suppose, by the western intrusion into the tropics, into the deserts and the jungles of those places that they think to be wild. It is not a new theme, but I think it continues in our own age in different forms. I am, I dare say, attracted to the same things in my own life, and therein lies a personal neurosis that I like to explore in objective characters.

Recommended Reading:
Some of My Favorite Writing on the Region

Tahar Ben Jelloun's *Leaving Tangier* (2009), which explores the bitter side of Moroccan emigration to Spain.

Paul Bowles', *The Sheltering Sky* (1949), *The Delicate Prey: And Other Stories* (1950), and *The Spider's House* (1955). The most famous of foreign writers expatriated in Morocco, Bowles' refined, chilling tales are masterpieces of observation, both of bewildered, self-destructive Westerners and of the Moroccans fatally enmeshed with them. Lesser known than *The Sheltering Sky*, *The Spider's House* explores the events leading up to Independence in 1956 through the lives of young members of the Istiqlal movement, while his thriller *Let It Come Down* (1952) is one of the indispensable Tangier books.

William S. Burroughs' *The Naked Lunch* (1959) and *Interzone* (1989). The chapters which deal with Burroughs' long and chaotic sojourn in Tangier are both brutal and hilarious.

Mohamed Choukri's *For Bread Alone* (1973). Choukri's brilliant narrative economy and intensity were formed by oral storytelling, and this work draws on his impoverished upbringing, as do *The Tent* and *The Time of Mistakes*.

Andre Gide's *The Immoralist* (1902), though set in Algeria rather than Morocco, evokes the French colonial period in the Maghreb and set the tone for many European fixations with the region subsequently. Gide's spare, haunting descriptions of the desert and the story of a young couple, one of whom is afflicted by TB, would seem to have influenced *The Sheltering Sky*.

Mohamed Mrabet's *Love with a Few Hairs* (1967), *Collected Stories* (2004), and his autobiography *Look and Move On* (1976). Most of Mrabet's works are orally dictated and transcribed (many by Paul Bowles), giving them a fresh, kinetic quality that is also reputedly due to *kif.*

www.vintage-books.co.uk